BROKEN PLEDGES

Kevin Kilgarriff

INTRODUCTION

Step onto any college campus in North America, and you'll find that the social scene is dominated by one thing - Greek Life. Fraternities and sororities are the nexus for students either seeking to be a part of a group or to just blow off some steam at a frat party after a tough week of academics.

Today, Greek-letter organizations mainly have a reputation for partying and hazing. The true history, however, dates back to 1776 when the very first Greek-letter organization, the Phi Beta Kappa Society, was founded at the College of William & Mary. At the time, unlike many modern day Greek organizations, groups like this were often founded with an academic purpose, often debating current events or literature, or simply helping its members grow into better versions of themselves in order to succeed in life.

Typically, these groups would adopt Latin letters for their names. Phi Beta Kappa, however, chose to adopt Greek Letters in an attempt to set themselves apart. ΦBK, it was expected, would be seen by everyone as being elite. The attempt was successful, and other groups soon followed suit. It became the first of hundreds of Greek-letter organizations that were founded on college campuses throughout the country over the years. Fraternities were created, allowing only males to join, with the first sorority appearing nearly one hundred years later in 1874, allowing only female members.

Social events soon became a normal part of Greek life, and it wasn't long before the social aspect of it was what Greek life

3

became primarily known for. The truth, however, ran much deeper. In reality, members wanted to be a part of something bigger than themselves. They were seeking a shared experience that only members could lay claim to. The result was a bond that would connect them for life. Greek-letter organizations weren't just social groups. They were Brotherhoods and Sisterhoods.

This bond evolved into an air of exclusivity. Becoming a member wasn't as simple as just signing up. Soon they began instituting a pledge period during which you would learn about the organization, as well as prove your worth, and at the end of which you would be able to call yourself a Brother or Sister of that particular organization.

It was during this time that the well-known practice of hazing would take place. Pledges would be placed into various situations that resulted in them being treated in a less than humane manner, both physically and mentally. The practice was most common among fraternities.

In the 1980's, hazing had reached a boiling point. Numerous hazing activities that included excessive drinking or harmful physical activities began to gain the attention of the public. In an effort to dissuade the Greeks from partaking in this behavior and having a negative effect on their school's reputation, colleges began to crack down on the practice and handed out severe punishments.

By 1993, Pennsylvania's South Cuthbert University had all but banned hazing within Greek-letter organizations. It would be another two years before the first Anti-Hazing law was passed. But for the most part, fraternities at SCU had steered clear of the most heinous activities that had been a part of their pledge periods in the past.

Hazing did still happen. But it was on a much smaller scale. Activities that could result in harm being done to the pledges were generally avoided.

But on one cool, April night, the SCU Chapter of Kappa Chi Rho changed life at the school forever. The question had been asked for years within the hazing discussion at SCU. How far would someone go to become a Brother of a fraternity? On April 7, 1993 - and again nearly thirty years later - that question was answered at South Cuthbert University.

They would do whatever they needed to do in order to get in...

...even if it killed them.

CHAPTER 1

APRIL 7, 1993
South Cuthbert, PA

"Membership built from only those insistent on the Brotherhood of all men!

A demand for only the highest moral standard!

The predominant responsibility of love and acceptance among all members!

Judgment only by...only by..."

Chase Dempsey's mind went black. The blindfold was tied tight around his head as he walked, making it difficult to concentrate. *"Oh shit...not now. Don't forget this now!"* he thought to himself.

"by..." The cool night air against his face, and the sound of dry leaves crackling below his feet, were making it nearly impossible for him to concentrate.

A deep voice screamed in his ear. "What the fuck Dempsey?! You've been pledging Kappa Chi Rho for eight weeks and you still don't know what the Landmarks are?!"

Chase's body shuddered at the sound. "I'm sorry, Brother..." He hesitated.

"Brother who?!" the voice screamed back. "Do you even know who I am? Am I supposed to let you into my Fraternity, and call you my Brother, if you can't even recognize my voice?!"

"Jason!" Chase quickly yelled. "Brother Jason! Brother Jason!". He stumbled mid-sentence,, barely stopping himself from

6

falling. He wasn't certain where he was. As near as he could figure, he was being led through a wooded area. Although, he had no idea how far he'd walked.

"Pledge Chris, are you gonna let your Pledge Brother hang out to dry?" he heard another voice call out. He was certain that this voice belonged to Brother Matt.

"No, Brother Matt!" Chase heard Chris Wilbanks call out at the top of his lungs. His voice faltered slightly as he also lost his footing. "Judgment only by innate worth! No one is denied entry into the halls of Kappa Chi Rho because of appearance or background!"

Chase was thankful to have Chris there with him. He had only known him for a little over two months at this point. But as the only two members of the Spring '93 Kappa Chi Rho Pledge Class, they had already shared more experiences than either had shared with practically anyone else in their lives.

Chase knew that pledging would be a unique experience. But it was light years beyond what he could have imagined. Eight weeks ago the concept of Brotherhood seemed to be overplayed by the Brothers of Kappa Chi Rho, or KXP in its commonly used Greek shorthand. He felt that they were just giving him the hard sell. After all, they need new members in order to survive as an organization. Chase figured they'd do whatever they could to get new pledges. He was mainly interested in the same social perks that he witnessed all of the Greeks on campus seeming to benefit from - lots of partying and lots of girls to party with. The idea of Brotherhood was appealing to him. But if he was being honest with himself, he just wanted to get laid. And with a nickname like "Crows", derived from the Chi and Rho in the name, it definitely had the effect of giving them a certain allure about them that seemed to help in that cause.

In order to join the Fraternity, however, he would need to go through the pledge period. This meant eight weeks of learning about the Fraternity, getting to know the initiated Brothers, and, of course, doing anything those initiated Brothers told him to do. In the hierarchy of the Greek system, pledges were at the bottom.

7

As Chase had heard on more than one occasion from the initiated Brothers, pledges were pond scum. At the end of the pledge period, he would have earned the right to wear the letters KXP and call himself a Brother of Kappa Chi Rho. He just needed to go through a load of bullshit to get to that point. Chase fully expected this going in.

What he didn't expect, though, was that the very act of pledging would be the catalyst for that feeling of Brotherhood. The past eight weeks have been comprised of bonding activities that he'd come to realize every one of the Brothers before him had partaken in. Chase and Chris had become closer than either of them could have imagined, simply by virtue of their shared experience and by the fact that they were the only two students that were pledging Kappa Chi Rho this semester. Spring pledge classes were often much smaller than the Fall classes, and there were definitely times during his pledge period that he'd wished he was a member of a larger pledge class so that he could have less of the focus on himself. Although, it wasn't as bad as he had expected it would be.

That is until tonight.

It was Hell Week - the final week of pledging. This meant living in the basement of 403 South Martin St., the KXP Fraternity House, for five days and enduring a steadily increased level of shit brought on by the Fraternity Brothers. Each night would be taken up by a different pledging activity. These activities were decidedly more impactful than what Chase and Chris had been through so far. Being blindfolded was nothing new. "Bring your blindfold" was a common phrase to hear when being summoned to the 403. In fact, they'd been blindfolded for all of the activities this week. But each activity so far had taken place in the house. They were activities meant to test their trust and loyalty. Chase knew that every person in the room had gone through it successfully, and he told himself that they wouldn't bring harm to someone that they'll want to call their Brother in just a few days.

"Just remember that no matter how dangerous any situation might seem, it's all just a head game," Chase could

remember Brother Potsy confiding in him. *"No one will ever actually do anything to put you in danger. You'll never get hurt. It's about trust."* Tonight was different though. Chase was having a hard time with that trust aspect.

The night started like any other. Which is to say that Chase and Chris were told to don their blindfolds and sit on the concrete basement floor in silence. They often sat there quietly until hearing the sound of the Brothers pounding down the old, wooden staircase. Chase didn't know how long they'd been there tonight. But it was definitely longer than they'd been made to wait ever before.

Finally, the footsteps came. It was louder tonight. It sounded like less people. The usual hooting and hollering was there. But it was less amplified. He heard the feet beginning to shuffle along the dirty, concrete floor around him, and he shuttered when a pair of hands reached under his armpits and yanked him to his feet.

"Move," was all he heard the voice say as his body was turned and shoved forward in one swift motion.

He took small steps, unsure of where he was going.

"Stop...reach your foot out for the step and walk up the stairs." He felt like it was Brother Matt's voice. But it was hard to tell.

He did as he was told. When reached the top of the steps, he was then ushered through the house. He could tell that he was being led toward the front door. The cool air slapped him in the face as he exited the house and was led down the front porch steps. He could hear the sounds of feet shuffling along the sidewalk. That was when he heard the first words that week that had actually caused him concern.

"Get in the trunk"

Chase stopped in his tracks, wondering if he'd just heard that correctly.

"What's the matter, Dempsey?!" he heard an angry voice say to him quietly. He recognized it as belonging to John

O'Malley, one of the older Brothers that he had always looked up to and felt like he got along well with. This was the first time he'd ever heard an angry tone come out of his mouth.

"Are you scared?!" he said angrily into his ear.

Chase did his best to stay calm. "Not at all, Brother John."

"Do you trust me?" John asked him. His voice was low and Chase surmised that since they were outdoors, they didn't want to be heard by any neighbors that might call the cops at the site of people being loaded, blindfolded, into a trunk.

"Yes, Brother John."

"Then get in the fucking trunk!" he said in a harsh, loud whisper.

Within a matter of seconds, Chase was in the trunk and heard the lid close over him. He was unsure for a moment if Chris was in there with him.

"Chris?" he whispered. "You here?"

There was no answer. He was met with only silence. His assumption was that Chris was in a separate car, also alone in the trunk.

Moments later, he heard both the driver side and passenger side doors close and the engine start. This was followed by the sound of the radio turned up to full blast and the car jerking into motion.

For the first portion of the ride, Chase tried to keep track of where they might be. He'd made a mental note of turns and tried to count the minutes. But it wasn't long before the car began driving in what felt like circles and figure eights. He assumed they were in a parking lot. Probably the Rec Center. But the maneuvers had been successful. He had now lost all sense of direction and time. He gave up. He waited. Unsure of what would come next.

Eventually the car slowed. Chase could hear the sound of gravel beneath them as they came to a full stop. When the trunk was finally opened and he was allowed out, he had absolutely zero sense of where he might be. The air was silent. Void of any traffic or sounds of nearby activity. He heard only the nighttime chatter of bugs and the sound of one other trunk closing a short distance away.. *Chris!*

This gave him hope. The bond they'd created gave him the feeling that together they could get through whatever it was they were about to face.

He felt a pair of hands grasp each of his shoulders and reposition him a few feet to his left.

"Put your arms out to the side," he was told. He felt an arm reach around each side of his waist and he shuddered instinctively. He soon realized he was having something tied around him.

"Start Walking!" shouted the voice from behind him as an arm shoved into the small of his back.

He began walking forward and could tell he was walking across a dirt covered area. It soon turned into grass beneath his feet. The grass gave way to the crunch of dead leaves and the terrain became less stable. Chase could feel whatever was tied to his waist pulling him from behind.

"That's your Pledge Brother tied to you Dempsey!" he heard a voice yell, and this time there was no attempt to avoid being heard. "Don't walk too fast! You two need to stick together. This is what Brotherhood is all about!"

The Brothers, of which he had no idea how many there were, were quizzing them as they walked - each of them calling out questions from the Esoteric Manual. They'd been tested on the material weekly by their Pledge Master, and tomorrow night they were expected to take their final National exam. Chase knew the material front ways and back. But remembering the answers while walking blindfolded through, what seemed like the woods, proved difficult. Chase told himself that it was by design, meant only to scare them. He told himself that the Brothers would never do anything that would harm them. They'd all gone through the same thing themselves.

Had they though? Or was this something new that one of the more sadistic Brothers dreamed up. He had to believe that it wasn't. It was the only way he could get through it.

11

"Ok stop right here," a voice called out. Chase had silently identified it as Brother Jay.

Chase and Chris both stopped in their tracks.

"Ok you two need to stand here," he heard Brother Jay tell them. "Count to one thousand in your head and then you can remove your blindfolds. Then it's time to find your way back to 403."

Chase heard leaves rustling and feet pounding on the ground as they ran off. As the sound grew more distant, he eventually heard muffled voices and the sound of car doors slamming. A moment later he could hear the sound of tires screeching as the cars sped off.

He stood motionless, counting in his head. He didn't think he wouldn't need to count all of the way to one thousand. But he didn't want to take that chance. He was well aware that the beauty of the blindfold for a pledge activity is that Brothers can sit quietly, undetected, and observe pledge behavior when they think no one is watching.

It was some time between one-hundred and two-hundred that Chase started to become less worried. His gut feeling was that all of the Brothers were already in their car and on their way home.

He was nearing two-hundred in his head and was finally ready to speak to suggest to Chris that they take off their blindfolds. The words were nearly past his lips when he heard the sound that would haunt him for the rest of his life - footsteps approaching from the distance.

"They DID come back?!" he thought to himself. He was now glad that he had waited and continued counting.

No words were spoken. He could hear the sound of leaves rustling at their feet and he could feel the presence of someone nearby. One more unidentifiable sound pierced the night before he felt a light tap on the side of his leg, and then once again hearing the sound of rustling leaves slowly moving further and further away. .

12

He stood silently counting. He now had no intention of taking his blindfold off a second before he reached one thousand. It seemed like forever before he reached the end.

998...999...1,000

Chase finally removed his blindfold and turned to where he thought he'd find Chris Wilbanks standing. Instead, he saw nothing but a rope hanging from his side, the end of which had been cut. There was no sign of Chris Wilbanks.

He spun around, frantically looking for Chris, but found nothing but trees and darkness. Chase Dempsey was alone in the woods. His friend was gone.

CHAPTER 2

"Get it, Daisy! Get it!" Steve Brinkman tossed the old, dirty tennis ball through the trees. Daisy, an Irish Setter and Steve's most trusted companion, ran excitedly after the faded fluorescent prize. As the ball bounced off of a tree trunk and careened to the left, she quickly changed directions and chased it down.

"Good girl!" Steve praised her as she dutifully returned with it in her mouth. Her tail was wagging quickly from side to side as she hopped around in place awaiting the next throw.

Every morning before work, Steve would bring Daisy here, weather permitting, to let her stretch her legs, and also to get some much needed exercise in for himself.

The path through the center of the woods has enough inclines and declines to get the heart racing. If he ever gets the extra energy, he can always go off of the path and move through the brush. He's always certain to not veer too far off of the trail though. Some steep drops can sneak up on you and take you completely by surprise. For that reason he has never brought Daisy here after dark, as much as he can tell that she wants to.

"Go get it, girl!" he yelled, giving the ball a strong toss.

Daisy raced after as soon as he released the ball from his hands. But she then suddenly stopped mid-sprint and changed course, moving in the complete opposite direction from where the ball had landed. She slowed her pace as she trotted further away from Steve. Steve squinted his eyes as the sun peeked through the trees.

"Daisy? Daisy Girl, get the ball!"

Daisy didn't look back.

"Daisy! Get back here girl!" Steve yelled as he broke into a light jog following her path through the woods. He eventually caught up with her at the edge of an embankment. "What's up? Find something more inter..." His voice trailed off, unable to make another sound, as his attention was stolen by the grizzly sight that lay before him.

Twenty feet below them, at the bottom of the embankment, lay the body of a dead man. He was on his back, with his feet leaning above him against the dirt wall of the embankment. His head was twisted awkwardly to the side, and a branch had impaled him through the chest. He was wearing a blindfold, which had been dislodged just enough to reveal one open, lifeless eye.

Steve stared down at the scene below him for a moment before speaking. "Daisy...we need to call the police."

CHAPTER 3

Nearly twenty-four hours after the incident in the woods off of Oakburne Road, the Brothers of Kappa Chi Rho were still unaware of Chris Wilbanks' whereabouts. Chase had spent close to an hour wandering around the woods looking for Chris. He never found a single sign of him. He eventually found his way through the two mile route back to 403. The reaction had been mixed at the sight of him returning alone. Some Brothers screamed in Chase's face, wondering why he would leave his Pledge Brother behind. Others had shown genuine concern, recognizing that something was definitely not right and that something terrible may have happened. Sammy Compton, the Chapter President, made Jay Pierce drive him to the drop-off point so that he could look for Chris himself. A short while later, they returned alone. They said they also tried Chris' dorm room, but there was no one there.

The prevailing belief amongst the Brotherhood was that Chris Wilbanks had cracked. That the stress of being dropped off in the middle of the woods was his breaking point and that he ran off. Chase wasn't so easily convinced. Chris Wilbanks was mentally tough. Even more so than himself. Numerous times throughout their Pledge period, it was Chris that talked Chase down off of the proverbial ledge when he was worried about what type of activities they might have to endure. Paddling was one of Chase's enduring fears, and Chris was constantly ensuring him that paddling was a thing of the past. Hazing had been massively discouraged in recent years, with stiff penalties being handed down when a Greek organization was caught participating in the act. The punishments proved to be a powerful tool. Serious hazing had decreased sharply as a result. At least physical hazing. There had certainly been things throughout the past eight weeks that one would absolutely consider hazing. However, never once were either Chris or Chase put in danger. Chase had no reason to think that being dropped in the woods would have broken Chris Wilbanks to the point of quitting.

Chase had spent the night alone on the basement floor, replaying the events in his mind and trying to determine what may have happened to Chris. He knew he'd heard someone else there. Anything beyond that was all speculation.

In the morning Chase was out of the house early, heading directly to Chris' dorm room to see for himself. He thought that perhaps Chris just wouldn't answer the door in fear that the Brothers would drag him back. His loud banging on the door clearly had woken Chris' roommate, who had not seen Chris since earlier in the week. Chase then made his way around campus throughout the morning. He checked the cafeteria, the gym, and each of Chris' classes. There was not a single sign of Chris anywhere. Shortly before Noon, Chase returned to 403 to find a large group of Brothers gathered outside of the house. He felt every eye on him as he made his way through the front door.

"What is going on here?" he quietly asked Brother Potsy.

Potsy turned to Chase, then glanced up the stairs to see if anyone was up there. "Come with me for a second," he told him.

Chase followed Potsy up the stairs. He'd follow him anywhere, in reality. Potsy was Chase and Chris' Pledge Master. The one in charge of their progression through the Pledge period. He was the Brother that Chase trusted most.

As the two arrived in Potsy's bedroom, Potsy closed the door behind them and turned to Chase. "Listen, we still don't know anything for sure. But..."

"Nothing before the word 'but' ever counts, Pots," Chase told him. "Tell me what's going on."

17

Potsy lowered his head and let out a sigh. "Sammy was over at IGC and overheard someone in Wilkinson's office saying that a body was found in the woods this morning."

Chase began shaking his head in defiance as he fought back tears. "No. Nope. It's not him. It can't be him."

"We don't know anything yet," Potsy reassured him.

"It's *not* him," Chase repeated. His voice grew louder.

"Listen, we're going to..." Before Potsy could finish his sentence, the door swung open as Brother Jay Pierce leaned in through the doorway.

"You guys better get down here," he told them. "It's on the news."

The three raced down the steps and into the living room where most of the active members of the Fraternity were piled in with their eyes glued to the TV screen. Action News at Noon was just beginning.

"Good Afternoon, everyone! I'm Monica Malpass. Today's top story, a body was found in the woods near South Cuthbert University. We go now to Dann Cuellar, who is on the scene. Dann?"

"Thanks, Monica. The body of a white male was found this morning by a man walking his dog through these woods behind me, just two mile off campus near South Cuthbert University. The deceased has been identified as Christopher Wilbanks. He was a student at South Cuthbert University. No cause of death has been determined yet, and it's not yet known if foul play is expected."

The screen now switched to show a man in a suit with a half a dozen or more microphones being held in front of his face. "Det. Mike Showalter - South Cuthbert Police Department" was the name that flashed across the bottom of the screen as everyone watched in disbelief.

"This is still an ongoing investigation. But this is what I can tell you at this point. The victim's body was discovered in the wooded area just Southeast of campus on Oakburne Road. He was found at the bottom of an embankment. Official cause of death is pending the results of an autopsy. But he had apparently fallen

18

down an embankment and died on impact. As I said, we are still investigating as to why he was in these woods. As more information becomes available we will transmit that to you in as timely a manner as is possible. Thank you."

A reporter could be heard yelling out a question from the side. *"Detective, is there any truth to the rumor that he was found blindfolded?"*

"I can neither confirm or deny that," he responded flatly.

"Do you suspect foul play?" the reporter asked.

"I also can neither confirm or deny that information. We will update you later. Thank you everyone," the Detective said before turning abruptly to leave.

"Oh, fuck me," Sammy Compton said to himself as he stood up. At 5'10", he was an imposing figure. Nicknamed 'Bull' not only for his stocky frame, but also for sharing a first name with Sammy the Bull, the renowned mobster. "How did this happen?!" he screamed at the group. His voice grew louder with each question. "How does a pledge die on Drop-Off Night? Why was he near that ridge?! You're supposed to stay away from there!"

"They were nowhere near it!" Jay Pierce shot back. "We dropped them in the same place as always. They were like fucking fifty feet from the road. You can see the friggin' road from where they were! That ridge is like a quarter mile away!"

"Well someone please explain to me how one pledge is tied to another pledge and then they end up a quarter mile the fuck apart." He called his attention to Chase, who was sitting in the corner of the room, still staring at the screen in disbelief.

"Demps..." Sammy sighed, recognizing that he's about to ask Chase Dempsey to relive a night that he'll forever want to forget, "...we need to know what happened. It's only a matter of time before they come wanting to talk to us...to you. We need to know what happened there."

How the fuck should I know? Chase thought to himself. He had no idea what happened. He'd been blindfolded and only knew what his remaining senses would allow him to know, which unfortunately was very little.

"I don't fucking know, man! It..." Chase paused as he realized that every Brother in the room had turned towards him. Every Brother that he had been looking up to as authority figures for the past two months. Every Brother that he was afraid to say no to. Every Brother that...well, that as far as he was concerned may be responsible for the death of Chris Wilbanks. At least just as responsible as Chase was.

"...it was dark! I was fucking blindfolded!"

"You had to hear something!" shouted a voice from the archway into the Chapter Room. Chase perked up immediately. It was a voice that he recognized. He heard the voice again in his head, over and over again and he repeated the events from last night.

You want to be my fucking Brother!?

"Well, you tell me John! You were there too, right?" Chase shot back. It was the first time in two months that he'd addressed anyone in the room without the moniker of "Brother" in front of their name. He exhaled as he felt the moment stretching out longer than he was comfortable with, and the weight of John's stare.

"I don't know what I heard, okay? I definitely heard things. There was rustling and...I don't know...noises. I have no idea what they were! But someone was there. After we were told to count to one thousand, someone other than me and Chris was there."

Chase watched as the collective group recoiled in exasperation. "Holy shit, we are going to lose our fucking charter," he heard someone say.

Sammy heard it too, and his expression hardened as he stepped quickly towards the center of the group. "Our Charter?! Our fucking Charter?!" he bellowed. "Are you fucking kidding me?! Yeah...we may lose our Charter. But big...fucking...deal. Fuck you! Chris Wilbanks is dead. Forget the fact that he was a pledge of Kappa Chi Rho. Chris Wilbanks..."

He paused to compose himself.

"...Chris Wilbanks was a 19 year old guy who just wanted to be part of something. And now his family is never going to see him again. And yeah, it happened as a result of..." Sammy stopped himself mid-sentence and rephrased. "...during one of our Pledge activities."

Chase could tell that Sammy was beginning to choose his language carefully, stopping short of blaming the Fraternity.

"But we, as human beings, should give zero shits about the fucking Charter. This is bigger than the Charter. If KXP suffers for this..." his eyes scanned the room "...well then so be it. Chris Wilbanks just wanted to be one of us. He just wanted to be a Crow. And he is never going to get that chance to walk the campus wearing KXP across his chest. He's never going to go home to his parents...proudly displaying the letters to signify his accomplishment."

Chase saw Jay Pierce stare down at KXP across his own sweatshirt. He scanned the dozen or more KXP baseball caps topping the heads of the Brother's in the room.

"EVER!" Sammy's voice jolted Chase back to reality. "Shit...if losing our Charter is how life decides to punish us for him being robbed of that and everything else he could have done in life...well hell...I think we should consider ourselves lucky."

Chase leaned forward with his head buried in his hands. At that moment, he felt anything but lucky. He wasn't exactly the last one to see Chris Wilbanks alive. The blindfold made sure of that. But he was the last known person to be in his presence. Chase knew that once word got out about that fact, everyone would blame him. And if he was being honest with himself, he wasn't so sure that they'd be wrong. Deep within his heart, he felt that he was in no way ready for the level of hardship that he would need to deal with from this point forward.

CHAPTER 4

TWENTY-EIGHT YEARS LATER

Friday, August 30th, 2021

"Remember, Scott, school..."

"...comes first. I know Mom." Scott Dempsey had a knack for finishing his Mother's sentences. It wasn't a knack, really. There was no trick to it at all. She could be more predictable than the hours of the day. After eighteen years of life, Scott had heard every one of her pre-packaged warnings a thousand times. "Don't worry, I'm not here to party," he reassured her before adding "...much."

"I think your brother partied enough for all of us while he was in school," Chase Dempsey chimed in with a laugh from behind the wheel.

"Yeah, well you'd better not take after him," Scott's mother, Suzanne said, turning around and looking over the seat with a wink and a smile. "You're not of legal drinking age, buddy."

"Mom, Pete had a 3.7 GPA last semester at Kutz," Scott argued jokingly. "Trust me, you guys have nothing to worry about with me. I'll even beat that!"

Chase and Suzanne exchanged a quick glance across the front seat. They knew that they didn't have anything to worry about. Scott was always well-balanced and never had any trouble prioritizing his own life. Growing up he managed to have a steady stream of A's, with a very occasional A-, and still have time for sports and friends. And he did this without ever getting into any real trouble. They had no reason to think college would be any different.

Their Honda Pilot cruised smoothly up Rt. 100, just minutes away from South Cuthbert University - Scott's address for the next four years of his life.

"It's beautiful out here. Scott, these trees look amazing when they're turning for Fall," Suzanne commented.

Chase motioned towards the roadway before them. "Scott, when your Mom and I first started at South Cuthbert, this was a one-lane road and the trees on either side formed an overhang that covered the road. It was like a natural archway."

Suzanne perked up. "Oh right, remember that? It was so beautiful. I'd love to live out here."

Scott leaned forward in between the seats to get a better look. "I bet it was like you were in a tunnel. Wait...did you say you want to live out here?"

"Don't let your Mom worry you, son," Chase said with a laugh. "We're years away from moving out of our current home. You can rest assured that here you'll be safely 'away at school'." He added air quotes for effect.

"Besides," Suzanne chimed in, "your Dad still thinks we're buying a Winnebago to live in and travel the country."

"It would be amazing!" Chase retorted. "Think about how much we could experience. We've barely left PA... and we're gonna be fifty!"

"Fifty?!" Suzanne asked. "When's that, exactly?"

"You know...eventually!" he said, absently waving his hand in the air.

Scott leaned back and laughed to himself as the two went back and forth. It was the kind of laugh he was used to having while listening to his parents banter. He was happy to be going away to college for the experience of living on his own. But he would definitely miss his parents.

The moment was interrupted by a slight lunge forward when the car suddenly came upon a traffic light as they entered the borough.

"Guess that's the end of that," Chase said. Up ahead he could see that it was more town than landscape - South Cuthbert Borough.

"God, I miss this place," Suzanne said as she looked out the window.

"What about you, Dad?" Scott asked. "You miss it here?"

"Me?" Chase asked, pausing before he answered. "Oh yeah...definitely."

Suzanne reached out and took hold of Chase's hand. His hand gripped hers tightly. Scott seemed blissfully unaware of the gesture as he examined the shops near the intersection.

South Cuthbert, PA, located about twenty-five miles west of Philadelphia, is home to South Cuthbert University. SCU is a State School and a favorite among Southeastern PA residents. In fact, Scott knew a number of high school classmates that would be joining him out here, including his roommate here, Jim Wooderson. Or Woody, as he was more commonly known.

The school is located in the Borough, which has a very small town feel to it. Streets are lined with Mom and Pop shops. The buildings and homes, for the most part, had an older look to them and it seemed to Scott that some of them must be a hundred years old or more.

As they moved through town, Scott noticed that they were at the intersection of Stone Boulevard and Cleer Street and remembered the joke he'd heard at Freshman Orientation that you come in Cleer and you go out Stoned. He also remembered pretending to laugh at it and thinking that it sounded like an old and lazy joke that had to have been made up decades ago. But people still keep it alive for some odd reason.

As they approached university grounds, he noticed that there were less businesses, more houses, and more students. Probably not freshmen, he thought to himself. Not if they were already walking around off campus. He noticed that some of them had Greek letters on their shirts. He saw that some looked like actual letters and others that were just unrecognizable symbols. Unrecognizable to him, at least. But he'd seen enough movies to know they were Greek.

"You guys were in a fraternity and sorority, weren't you?" he asked his parents.

There was a pause before Suzanne answered. "Yep, I was in D Phi E and your Dad was in Kappa Chi Rho. Why?" she asked, turning back with a smile. "You thinking about pledging?"

Scott let out a light laugh. "Eh, I don't know. Probably not. I don't think I would want to deal with the hazing."

Chase sat quietly in the driver's seat, gripping the steering wheel slightly tighter with each moment. Suzanne glanced over and noticed his tell, then stepped in. "Well, I don't think that hazing is that bad anymore, Scott. They have really cracked down on that in recent years."

"Really? Have they, Dad? I imagine it was tough when you were there, right?"

Chase took a deep breath, then painted a smile on his face. It was the same smile he'd put on a hundred times before.

25

"Yeah, I'm sure that any serious hazing is a thing of the past now, bud. They probably aren't able to do anything serious without fear of getting in trouble and losing their charter."

"You really think so?" Scott asked.

"Yeah, totally!" Chase was now hiding deep below his manufactured exterior. "I would bet that it'd be Brothers making you run to get them food and shit like that. Maybe some roman chairs while you recite things from the Esoteric Manual. They'll make you drink for sure."

"Chase!" Suzanne protested with a laugh.

"What? They're totally gonna do that. They're not supposed to. I'd say they are more likely to go lightly in that area these days. Schools are cracking down hard on that now. Too many incidents. But I can tell you that it's not gonna be like paddling or standing around naked or anything like that."

Scott sat wide-eyed for a moment before his attention was diverted as his Dad turned right down Wilkes Avenue and he could now see the campus buildings come into view.

"I still can't get over how much all of this has changed," Suzanne said.

"You got that right," Chase replied. "Hey Scott, this parking garage here didn't even exist when we were here. In fact, a lot of these buildings didn't exist when we were here. I used to live in the house right on the other side of this parking garage. Back then that was just a flat parking lot. My bedroom window had a clear view of campus. Right now I'd be looking at a concrete wall. I remember the first day of school, my roommate turned his speakers out the window at 7:30 in the morning, turned the volume all the way up and blasted "Reveille". Woke up half the campus," he told him laughing.

Scott chuckled at the thought. Though not as hard as his Dad did. He normally found himself faking a laugh whenever his

26

Father told him, what he thought would be, a funny story. But he had to admit that this was one of his better ones.

"Ok, Oreland Hall," Chase said. "Sucks that you and Woody couldn't get into the new ones. I spent my first year in Oreland. It's very...antiseptic."

"Yeah, you're not kidding," Scott said as he helped to search for a parking spot. "The dorms they had us in at orientation were much nicer than what I've seen of these old ones." Scott interrupted himself and leaned forward quickly between the front seats pointing. "Spot! Right there on the left."

"Yep, I got it," Chase said as he pulled in.

There were two dorms along Wilkes Avenue. Coan was on the corner of Wilkes and Central, with Oreland immediately next to it. Both were eight stories high with three wings jutting out like spokes from the center. Scott had wandered into Coan the month prior during orientation to look around, and he remembered that it seemed pretty sterile with cinder block walls, all painted white. Low grade carpets covered the hallway floors. The tile floors in the dorm rooms reminded him of his high school hallways. He figured that since they were all identical from the outside, that he could expect Oreland to look pretty much the same on the inside as Coan.

The sidewalks were busy with families unloading their cars and carrying things towards the entrance to the dorms. The parking spot they had happened to find was just feet away from the walkway leading up to the front door of the dorm. Chase popped open the tailgate and began unloading all of Soctt's things.

"Hey, I hope you plan on keeping all of that on your side of the room!" they heard a voice call out. Scott recognized the voice immediately. "Woody! What's up bud?"

Walking towards them, and pulling a cart behind him, was Woody, Scott's high school friend, and now roommate.

"How ya' doin', Demps?" Woody called out. He had a big smile and an obvious look of anticipation on his face.

"Not bad, man! You ready for this?"

"I sure hope so!" Woody joked. "How's it going Mr. and Mrs. Dempsey?"

Chase and Suzanne came around from the other side of the car to greet Woody.

"Woody, how's it going?" Chase asked as he walked over to shake his hand. "Ya' got a cart, sweet!"

"Yeah, you guys had perfect timing actually! My folks just left and I was bringing this down when I saw you."

"Awesome!" Scott said. He quickly began loading the cart with his belongings.

Chase and Suzanne followed suit and between the four of them were able to get a fair amount of Scott's things into the first trip.

"*Perfect*," Scott thought to himself. "*Let's not make this take any longer than it needs to.*" As much as he loved his parents, he was not immune to being embarrassed by them.

Stepping off of the elevator, Woody led the group towards their destination. "We're in 444. It's down this hallway, second to the last door on the left."

Arriving in the room, Scott found that Woody had already taken the bed closest to the window and the desk on the left, which was fine with him. They began unloading Scott's things, with Suzanne taking extra care to try not to be too motherly. Her face was contorting itself into various shapes as she held back on offering advice regarding where to put things.

It took only one more trip to get everything up to the room. Suzanne had packed enough food to feed him for a solid two weeks. The food comprised nearly half of what they needed to carry to the room.

"Well, I guess that's it!" Scott said as they brought in the last of his things.

"Do you need help unpacking?" his Mom asked, not quite ready to let go of her youngest child.

"No thanks," Scott replied. He was too wrapped up in his new room to even take notice of her demeanor. "I think I'm good now. I can take care of all of this. Might take me a while to really get it how I want it."

"Oh...Okay." She tried her best to hide her disappointment.

Chase, on the other hand, was well aware of what she was going through and knew that prolonging it would only make it more difficult. "You know what. He's got a lot to do, Suz. We should probably just get going and let him get started."

"Um, yeah. You're probably right," she reluctantly agreed. "But, Scott, let me get a picture of you two first! Class of '25!"

Scott jokingly rolled his eyes at Woody and his Dad. "Fiiiinnneee," he said, doing his best to sound exasperated.

The two stood together while she snapped the photo with her phone. Scott was pretty sure that he blinked, but decided not to say anything. He then walked his parents out into the hallway and gave them both hugs.

"Thanks guys, both of you. I'll do well up here. I'll make you both proud, ok? I promise."

Suzanne smiled. "You make us proud every day of your life. You just do your best here and always try to do the right thing. *That* is what would make us both proud."

"Ok," he said with a smile. "I will."

"Good luck, bud." Chase said as he gave him a hug. "Love ya'. If you need anything, you call me. Got it?"

"You too Dad," he said as he patted him three times on the back, per his usual. "And yeah, I will totally call you. I promise."

Scott watched as his Mom and Dad walked down the hall and disappeared into the lobby as they turned towards the elevator. He smiled slightly and went back into his room.

"Okay, WoodMan. Time to get started!"

And with that, the first chapter of the rest of Scott Dempsey's life had begun.

CHAPTER 5

With Scott's parents now on their way back home, the unpacking and organization began without abandon.

"Toss me some of that putty stuff." Woody called across the room.

They knew that the walls in their dorm room would be nothing but cinder blocks and that they wouldn't be able to put thumbtacks in them. So Scott had brought a ball of putty to use for hanging their posters. He threw the wad across the room to Woody, who was perched precariously with one foot on the bed and one on a stack of plastic bins while he hung a poster of a bright yellow McClaren. For the next year they'd be staring at this, along with a vintage Corvette, a Nirvana poster and one depicting the album cover of Pearl Jam Ten. The two of them had learned early on in their friendships, some three years back, that they both shared a love for 90's grunge and fast cars. 444 Oreland Hall would be an homage to both.

They both connected their devices to the Wi-Fi and set up the TV and the Roku Stick. Woody had called the far left corner for all of his Hockey gear. It was a smell that Scott had conceded to when they agreed to be roommates. Within a couple of hours, all of their things were put away and Scott fell backwards into his beanbag.

"Whew! That was a lot more work than I thought!"

Woody laid back onto his bed and stretched out.

"I don't know about you. But I need a beer," he said with a laugh.

"Yeah, we're gonna' have to figure that shit out," Scott agreed. "Who'll get that for us out here?"

Almost as if it were on cue, their answer appeared in the open doorway.

"How you guys doing? My name's Billy Archibald. I'm in the next room over. You can call me Archie."

Archie leaned through the doorway with a hand grasping either side of the door frame to hold him up. His stocky frame looked like it might take the door frame with it.

Scott and Woody stood up and walked over to meet him.

"Hi I'm Woody. This is Scott."

Scott reached out and shook Archie's hand. "Hey, Scott Dempsey. Call me Demps."

"Nice to meet you guys! You guys new here? Freshmen?"

"Yeah," Scott replied. "Barely been here two hours."

"Awesome, welcome! You guys are gonna' love it. Listen, one of my Fraternity Brothers is having a party tonight up on Miner Street. You guys interested?"

The two of them glanced at each other. Their parents probably hadn't even gotten home yet and the two of them were already invited to a party.

"Yeah, sure!" they both said, nearly in unison.

"How do we get there?" Scott asked.

Arch waved the questions off. "Don't worry about it. You can walk up with me and Schoff. He's my roommate. He's in the fraternity too."

"What frat is it?" Scott asked.

A wry smile appeared on Archie's face. "Well first of all...it's not a frat. It's a Fraternity."

It sounded to Scott like it was said half jokingly. But he got the feeling that the other half was deadly serious.

"Kappa Chi Rho," Archie continued. "KXP. You'll see the letters around campus. See, check it out."

Arch turned his leg towards the two to reveal a KXP tattoo on the outside of his ankle.

"We're called The Crows."

"Aaahhhh," Scott and Woody nodded as the point finally dawned on them. Chi...Row. ChiRow. Crow.

"Well listen, we'll probably head up around 8:30 or so. So be ready."

"Alright cool, thanks Arch. Nice to meet ya'," Woody said.

"Yeah thanks!" Scott chimed in to make sure he was heard too.

Just a few hours after he had embarked on an anti-Greek rant in the car, Scott was suddenly taken in by the idea of a fraternity. He had no idea what was involved, what the reason was for their existence or what it meant to be in one. But the confidence that Archie had just conveyed when speaking about it and made everything sound incredibly enticing to him. He immediately wanted to know more. Throw in the fact that he was sporting a cool tattoo, and it was settled. Scott Dempsey was officially intrigued.

CHAPTER 6

Archie and Schoff's room seemed to be the meeting place for everyone before they headed out to the party. Scott and Woody had just walked out of their door, and were gathering in the hallway outside of Archie and Schoff's door, when Webber came walking down the hall. Webber was the Resident Advisor on their floor and also a Crow. A few minutes later Demps heard the sound of females laughing from the other end of the hallway. He turned to see three very attractive girls heading in their direction. He was loving college so far.

"Let's get this year started!" one of them called out excitedly. "Whoooo!!!"

"Woo hoo! Fucking right!" Arch yelled back from his doorway, surprising Scott. For a second Scott had thought that the girls might be talking to him.

"Hey, this is Demps and Woody," Archie said to the girls. "Guys, this is Sydney, Shelly and Mags."

"Are you guys freshmen?" Sydney asked.

"That's what they tell me," Scott replied. Woody laughed and nodded, trying not to seem too awkward.

"Well stick close to us and we'll take care of you," Mags chimed in.

"Fine by me," Scott said with a smile, pretty certain that he nailed his first female interaction of college.

Miner Street was a few blocks North of campus. Well, at least Scott thought it was North. He wasn't exactly sure which direction was up yet. He'd barely even seen any of the actual campus yet and he was already headed *off-campus*. The group was walking up the street when it occurred to Scott he really didn't know where they even were.

"So whose house are we going to?" Scott asked.

"Dommie Watkins. He's a Crow too." Archie called back from the front of the group. He was a few steps ahead of everyone and turned back slightly while answering. He was a quick mover with lots of energy. Scott felt as though he needed to speed-walk just to keep up. In fact, he had the feeling that everyone was, and that Archie was used to it.

Their small army of party-goers was trekking up South Darlington Street. Most of whom Scott and Woody either barely knew or had just met fifteen minutes prior.

"Hey, Arch, how many kegs is Dommie having?" Shelly called out from the back.

"Two I think. Plenty though, I'm sure. Plus, you know...whatever else," Archie yelled back with a knowing laugh. "And there's also a Late-night at the Brown House."

Late-Night? That's a new one! Scott thought to himself. College was definitely going to be a new world for him. A week ago there were no "late-nights". Sometimes a friend's parents would go away and they'd have a party. Otherwise it was just drinking in the woods and trying not to get caught.

"Where's the Brown House?" he asked, trying to sound like a Late-night was an everyday occurrence for him.

"It's only like a half block off campus," Sydney answered while latching onto his arm, startling him a bit more than he would've expected. "Not far from your dorm. We'll hit it on the way home."

"Oh ok, perfect!" he said, glancing at Woody. The two of them had entered completely new territory.

35

CHAPTER 7

Holy shit.

That was all that Scott could think to himself when he walked into the party. He was absolutely no longer anywhere near being in Kansas anymore, and was officially in a world separate from what he used to know.

Scott was used to walking into a party at home. That was nothing new. But at home the parties mainly consisted of his own classmates, or people younger than him trying to glom onto the group and get some cred. At home every kid looked alike. They were all clones. The hairstyles were all identical, along with the clothes and the drinks in their hands. And the house was usually well-decorated and clearly owned by adults that were, for whatever reason, not present at that particular moment in time.

But here, in a house that was rented out by six 19-22 year olds that Scott had never met, he could sense immediately that this was definitely not one of those parties. The house was packed with people of all different sorts. Each with different clothing styles. Different haircuts. Different ethnicities. Different age groups. It was like nothing he'd seen before.

"You ok there?" he heard a female voice ask with a chuckle. He didn't recognize the voice at first. But the tug on his arm made him swing around to see the face of Sydney Moore. "You look scared," she said with a laugh.

Scott quickly considered the idea that she might be right and forced himself to relax and smile back at her with a laugh.

"Oh, so I guess you're going to be the cool sophomore that makes fun of me? I was wondering which one of you that would be."

"Ha ha, no that would typically be Mags," she said, pointing towards her friend. "She's the fun-loving asshole of the group. Don't get me wrong. She's awesome. But she'll razz the shit out of you. Don't take it seriously though. If she's doing it, it means she likes you. Me though, I'm more of the 'stick with me and I'll show you how to survive' type gal." She winked at Scott and he could immediately feel a connection with her.

He let out a laugh while scanning the room, then gave her a sideways glance, "Well then I guess I'll just need to stick with you."

The two locked eyes for a moment, but were suddenly interrupted by a loud group of screams from the other room.

A huge grin came across Sydney's face. "Oh my God! No they are not!" Grabbing Scott by the hand she pulled him through the crowd towards the commotion. "Follow me!"

He felt like he was barely touching the floor as she guided him across the room. Turning the corner into the kitchen, he again heard the crowd erupting as he caught a glimpse of a body flying horizontally through the air. Following Sydney to the front of the crowd, he could now see six guys, lined up in rows of three across from one another, next to the keg, with their arms locked.

The crowd began chanting "Schoff! Schoff! Schoff!". Scott turned to see Schoff standing on the far side of the hallway leading into the kitchen with his arms raised. Schoff let out a loud, primal scream, then broke into a sprint and took a diving leap landing in their locked arms. The six of them then hoisted Schoff's legs into the air as a seventh man shoved the tap from the keg into his waiting mouth.

"Diving Keg Stands!" Sydney yelled, jumping up and down in delight while she grabbed Scott by his arm.

Keg stands were nothing new to Scott. In high school the Harrington brothers were famous for hosting barrels in the woods behind the school. Scott had done more than his fair share of keg stands at those. But running across the room and diving into one was completely new to him. This was a game changer for him.

"One, two, three, four..." the crowd started counting in unison. Scott joined in as Sydney counted alongside him. "...Sixteen. Seventeen. Eighteen. Nineteen...Ohhhh!"

Scott threw his head back along with everyone else when Schoff tapped out and was brought down to his feet.

"Who's next?!" Archie yelled out as Schoff worked to get his bearings.

Before Scott could even scan the room to see who the lucky person would be, he heard the answer.

"This guy right here!!!" Sydney screamed at the top of her lungs.

He felt his heart drop as he saw every face in the room turn towards him. His eyes went immediately to Sydney.

"I'm gonna fucking kill you." he said with a smile.

"Welcome to SCU!" she shot back as she jumped out into the middle of the kitchen and addressed the crowd.

"Hey guys! Scott Dempsey here is a freshman. This is his first college party and this diving keg stand is going to be his first fucking beer at South Cuthbert University! Let's make this count!"

Everyone in the kitchen, and other rooms from what it sounded like to Scott, began screaming out in approval for this incredible opportunity.

Scott felt a dozen hands shove him from behind and usher him through the kitchen door into the hallway. He turned around to see the image of the keg in the kitchen and a path lined with drunken college students between him and destination.

"Go! Go! Go! Go! Go!" they chanted as he mentally prepared himself for the feat. Scanning the hall once more, he caught the eyes of Sydney Moore standing at the end with a smile on her face. An energy burst through him and his foot catapulted him from his sedentary position and into a full sprint. He could hear the cheers as he picked up speed. They grew even louder as he planted his feet and took off into the air. When he landed in the arms of the six men he was trusting to catch him, the seventh almost simultaneously shoved the tap into his open mouth and began the flow of beer into his throat.

His heart was filled with joy at the sound of the cheers that erupted from the crowd. He'd been at college for a matter of hours, and his first beer was delivered via a diving keg stand to the joy of everyone around.

Scott Dempsey was an immediate legend.

The crowd counted off the seconds for him, finally maxing out at twenty-five before he tapped the arm of the one controlling the tap. The crowd was elated as the scene unfolded.

"Whooooo!!! Fucking Demps! That was awesome!" Archie called out, offering up a high five as he crossed the room while Scott was lowered to the floor.

"Guys, this is Demps." he said to the group of guys standing around the keg. "He lives in the room next door to me and Schoff."

Demps did his best to gather himself and take in exactly who he was meeting as the group each introduced themselves one by one.

"Demps this is Dommie, Craig, CJ, Matt, Ryan and Jimmy Cacc."

Archie pronounced Cacc like cock. Jimmy was quick to clarify, in a thick New York accent,

"Cacc's short for Caccavelli. It's not because I've got a huge schlong."

"Yeah that's for sure!" CJ joked.

Scott was sure he wouldn't remember any of their names. But he recognized that they all had the letters KXP either stitched across their chests or adorning their baseball caps.

"You guys are all Crows?" he asked.

"Fucking right!" Dommie responded. "Stick with us man. We'll show you the best time here."

Scott smiled. He one hundred percent believed him. "Sounds good to me," he said, wiping the last drops of beer from his chin. "So whose house is this anyway?" he asked.

"It's CJ, Dommie and Matt's place," Archie answered. "Derek and Bierman live here too. They're in the other room."

Scott began to peer through the doorway, as if he'd have any idea which of the fifty or more people in that room were Derek or Bierman. He was interrupted by the feel of a hand lightly grabbing him by the shoulder.

"These guys aren't causing you any trouble are they, Demps?"

He turned to see Sydney sidling up next to him. Her green eyes peered right into his and her face was so close that her hair rested on his shoulder.

"Oh, well hello there!" he said with a smile. Doing his best to turn on the charm. "These guys? No, these guys have been great! They didn't drop me, so right now they're my best friends here!"

They all laughed and Dommie gave Scott a fist bump. "Haha, yeah man, it's all about trust. And shit man, you've been at South Cuthbert for, what...five minutes? And you're already getting in with awesome chicks like Sydney? That's my boy! Moving fast!"

"Who says he's moving fast, Dommie? Maybe I'm moving in on him!" she shot back with a smile and wide eyes.

"Ohhhh!" they all said loudly and in unison.

Scott laughed and was enjoying the friendly back and forth between Sydney and the group. It was clear that they hung around each other a lot.

"Demps, let me pour you one," CJ said as he skillfully worked the tap and filled the red Solo cup. "Here you go man, no cover charge for you. You earned it."

"Thanks much...CJ, right?" he asked, hoping he got it right.

"Yep, you got it man. Impressive!" he replied with a laugh.

Sydney then grabbed Scott by the arm and pulled him to the side. "Come on, Demps, I'll introduce you around. I don't want these assholes to be your main impression of this school."

She laughed and shot a playful glance at them over her shoulder as she led Scott into the other room.

"Ooohhhhhhhh!" they all sounded out again in response.

"Go get her, Demps!" Scott heard one of them yell as the rest howled with laughter.

Get her indeed. So far he's had nothing but good interactions here at South Cuthbert. Archie and Schoff seemed to be the coolest neighbors he could ask for. The Brothers of Kappa Chi Rho were very welcoming to him, and he felt immediately at ease with them. He also had felt a clear attraction to Sydney Moore since the moment he'd laid eyes on her.

The attraction was only growing stronger as she walked him around the party and introduced him to everyone one by one. She had everything he could possibly want. Funny, smart, beautiful. She was magnetic. Everyone seemed to be drawn to her, and here she was for some reason latching herself onto him.

In reality, it probably should've come as no surprise to Scott. His chiseled, scruff-lined jaw and 6'1" athletic build were easy for her to notice. Plus, his charm and sense of humor could put anyone at ease within moments. But there was a side of him that never believed those things about himself, and it was that part of him that had him in awe that he was currently spending his time with this beautiful girl. No. He had to remind himself that he is in college now. This woman.

The rest of the night went as well as Scott could've hoped. He eventually found his way back to Woody, who was hanging around with Archie and the rest of the Crow Brothers. Sydney had reconnected with Mags and Shelly and the three of them joined the group as well.

They played drinking games - Anchorman, Boat Races, Quarters. Scott showed off some impressive skills that not even he knew he'd had.

There were more Freshman guys there than he thought he would have seen. He felt that the Fraternity Brothers would each be tasked with inviting as many Freshman girls as possible, of which there were definitely plenty. But he also found himself making friends with a number of guys that weren't members of the Fraternity.

He came to find out that each of them came with a Crow, just as he did. He started to realize that this wasn't just a party. It was an unofficial recruitment event. Which was fine with him. If this was going to be representative of his college existence, he had no problem with that. This was the most fun he'd had in recent memory. He just hoped that he *could* remember it. Because it was also the most drinking he can ever recall doing.

He was becoming more and more aware of his balance, or lack thereof, and he felt Sydney's hand resting on his back to steady him.

"You ok there, hun?" she asked with a smile

"Oh yeah," he said, with a wave of his hand. "I'm fiiiiinnnee. No need to worry about me."

"Haha, sure." She stared quietly for a few seconds, as if contemplating something. "Tell you what, how about we get outta here?" She looked him in the eye and smiled.

Scott was more than happy to comply. The two made their way towards the door without telling anyone they were leaving. Scott caught Woody's eye along the way and Woody gave him an approving nod.

Scott and Sydney made their way down South Darlington Street. He was impressed with how well she seemed to handle her alcohol.

They reached Wilkes Avenue and Scott instinctively began to head towards Oreland Hall, when Sydney took him by the arm.

"How about we head back to my place instead?" she said smiling.

"Oh?! Ok...sure! I'm...I'm..that's..." he started to respond nervously. "What I mean is, yep!"

Sydney let out a loud laugh and looked at him. "You're really cute. I like you."

She stood up on her tippy toes, stretched her neck as far as her 5'7" frame would allow and kissed him. Scott returned the kiss, leaning down to ease the strain on her. The energy between them was palpable and the two embraced as they began to kiss more passionately.

"Exactly how far away are you?" he asked while pulling away for a moment. Sydney burst out laughing before responding.

"Just a few minutes in that direction," she said while pointing. "Over on Elm."

"You're not in the dorms?" he asked.

"Nope, I'm in a house with Mags, Shelly and two other girls from AST. That's our sorority." She paused and smiled. "But I have my own room."

Scott smiled knowingly as the two kissed once more and started walking towards her house. Their pace quickened with each step.

Arriving at the house, they stepped inside the door and immediately embraced. Unable to let go of one another, they clumsily made their way up the stairs and fell into Sydney's bed together.

The two stopped kissing long enough to look into each other's eyes. The energy and attraction could be felt by both of them. It was clear that this wasn't going to be just a fling.

Sydney leaned in and gave Scott small kisses, each time returning to meet his gaze. She smiled and said the words that cemented it for Scott.

"I think that you and I are going to be good together."

CHAPTER 8

TWO MONTHS LATER
Sunday, October 24th - 7:30 AM

The loud hum of Scott's phone vibrating violently on Sydney Moore's nightstand was barely enough to pull him out of his deep sleep. He squeezed his eyes shut as the morning sun squeezed into the room through the space between the shade and the window frame. A light thumping could be felt inside his cloudy head. He had spent the night prior hanging out at CJ's apartment with some KXP Brothers and the rest of his Pledge Class. He then met up with Sydney to spend the rest of the night at her house. So much of his time these days was spent doing Kappa Chi Rho pledge activities. The last thing he wanted in the world right now was to interrupt his time with her.

His eyes opened slowly and he pulled his hand out from under the pillow. Reaching over to the nightstand, he picked up the phone to find out who it was that was calling him so early in the morning.

The words 'BROTHER ARCHIE' flashed across his screen. All of the Crow Brothers were listed in his Contacts as 'BROTHER' so as not to ever take the chance of missing a call from one of them. Even the perception that he had ignored a call from a Brother could result in him dealing with a world of shit. Archie, who was the Pledge Master for his Pledge Class, was the least likely to give him hell for a missed call. But he knew just

44

from the sight of his name that any chance of having time with Sydney this morning was over.

He felt Sydney's body spoon up behind him.

"Oh no, don't answer it," she pleaded, squeezing his body tightly and attempting to hold his arms down.

Scott smiled at the notion that someone who had been through pledging a Sorority, and would likely lose her shit if one of her Sorority's pledges ignored her call, would suggest not answering it.

"Are you kidding? You know I have to."

"Pledging is so stupid. Why do you guys do it so differently than we do?"

"What," he chuckled, "you mean why don't we wrap each other in toilet paper to show how connected we are to each other?"

He clicked the green "Answer" icon on his screen and prepared for his day to begin.

"Hey, Brother Arch," he said with as much respect as he could muster at this hour.

"Hey, Scott, we need everyone over at the house right now," Arch demanded. His tone was more hurried than Scott had ever heard from him. Especially for this early in the morning.

Scott quickly pulled himself halfway into a leaning position, propping himself up on his elbow. "Uh, yeah sure. What's up? Everything ok?"

"Just grab your Pledge Brothers and get over to the House right away. I'll explain when you get here."

Scott closed his eyes, trying to will himself back to sleep, hoping that this phone call was nothing but a dream. "Ok, sure. Let me get on the horn to everyone and we'll see you in a bit. What is this about though? Are we in trouble?"

There was a pause on the other end before Arch replied. "No, you're not in...listen. Just grab everyone and get over here. And..."

Another pause.

"...and Coleman and Wilby, don't worry about...uh...getting them. Just you and the rest of the guys."

"What?" Scott asked, a bit confused. "Are they there already?"

"You only need to worry about the rest. Just get here right away, ok?" Archie demanded.

He had hung up before even giving Scott a chance to reply, confusing Scott even further. Scott had only known Archie for a couple of months. But from what he's seen from him, the behavior he had just exhibited was highly unusual.

It was only seven weeks ago when Rush Week had begun. Rush Week consists of a series of school sponsored events giving students the opportunity to meet with any or all of the Greek Organizations on campus. It allows the students to meet the Brothers of each Fraternity and see if they feel a connection with any specific groups. The Fraternities then have the opportunity during this time to meet the students, give them information about their respective organizations, and to also determine who they'd like to invite to officially join.

If someone were to be invited to join, it was not just a matter of suddenly being a member. In order to become a Brother of a Fraternity, one would need to go through a Pledge Period. This typically consists of eight weeks of learning about the organization and becoming more acquainted with the initiated Brothers or Sisters. This was also the period of time when the common practice of hazing would take place.

The Crow's decision to invite Scott to pledge was also an easy one. Scott's fun-loving personality made all of the Brothers love him. And his good looks and personality made it clear that he'd be a big help in drawing plenty of girls to their parties. Which, once Rush was over, was really the main goal. Inviting non-Brother males to a Fraternity party was high on the list of banned behavior. With the exception of non-Brother roommates or close friends, which sometimes even were members of other Fraternities, the vast majority of tickets sold for a Kappa Chi Rho party were sold to female members of the student population.

During the eight-week pledge period, pledges would be given a Pledge Pin, which would be expected to be worn at all times, as well as a name tag identifying them as a Pledge of Kappa Chi Rho. The name tag was only required Monday through Friday between the hours of 8am and 8pm.

Pledges would also receive a Pledge Paddle, adorned with the Fraternity letters and the Kappa Chi Rho Coat of Arms. They'd be required to obtain the signature of every active Brother on the back of the paddle before the end of the eight-week period. Finally, they would receive an Esoteric Manual, which contained the history of Kappa Chi Rho and of the information surrounding their service goals and core values. Each week, the Pledge Master would assign a portion of the manual for them to study, and then tested them at the end of the week.

The process was taken seriously and, as such, leadership within the Pledge Class was required in order to help them govern themselves, as they were not yet official members of the organization. The Pledge Class would be required to elect from their members a President and Vice President that would be expected to lead them when their Pledge Master was not around.

Scott's Pledge Brothers, 12 in all, felt the same natural attraction to him that everyone else always seemed to feel. He was an obvious choice for them as President of their Pledge Class. As a result, whenever the Pledges presence was required suddenly at the Fraternity house, Scott's number was the first one the Brothers would call.

These days, more often than not, Scott was finding that Sydney was by his side whenever that call would come. They've become inseparable since they met and Scott had taken to sleeping at her house most nights. Woody had been joking that he loves living on his own.

For Scott, he'd felt like he'd won the life lottery. It wasn't his first serious girlfriend. After all, he'd spent most of his Sophomore and Junior year of High School dating Meg Haney. So he was no stranger to relationships. But this one was different. Sydney was different. He'd never felt so at ease with someone as he did with her. Life with her just worked. And as far as he could tell, she felt the same way. The arm wrapping around him and squeezing his upper body right now was telling him that he was correct.

"Mmmm...please don't go," she groaned, dragging out the word 'go'. "Tell them I tied you up and wouldn't let you leave."

"Ooh, sounds tempting. Can I get a commitment on that for later?" he said, rolling over to come face to face with her.

"Nope, sorry. Limited time offer. Now or never. But I have to warn you that I'm pretty horny. So if you leave, I may have to grab the first guy that I see walking past the house and call him in here."

"That's pretty messed up. But I have noticed that the bartender from Jake's has been walking his dog past here every morning around this time."

"Duane? Oh, he's pretty hairy. That's super hot," she said while laying small kisses on his cheeks.

"Ok, well it'll be awkward seeing him all the time when I turn 21. But, I've got a few years to get over it. So I'm gonna have to chance it." He kissed her and rolled over to the edge of the bed. In one swift motion he reached his hand to the ground, grabbed his pants, stood up and thrust his leg into them.

"Call me later?" She smiled at him with the sly, questioning grin that he remembered being the first thing that made him want her.

"Absolutely," he said as pulled his T-Shirt over his head. Then, sliding on his shoes and leaning in towards her, he gave her one last kiss. "I love you."

"I love you too," she whispered.

It was so new for them to say this. But it felt like they'd been saying it for years.

"Have fun being all rowdy and masculine, Pledge!"

"Oh you know it," he said quietly with a smile while leaving the room. He didn't want to wake her roommates. "Try to get some more sleep. I'm sure you've got a full day of harassing your own pledges ahead of you."

He headed down the steps and exited to the street. Taking out his phone, he began the process of gathering together the rest of his Pledge Class.

CHAPTER 9

Scott walked quickly along Elm Street as he typed into the group chat they'd set up for their Pledge Class. He decided that they'd follow the typical protocol, which was to meet outside of the parking garage on the corner of Central and Wilkes and walk over together as a group. And only as a group.

They had learned the importance of unity early on in the pledge process, and they had learned it the hard way. The first time that they were all summoned to the house, they each showed up either alone or in small groups. It took forty-five minutes before all twelve of them were present. The question asked of each of them when they entered the house was "Where are your Pledge Brothers?"

They were immediately sent into the Chapter Room to do push ups until the others arrived. The ones that arrived first found themselves doing push-ups until the last ones arrived.

Scott had arrived first. He lost count after one hundred push-ups. And that was roughly when he stopped trying to do real push-ups too.

Ever since that night, whenever the Pledge Class was required to be somewhere, they showed up together. If one was missing, they all were missing.

Unity. Brotherhood.

So today they would all go over together. All of them except for Coleman and Wilby, at least.

Why would Archie say to come without them? Scott wondered.

He had to assume that they crashed at 403 last night. But if so, why weren't they answering on the group chat?

The Pledge Class consisted of twelve men that semester. There was Scott, of course. He was joined by:

Woody

Wick (short for Chadwick)

Ethan (Addressed most often just as 'E')

Jamie (affectionately known as Phatty)

Casey

Robbie

Chewie (who was 6'7" and had brown hair down to the center of his back)

Danny Garabedian (AKA Badass Danny G)

Phil Trout (or just Trout)

Fran Coleman (or simply Coleman)

and Will Bonnetti (shortened to Wilby)

Two months ago none of them had ever even met before. Today they were Pledge Brothers that have embarked on an adventure that would take them to places they'd never imagine possible on their own.

The other nine members of the Pledge Class arrived at the meeting point surprisingly quickly, considering the early hour on a Saturday morning. It was a product of the fear instilled in them the past six weeks for not being available.

Scott explained to everyone that Archie's instructions were to come without Coleman and Wilby.

"Where the hell are those assholes?" Wick asked. "I don't feel like reciting the names of all of the active Kappa Chi Rho chapters just because we showed up without them."

"They're probably there already," Scott assured him.

"They're probably fucking still passed out," Robbie said leaning back onto the stop sign, exasperated. "They probably did something stupid there last night, like shit in the bathtub or something, and now we'll all have to pay the price for it."

"Well shit, have they replied on the group chat? Should we wait for them to, at least?" Casey asked.

"As long as we..." Scott was interrupted by the ring of his phone.

"Is that them?" Trout asked, almost grabbing the phone from Scott's hand.

"Easy, asshole!" Scott exclaimed, yanking his arm away. "I've got it."

He looked down at his phone. "It's Arch."

He answered the phone and put it on speaker. "Brother Archie, what's up?"

"Where the fuck are you guys?" Archie yelled back.

"We all just got to our meeting point. Are Coleman and Wilby there already?"

"Shit. Get over here now!" Arch yelled. Scott and the rest of his Pledge Brothers recoiled in surprise

Scott attempted to reply. "But Br..."

"No, don't worry about waiting for...just get here...right...now." Archie paused. "The ten of you. The ten of you get here right now. Don't wait. And don't worry about... just get here now. You don't have to worry about it just being the ten of you. Trust me."

They now suddenly heard what Scott was unable to convince them of. Archie was not acting like himself. Something was clearly not right. But Scott decided, as President of the Pledge Class, that he needed to take the lead and move things forward.

"Alright, well you heard him, guys. Let's get moving. Trout's probably right. Those guys are probably still passed out. Let's get over there and we'll find out what the hell is going on. If we need to answer for something that they did, we might as well get it over with so that we can get on with our day."

"Dude, what if this is a test?" Danny G. pointed out. "What if Coleman and Wilby are at the house right now and just aren't allowed to call us. They're setting us up to show up without them. This could all just be a test to see if we actually show up without them. Then we walk in and it's like BAM! Two Hundred push-ups!"

"Oh would you shut the fuck up?" Phatty yelled out. "That is the most ridiculous thing I've ever heard."

"I can't believe I'm saying this," Scott chimed in. "But Phatty's right. That's fucking ridiculously elaborate. I don't think that they would set us up like that in order to pin any of us against the rest of the group. We need to take Arch at his word. It's not just about unity. It's about trust. A Brother told us to come without them. We need to trust that he's not screwing us over."

He looked around at the group, half of him was waiting to see if his statement made sense and the other half was waiting to see if anyone had the guts to speak up against it. He heard nothing from them.

"Alright, let's go. We're going."

Scott began walking. The group soon followed in line behind him and they started on their short journey to the 403.

"Shit, I hope we're not drinking." Phatty looked like he might lose his breakfast if he even had to *hold* a beer. "CJ had me shotgunning beers with him all night last night. Dude can fucking drink!"

"They probably just want us to clean the house." Casey yelled out. "Some of them probably left CJ's apartment and went back to the house. They probably got all shitty and fucked the place up and don't feel like cleaning it up themselves."

"I hope that's all it is," Phatty responded. "Cleaning I can do. But shots...not so much."

As they neared the bottom of the street, Scott saw red and blue lights flashing off of the sides of the houses. He recognized them immediately as police lights.

"Um...I don't think we're doing shots." Scott said quietly to the group as he slowed to a stop. They peered around the corner and 403 came into view. The situation appeared much more dire than expected. "And I don't think we're here to clean either."

CHAPTER 10

The scene was the last thing any of them would have expected to see. The group took a moment to examine what they were seeing. An ambulance and three police cars lined the curb in front of 403. A small group of police officers stood on the porch. On the sidewalk they could see a group of ten or more Crows milling about. Some of them they didn't even recognize and were likely older Brothers that had shown up just to hang out for the weekend. They all had looks of concern on their faces. Ten yards down the street, away from the others, Archie was speaking with a man in a suit. Scott could see a badge on the man's suit coat. Archie had his hands up to his head and seemed distraught.

"What the fuck is...?" Casey didn't even get his whole sentence out before Phatty interrupted.

"Guys, I got a bag and a pipe on me. I can't go over there."

"Dude, there's a fucking ambulance there!" Scott chastised him. "Get over yourself. Something's wrong and you're worried about getting busted for weed? And since when does that even happen?"

He turned to the group and walked backwards towards the house as he addressed them. "Alright guys? All of you. Something happened. This is not about us. Now let's go."

He turned back towards the house and picked up his pace. No one objected. They all followed in line behind him.

Scott saw Archie point in their direction, calling the police officer's attention to them. The two began walking towards them and Archie called out and motioned to them. "Guys, over here!"

54

The group all walked over without a word. Some of them nervously glanced at the Police Officers, wondering what could have happened.

"Guys, this is Lieutenant Quinn from the South Cuthbert Police Department," Archie said motioning to the man in the suit. "The Borough, not the school," he clarified in order to call attention to the gravity of the situation.

Lt. Quinn nodded to the group. He opened his mouth to speak, but then stopped himself. He looked over at the house and back to the group. "Guys I'd like to speak to you, if you don't mind."

"Actually, Lieutenant," Archie interrupted, "it might be better to do this in private. This house over here, two doors down, 407, some of our Brothers live there as well. It might be better to do this inside."

Lt. Quinn glanced up at the house and nodded to Archie in agreement. He began walking towards the front steps. Scott and the rest of his Pledge Brothers exchanged worried glances as they stepped in line behind him and entered through the front door of 407.

Walking past the Brothers on the porch, Scott could see from their faces that something terrible had occurred. As they moved through the foyer and into the house they could see other Brothers scattered about with similar looks on their faces.

Lt. Quinn led the group into the Living Room. Archie came in with them along with CJ, the Chapter President.

The Lieutenant scanned the group. He looked at CJ, "Everyone in?"

CJ nodded. "Yes sir."

Archie stepped forward. "Sir, if you don't mind, I'm their Pledge Master and I'd like to be the one to tell them."

Scott's eyes widened immediately and his head quickly turned to Archie. *Oh my God, tell them?* He thought to himself. Coleman and Wilby's names immediately ran through his head. *Tell us what?*

"Sure that's fine," Lt. Quinn responded. "Go right ahead."

Archie nodded and turned to the group. "Alright guys, there's no easy way to say this. So I'm just gonna say it. There was an incident last night. Wilby's been taken to the hospital. It seems pretty bad."

There were audible gasps from the group and they began hurling questions at Archie. He raised his voice to interrupt the barrage. "Guys! GUYS! That's not all. Let me finish! Also..."

He paused and looked at the ground before looking back up to continue. "And guys... Coleman's dead."

The room fell silent. They all shared the same look of disbelief. This wasn't possible. They'd just lost a Pledge Brother? They had just been with him last night – just a few hours ago.

Robbie clumsily stepped backwards while reaching for a chair behind him and falling into it. A look of shock stretched across his face. Casey's hands went immediately to the sides of his head, as though he could somehow remove the information he'd just heard. Phatty stumbled across the hall and into the bathroom, where he'd barely made it to the toilet in time to make good on his promise from earlier to vomit.

Scott's hands covered his mouth and tears began to fill the corners of his eyes. He mustered the strength to force out the question everyone was trying to ask. "What happened?"

Lt. Quinn stepped forward to field the question. "It's not clear at this point. They were found over in your Fraternity house, two doors up. Your friend...Coleman..." He paused as if unsure if he should address him in the same way that Archie did, instead of his full name. "...he was pronounced dead there at the scene. Will Bonnetti, though...Wilby... he was found unconscious and unresponsive. He had lost a lot of blood. But he is alive. Both appear to have been attacked. Possibly with a knife."

"This doesn't make any sense." Wick shook his head and walked to the front of the group. "What happened to them? We were just hanging out with them last night. They were fine."

Lt. Quinn nodded in agreement. "Right, we've heard word similar to that from the others here. And my understanding is that all of you were with them last night. So we're going to need statements from each of you so that we can piece this together. The more we know, the better. And guys, I get it, this is college. Shit happens here that you might not want a cop walking in on. But please be completely truthful and open with us. The more information we have the better chance we have at figuring out what happened here. We aren't going to drag anyone into the station if a bong or a joint ends up in your story or if you were drinking and you aren't twenty-one yet."

Scott had figured as much. It'd been all of ninety seconds since he'd heard this terrible news. But his mind had immediately begun to race through a list of thoughts and questions, ranging from what could have possibly happened to them, and more selfishly, could he and his Pledge Brothers be in any trouble. This included the fact that the unspoken truth here was that if they didn't know what happened yet, then every person in this room was being considered as a possible suspect, including himself.

CHAPTER 11

Descending the wooden steps into the basement of 403 S. Martin Street, Lt. Quinn was reminded of Clarice Starling getting ready to come face to face with Wild Bill in *Silence of the Lambs*. Even with the makeshift lights they'd brought in for better visibility, it was still as creepy a setting as Quinn could remember ever being in. The only thing that the lights seemed to achieve was to highlight the dirtiness and dinginess of the room. He couldn't fathom how students chose to party in this filth.

As he reached the bottom of the stairs he once again came face to face with the true reason for the lights, along with his own personal Clarice Starling.

"Hello, Clarice." He said doing his best Hannibal Lecter.

"Ha, no shit, right?" Detective Dakota McKue didn't even take her eyes off of the body of Fran Coleman. "This basement is fucking creepy as shit."

"So what've we got?" he asked.

"Well, nineteen year old male. His ID, as you know, says his name was..." she glanced down at her notepad. "...Francis Coleman. I'd estimate he's been dead maybe six or seven hours. We'll need an autopsy to determine the official cause of death. But it appears to be pretty clear to me to be knife wounds. Multiple."

"And he was found down here." Quinn added. "But the other kid was found upstairs in the kitchen? Why do you figure that?"

"Well, the Bonnetti kid...he's the kid upstairs...I got here just as he was being brought out by the paramedics. He was covered in blood. But it all appeared to be on the front side and arms."

"Defensive wounds."

"Right...and I don't see any defensive wounds on this guy here. He took multiple puncture wounds on his side, back and on the side of his neck. He likely was killed right here and didn't even see it coming."

Lt. Quinn begins to piece together a probable progression of events from what they know. "So he gets killed down here. The killer then runs up the stairs and runs into the other one in the kitchen, at the top of the stairs and has to go through him to get out of here."

Detective McKue agrees. "Yep, but the killer was too surprised by him to have the presence of mind to make sure the job was done. Which would also mean..."

"Will Bonnetti saw the killer," finished the sentence for her.

"You got it."

"Well then we need to hope he makes it," Quinn stated matter of factly. "He might be our only hope for a positive ID."

"Funny you should use that word," McKue quipped.

"What word's that?"

"ID," McKue replied. "I found this lying next to Francis Coleman's body."

Detective McKue held out a South Cuthbert University Student ID. The name on the ID read "Scott Dempsey".

CHAPTER 12

Once Scott, along with the rest of his Pledge Brothers, had finished speaking with Archie and Lt. Quinn, the group began meeting one by one with uniformed officers to give their statements. They had each walked through their own whereabouts from the previous night, along with the last time they'd seen both Coleman and Wilby.

The answers were all roughly identical and included the same general points. There was a party at the Theta Chi house. That had taken a lot of the girls away for the night. But the Crows got along well with Theta Chi. So some of the Brothers were invited to the party. The pledges were never included in this though. For no other reason than because they're pledges. So the pledges snuck some beers into Trout's dorm room and hung out there until around 11pm. At that point they met everyone at CJ's apartment for a late-night. CJ had been at the Theta Chi party and invited some people back to his place. He probably had about thirty people there. This included Coleman and Wilby, and everyone's memory seemed to match up on the point that the two of them left together around 1:30 AM. They were believed to be heading back to their dorm room. No one's statement made a mention of seeing either of them after that point.

The ten of them now sat quietly in the living room of 407, waiting to see what came next. Scott looked around the room and realized that it was the first time in the past month and a half that there had only been ten of them. They'd grown accustomed to doing everything together. All twelve of them. They were learning the values of Brotherhood. Learning to be there for each other. It's what they were doing now...being there for each other. Only it didn't feel right.

"We let them down." Scott said. His head was hung low and he was fighting back tears.

"Got that right." Danny G. agreed.

"Dude, how?" Casey asked incredulously. "We don't even know what happened! How the fuck can we blame ourselves?"

"Well we sure as hell aren't being there for Wilby right now!" Robbie yelled. "When the hell can we get out of here?"

"They only have Chewie left to be interviewed, alright?" Scott said. The annoyance was clear in his voice. "Then we go...together."

"Yeah well, with all due respect, dear leader..." Robbie was never one to hide the fact that he wasn't happy that Scott was picked over him as Pledge Class President, "...I feel like we're all big boys and should be able to leave so that we can check on our friend."

"Oh shut the fuck up, Rob." Ethan chimed in. "Just let the president shit go. It's been a month and a half for Christ's sake."

"Can we all just shut the fuck up!" Scott yelled. "Coleman's dead. Wilby's... I don't even fucking know what. We need to stick together and be here for each other. So we wait. We've got one more person that they need to speak to. Then we're out of here."

Lt. Quinn interrupted the group as he walked in the front door of 407 with a woman walking behind him.

"Scott Dempsey?" he asked out loud as he scanned the group. "Which one's Scott Dempsey?"

Scott turned around with a surprised look. "Yeah...that's me."

"Can we speak to you for a minute, son?" Quinn asked, motioning him into the kitchen.

Scott froze. Why would they want to speak to him again? He'd already given his statement. He considered questioning whether they had the right person. But he'd heard enough from his

Dad, a Homicide Detective in Philly, that the ones that appeared to have something to hide, most often actually had something to hide. He decided not to convey that image and stood up.

"Sure, of course," he said politely

He stood up and made his way past his Pledge Brothers. He could almost hear their thoughts, wondering the same thing that he was wondering. He knew this would arouse suspicion with the group.

As he moved through the room, Robbie stepped into Scott's path.

"Guess they actually still need to speak to two people still, huh Scott?"

CHAPTER 13

Lt. Quinn and Detective McKue led Scott into the kitchen of 407. "Scott, have a seat." Quinn motioned to the old beat up table in the corner. None of the chairs matched.

"Scott, as a reminder, I'm Lt. Quinn. I believe that we may have met briefly earlier. This is Detective McKue. We'd like to ask you a few more questions."

"Yeah, of course," Scott replied as he sat down in the closest chair. He was nervous. Why was he being singled out? Everyone had already given their statement, including him. What did he say that made them want to speak to him again?

"Scott, how old are you?"

"18, sir," *Odd question,* he thought.

"Can you tell me where you were last night?" Detective McKue asked abruptly. She was tough looking. She wore a pair of tight slacks and a form fitting blouse that showed that she kept herself in shape. She was probably a foot shorter than he was. But he felt like she could take him in a fight. The gun on her hip only added to that. And her current demeanor completed the trifecta.

"Yeah, sure. Just like I told the other Officer..."

"Yeah well, we're asking you now," she snapped back.

"Right..." Scott was visibly taken aback. "So I started out the night hanging out in Trout's room. Trout's my Pledge Brother. He's in the other room. And around 11pm we went to CJ's apartment."

"Is it true that you got into a fight with Coleman last night?" Lt. Quinn asked.

"What?" Scott was not liking the path that this seemed to be going down. "Uh...yeah...yeah. We did...at CJ's place. Well, just an argument. Not a fight, really."

"What was it about?" McKue interjected.

"It was stupid. We were drunk. Started off as pledge stuff."

"Pledge stuff?" She was not big on waiting for an answer.

"Yeah, that's how it started. He didn't like how I was acting as the Pledge Class President. But, really, I don't think he liked that I'm dating Sydney. He went to high school a year behind my girlfriend. I think he was jealous."

"What makes you think that?" Quinn asked.

"Well it was no mystery." Scott said matter of factly. "He's told me that he doesn't like us dating. She told me that he didn't know her that well. Just an acquaintance. It was pretty clear that he liked her too though." Scott was growing wearier with each answer. None of this was painting him in a good light, and he was painfully clear on that point.

"And you two got into a fight?" McKue asked.

"Well like I said, I wouldn't call it a fight." Scott clarified.

"What would you call it?" Quinn asked.

"I don't know...a scuffle? He pushed me. I pushed him back. And then some guys stepped in."

"What time did you leave CJ's?" McKue asked. The questions were coming more quickly now.

"Around 1:45," Scott answered just as quickly. He didn't want to appear unclear in his answers.

"Around?" she fired back.

"Yeah, I don't know exactly. But it was pretty close to that I guess."

"Did you leave alone?" Quinn jumped in. They were beginning to seem to be treating him like a ping pong ball. Bouncing him back and forth between one another.

"Yeah, I did."

"And where did you go?" Mckue this time, right on queue.

"I walked to my girlfriend's house and spent the night there."

"Where does she live?" It was McKue again. Scott was thrown off by the sudden break in cadence.

"She's over on Elm. Over in the direction of College Arms. I don't actually even know the address."

"You don't know your girlfriend's address?" Quinn jumped back in.

"No, we've only been dating for a couple of months. She brought me there the first time and I never needed to mail anything there. So..."

"You l' smart with us, asshole?" McKue shouted.

"What? No!" Scott yelled back at her.

"What time did you get there?" she quickly fired back.

"I don't know...probably ten or fifteen minutes after I left CJ's. I didn't notice the time when I got there."

Quinn stepped to his left so that he was now directly in front of Scott. "Did you see either Francis Coleman or Will Bonnetti after you left CJ's last night?"

Scott lifted his head and looked him directly in the eyes. "No sir."

"You didn't see either of them?!" McKue asked with a raised voice, clearly upset now.

"No!" Scott yelled back. There was no ambiguity left in the matter. He knew they felt that he was involved. "Look, I don't know what you two are thinking. But I had nothing to do with this!"

He stared at Quinn and McKue as the two paced the kitchen floor and exchanged glances. The silence between them extended longer than Scott was comfortable with. He was ready to scream out again about his innocence when Detective McKue turned back toward him and dropped the last possible question he ever could have expected he'd hear.

"Scott, can you tell me how your student ID might have wound up next to Coleman's body?"

Scott felt the bottom drop out of his stomach. Did he just hear that correctly?

"Excuse me?"

"I think you heard her, Scott," Quinn said to him before repeating the question. "Why was your student ID found next to Francis Coleman's body?" Quinn stretched out the final words purposely and forcefully.

"No. No. No! What are you talking about? That's not even possible!" Scott began to reach for his wallet. But Quinn and McKue instinctively put their hands on the weapons and took a defensive stance.

"Don't you fucking move!" McKue yelled.

"Whoa, holy shit!" his hands immediately went into the air. "I'm getting my wallet out. Oh my God, what the fuck?!"

"Alright," Quinn relented and raised his hand to McKue in a relaxing motion. "Go ahead, Scott. But, I don't think you're going to have any luck there."

Scott relaxed his body as best he could and lowered his hands. He feared that they were somehow right. He reached into his pocket and pulled out his wallet. Slowly flipping it open, he stared in disbelief at what he was seeing. Where he would normally see the South Cuthbert University logo peeking out of the top slot, he instead only saw the VISA logo from the credit card he'd signed up for two weeks ago outside of the cafeteria. The look on his face told Quinn and McKue all they needed to know.

Quinn continued. "I'll ask you again, Scott. Is there any reason that your student ID might have been found next to Francis Coleman's body?"

"No...this isn't possible," Scott uttered. He then looked up at the two and adopted the defensive tone. "No! I have no idea how that would have gotten there!"

"So let me get this straight." McKue said, stepping in front of Quinn. "You and Coleman get into a fight."

"It wasn't a fight!" Scott interrupted.

McKue continued without ever pausing to hear him. "Coleman leaves with Will Bonnetti. You leave...alone...not long after. And the next time anyone sees them, Coleman is dead, Will

Bonnetti is in the hospital, and *your* student ID is found next to Coleman's body."

"No...Nope. I didn't...you're not..." Scott was in too much of a shocked state to even compose a complete refusal of what she was asserting. He couldn't believe that he was actually being accused of murder.

Quinn reached down and pushed the left side of his suit coat to the side and back, exposing a pair of handcuffs. He pointed to the wall with his other hand as he took the cuffs from his belt. "Scott, please stand up and turn around with your hands above your head."

Scott sat for a moment. His eyes were like saucers and his mouth was agape. He spoke not a word and quietly stood, faced the wall and did as he was told.

Detective McKue dutifully followed along. "Scott Dempsey you are under arrest for the murder of Francis Coleman. You have the right to remain silent. You have the right to an attorney. If you can not afford an attorney, one will be appointed for you. Do you understand the rights that have been read to you?"

Scott barely heard a word she had said. He could not fathom the fact that he was now being placed under arrest for murder. A flurry of thoughts ran through his mind as he felt the blow of the handcuffs crash against his wrist, and Quinn grabbing his arms to force them behind his back.

"Do you understand your rights?" Quinn repeated.

Scott stood silently.

"I'll take that as a yes," Quinn said before yanking him backwards towards the middle of the kitchen.

Scott straightened his back and gained his footing. He then looked up to see Archie standing in the doorway. His mind reeled at what Archie and his Pledge Brothers must be thinking. Even worse, what his Mom and Dad will think of him when they hear that he's been arrested for murder.

CHAPTER 14

WARRINGTON, PA

"Hey Suz, do you have any idea where my Chewbacca T-Shirt might be?" Chase Dempsey called into the bathroom as he rifled through his dresser.

"How the hell would I know? What? Do you think I'm wearing it?" she joked. "Did you pack it?"

"No, I didn't pack it" he yelled back in a condescending tone, completing the sentence to himself in a whisper "...at least I don't think so."

He continued, now at full volume. "I want to wear it on the plane since we're going to Hollywood Studios as soon as we get there." He dug deeper into his drawer. "I swore I saw it here."

It had only taken Chase and Suzanne a few days to get used to life as empty nesters after Scott left for college. They'd quickly adjusted to life on their own, enjoying some nights on the town and freely walking around the house naked.

Then, one day, they suddenly found themselves having sex in the kitchen. It was the first time they'd done it outside of their bedroom in over twenty years. It was an invigorating experience for both of them to fully enjoy the new-found freedoms that they've been given. Afterwards, they both sat on the tile floor, leaning up against the cabinets, and Suz turned to Chase with a wry smile and said, "Let's go to Disney!"

Within a matter of hours they had a trip booked with a stay at the Grand Floridian Resort & Spa. They had gone to Disney once before as a family when Scott and Pete were younger. They stayed in one of Disney's value resorts to save money. But they had seen the impressive Grand Floridian every day while riding the Monorail to the Magic Kingdom. Ever since then, the Grand Floridian was on their bucket list.

It was certainly a plus for Chase that they had recently opened the new Star Wars themed area in Hollywood Studios, and today was the day he'd finally get to live out his childhood dream of piloting the Millennium Falcon. To do that properly, however, he needed his co-pilot. He needed his favorite Chewbacca t-shirt.

"Do you remember when we had the boys there and all Scott wanted to do was hang out in that arcade in the lobby of the hotel?" she asked as she packed her toiletry bag.

"I swore I put it on the bed right here," Scott said, retracing his steps. He had more important things to do right now than reminisce.

"We had to promise him we'd let him go on Space *Mountain* three times in a row just to get him to step away from Space *Invaders*."

"It's the green one with him standing and holding his Bowcaster."

"I wonder how he's doing. I hope he's doing ok."

"Found it!" Chase yanked the shirt from the back of the drawer and held it up victoriously. "Did you put this back there?"

"No," she answered. "Are you even listening to me?"

"Yeah, of course. Honey, Scott's fine. You don't need to worry about him," he responded dismissively. But with another glance, he began to recognize the look that he had been expecting for the past month. It was the inevitable fall from grace. The moment of coming down from the high of being empty nesters.

He tossed the shirt down on the bed and walked towards her with his arms open. She fell right into them like a child.

"He's doing great," he reassured her. "He's at college! He's loving life right now! Dude has probably gotten drunk and laid more than we have since he left."

"Stop that!" Suz playfully slapped his chest. "He has not! Not my sweet son."

"And we've been doing that a lot!" he continued.

"Oh my God, shut the fuck up!" she leaned back and yelled at him while holding back a laugh. "He is not doing that! He is at the library every night and is being his good sweet self."

"Ok you're right. I'm sure that's what he's doing," he said, pulling her back in towards his bare chest.

"You're rolling your eyes aren't you?" she asked, already knowing the answer.

"*So* far back into my skull," he joked.

They both laughed and separated themselves unwillingly. As much as Chase wanted to stay at home in bed with her, they had a flight to catch. He couldn't pass up his chance at doing the Kessel Run in less than twelve parsecs.

"Alright, we need to get moving before you convince yourself that leaving here is a terrible idea." He flashed her a smile and started to put on his Chewbacca t-shirt. He barely had it over his head when was interrupted by the ring of his cell phone. They both looked down at the bed, where his phone lay, and saw Scott's name flash across the screen.

"Oh speak of the devil!" he said to her as he reached for it. "He's probably calling to tell me how many chicks he bagged last night."

"You're such a dick."

Chase hit the screen and answered the call on speaker with a laugh. "Hey buddy, what's up?"

"Hey Dad...you got a sec?" Scott's voice was quiet and pensive. "I...uh...I need to tell you something. I need your help."

CHAPTER 15

When Chase and Suzanne had first driven Scott out to South Cuthbert University, it took them an hour and a half. They had taken their time getting there. Chase even took the scenic route to give Scott an appreciation for the area. They were in no rush to launch Scott out of their atmosphere.

Today, they made the trip in forty-five minutes. The pedal was to the floor and their eyes were glued to the road. Today the scenic route did not exist, and the last thing Chase was worried about was getting pulled over. He definitely didn't harbor any concerns about being given a speeding ticket. No cop worth his salt would give a ticket to a fellow cop.

Chase's original plan, when he had chosen to major in Criminal Justice, was to join the FBI. But after his experience with Chris Wilbanks' death, he felt that the life of a Homicide Detective was calling him. He never could have dreamed that a homicide would one day bring him back to SCU.

The details were sparse at this point. One of Scott's Pledge Brother's had been killed, another was in the hospital, and the police were blaming Scott. He was now in custody at the South Cuthbert Police Station.

Not only did Chase know there was no way this could be true, but he couldn't even begin to wonder what the odds could be of this happening to his son. His mind was reeling with questions. Why was this happening to his family? Did he bring this on his son with his own actions?

He was hesitant to even ask the last question. He was terrified of what the answer might be. His mind replayed his own terrible experience in fast forward as he navigated his way through South Cuthbert. He remembered the sounds he heard that fateful night. His helpless feeling as he searched for Chris Wilbanks in the dark. The verbal attacks he received on campus from the people that believed all of the newspaper stories, even after he was no longer considered a suspect by the police. But mostly, he remembered the anxiety and panic attacks that he experienced both day and night as a result of the horrific ordeal. He tried to tell himself that this wasn't real and that his son wasn't about to be subject to the same hell that he went through so many years ago.

As the South Cuthbert Police Station came into view he felt a tightening in the center of his chest. The rush of feelings going through him combined into one giant ball of anxiety as he turned into the parking lot.

"It's gonna' be fine," Suzanne said, putting a hand on his shoulder. "This is all just a misunderstanding."

Chase knew that she recognized the signs of his panic attacks coming on – raised shoulders, arms pulling in towards the body as he attempted to turn the wheel, heavy and quick breathing through his nose in an attempt to stop the attack from overtaking him.

"Come on...pursed lips," she said quietly.

Pursed lips. Those were her magic words.

When Chase and Suzanne had first met, Chase was suffering from chronic and sudden onset of panic attacks. He continued to do so for years after. A direct result of going through what he now feared his own son was about to endure. He had spent two months officially suspected by the South Cuthbert Police Department for murder before it was clear that he had no involvement and was only a victim of being in the wrong place at the wrong time.

Once he was cleared of any wrongdoing, he remained active within Kappa Chi Rho at SCU. The Fraternity had its charter suspended for a year and was forbidden from partaking in any Fraternity functions, including the initiation of new members. Which meant that Chase waited a full year after Chris' death before becoming an official Brother. The majority of the members of the Fraternity believed Chase and welcomed him with open arms. Still there were a handful of Brothers that refused to remove their suspicions and never accepted him, even after he was sworn into the Fraternity.

It was the ones that did accept him, however, that made his life at South Cuthbert University, and his life overall, bearable. Many members of the Fraternity made it a point to refer to him as a Brother long before his initiation, given everything he'd been put through. Their kind words were his safe haven.

He tried to live the life of a normal college student. But it was nearly impossible to shake the stigma that he had been connected to so early on in his college career. There were people that would never stop blaming him for Chris Wilbanks' death.

Mike Sullivan, a Brother from Sigma Phi known by most as Sully, was one of the most vocal about it, never relenting in his attacks during Chase's time there. Many times Chase nearly caved to Sully's attacks. Even the school newspaper would sometimes resurrect the past and question what may have happened to Chris Wilbanks. Chase's name would always be included in the stories. Never in a positive light.

He often considered leaving school and finishing his education at DelVal, a local commuter college closer to home. But he refused to let them win. He knew he was innocent, and screw anyone who thought differently. Their ignorance was their problem, not his.

He was a month into his senior year when he nearly let their mocking tones crack his weakened armor. But a chance encounter in the archway going through Williams Auditorium would change his mind, and his life, forever.

Suzanne McCollough was a girl that everyone knew. She was 5' 6" with green eyes, an athletic frame, and a brunette head of hair that encased one of the smartest brains in the SCU Greek system. As a Sister of Delta Phi Epsilon, or D Phi E for those most familiar with the Sorority, she was well known as a girl that everyone dreamed of being with. But it was also well known that, for most, it was likely just a dream.

She was considered untouchable for no other reason than because she seemed uninterested in most of the guys at school. She certainly dated her fair share. She wasn't averse to the opposite sex. But she was very particular in whom she decided to spend her time with. The typical drunk Fraternity Brother was not her type. In fact, she seemed to go out of her way to avoid them. She did not join a Sorority just to hang out with Fraternities. She definitely had joined it for the experience of Sisterhood.

So it was a major shock to Chase Dempsey when Suzanne McCullough stopped him to say hello as the two passed by each other while walking through the archway of Williams Auditorium.

"You're Chase, aren't you?" she said as she raised her hand, pointing awkwardly as she walked towards him.

Chase was visibly surprised by the interaction. "Uh...um...yeah...Chase...Suzanne?   No...Chase...I'm Chase. You're Suzanne. Right? Yes...Chase."

"Are you sure?" she said with a laugh. "Yes, I'm Suzanne. You're Chase...Dempsey...from KXP?"

"Yeah, that's me," he said with an awkward chuckle

"You sound a little more sure about it this time. So that's good," she said with a smile.

"Yeah pretty sure," he said, forcing himself to relax. "...most days at least."

"Is today one of those days?" she asked.

The two exchanged a glance that Chase recognized as a glance that you don't often get a chance to partake in. Some people never experience it. He was smart enough to realize he may never see it again, and he took full advantage and looked Suzanne right in the eye.

"Yeah...yeah...today I'm certain," he responded in a calm voice.

Why she stopped him that day to talk, he never knew. He didn't want to know or need to know. All that mattered was that

Suzanne McCollough was talking to *him!* At that time, part of him wished it wasn't happening inside this fifty foot long archway where no one else could see. But as time went on and the two grew closer, he came to realize that the location on that first day didn't matter. Everyone would eventually know that she was with him. Chase and Suzanne would be an item. The untouchable Suzanne McCullough was now off the market.

This, however, only added to his anxiety. He had been only months away from disappearing into obscurity forever. Soon he would graduate with a degree in Criminal Justice and prove to the world, or at least himself, that he was better than they thought he was. He'd stuck it out long enough for the whispers to distance themselves from him. He had a core group of friends within KXP and the extended Greek System that knew him for who he was. They had gotten past the rumors, and so had he. Or so he had thought.

Now he was in the limelight again. He was now dating the great Suzanne McCullough! And the attention began to take its toll. Soon the panic attacks returned in full force. Many a night he'd spent frantically pacing the floor trying to gather himself and avoid the eventuality of hyperventilation.

Three years prior he began experiencing massive panic attacks that would reach a point of climax where Chase found himself unable to breathe. He was forced to deal with it himself. But now that he was with Suzanne it was different. He chose to lean on her and it proved to be a good choice. She was his rock. She was the one person in this world, above all else, that could talk him back from the proverbial ledge. She instinctively knew how to connect with him and ground him in reality. It was a characteristic he'd been desperately craving in a partner. In Suzanne, he'd found his Rock of Gibraltar. An immovable figure in his life that would be there for him at all costs.

"Pursed lips," was the first thing she had said to him during the first panic attack that he had in front of her. Helping him seemed to come naturally for her. She didn't jump back in shock, unsure how to react. She was immediately calm enough for the both of them.

"Pursed Lips," she told him again. "Pursed lips and exhale slowly." She jumped right in and didn't retreat. Chase knew that for the rest of his life he wanted to hold onto her with both hands.

CHAPTER 16

"Pursed Lips."

Suzanne Dempsey's word's brought Chase back to reality as he pulled into the South Cuthbert Police Station parking garage. He pulled into a parking spot and followed her suggestion, just like he always did. He soon felt his heart rate slow, and before long he was back to his normal self. Or at least as normal as anyone could be in this situation. His hope was that this was all just a misunderstanding and that Scott would be on his way home within an hour. But his experience as a Homicide Detective told him differently. If Scott was in custody, then they had what they felt was a good reason for keeping him there.

Chase knew the South Cuthbert Police Station better than most alumni ever would. Many students would never have a reason to ever even know where it was located. To most, the South Cuthbert Police Department was only a concern for them when they were at a party and drinking while underage – a common worry for many students. Chase had always laughed at the idea that screaming the words "The LCB's here!!" could clear out a party a thousand times faster than just declaring the party over and asking people to leave. Chase wasn't even sure that the Liquor Control Board even existed. But he sure as hell knew that if it did, they didn't care about a party on Martin Street in the middle of South Cuthbert, PA.

The South Cuthbert Police, however, did absolutely exist. Chase had spent his fair share of time inside the South Cuthbert Police Station. It was an experience that he fought every day to forget. As Scott grew closer and closer to college age, the dream of that ever happening seemed to come closer to dying off. He hoped against hope that Scott would choose any school *but* South Cuthbert. But he vowed to never tell him that he couldn't follow his instincts. He didn't want to impact any decisions his son might make. That decision, as it turned out, proved to quash his wish to forget his days at South Cuthbert. If the day that Scott decided to apply to South Cuthbert University was the nail in the coffin, then the day that he was accepted as a student there was the hammer that drove the nail in.

Today appeared to be the culmination of the worries that had been setting up camp in the back of Chase's mind ever since Scott made his decision to attend SCU. Chase tried, unsuccessfully, to tell himself that it was an irrational fear. People didn't just randomly go to school and find themselves embroiled in a murder investigation. He told himself that his own situation was an outlier. The chances of that happening to any one person were so slim, that the odds against his own son being caught up in one as well had to be astronomical.

But here he was. His son had been thrown into the same hellish world that he had to endure so many years before. He wondered silently to himself if the family was somehow cursed. What other explanation could there be?

The Desk Sergeant pointed Chase and Suzanne in the direction they needed to head in order to locate Scott. As they made their way down the hall, Chase assumed that the next familiar face he'd see would be his son's. That would, unfortunately, prove to be false.

As Chase and Suzanne turned down the hallway towards the interrogation rooms, standing at the end of the hallway, directly in their path, was Mike Sullivan. The two hadn't seen each other in over twenty years. Prior to that, to say their relationship was tense was an understatement. Sully was inexplicably the most vocal proponent of the idea that Chase was responsible for Chris Wilbanks' death. As far as Chase knew, Sully and Chris barely even knew each other. But that never stopped Sully from grasping at any opportunity to spread lie after lie about that night.

"Sully?" Chase showed his confusion as he slowed his pace. "What're you doing here?"

"Chase," Sully nodded. "It's been a while."

He glanced at Suzanne, "Suz."

"Mike," she responded tersely, refusing to use his nickname and grant him any level of friendship.

Sully motioned over to a woman standing behind him and introduced her. She was wearing yoga pants and a tight zip up sweat jacket that accentuated her impressive figure. "This is Lynn Clowry, my Assistant."

"Assistant?" Chase asked with a confused tone. "Sully, why are you here?" he asked again, this time more forcefully.

"I'm the Director of Greek Life here, Chase. We've got a serious situation here involving a dead student and your son appears to be stuck smack dab in the middle of it. What are the odds of that?"

"You motherfu..." Chase began to step towards Sully, but was held back by Suzanne.

Lynn Clowry did the same with Sully as he moved to defend himself. "Ok, that's enough, fellas! Let's move on! Let's move on!"

"Yep! Definitely enough!" Suzanne agreed loudly as she pulled Chase away and began moving him down the hall.

"Good talking to you Sully!" Chase yelled as he walked away reluctantly.

"Big shock, Demps!" Sully yelled down the hall. "Like Father, like Son!"

"Nope! Don't even listen!" Suzanne said quietly to Chase, as she continued to pull him down the hall and forced him to turn the corner.

Chase was incredulous. "What a fucking asshole. How the fuck did he become Director of Greek Life? That asshole?! He knows nothing about brotherhood!"

"Don't even worry about him," Suz said dismissively.

"Did that woman look familiar to you?" Chase asked. "What was her name? Lynn?"

"What? No," Suz responded confused as to why he would ask that. "No, never saw her before. Past conquest of yours, maybe?" Suz asked with a smile, trying to lighten the mood.

"Huh?" he asked.

"Maybe you had a one night stand with her? You know...Pre-Suz." She said with a smile.

Chase recognized that she was trying to relax him. He was about to walk into potentially the most unnerving situation he may ever be faced with. Running into Sully right before it was not an ideal prepper.

He forced a smile. "No, no I'm pretty sure that I would've remembered her."

Suz shot him a surprised glance.

"Don't get me wrong." He responded. "It's just that, well, before you I didn't exactly have many girls knocking down my door."

"Yeah, yeah, yeah. Whatever you say, Mr. Dempsey," she said, squinting her eyes playfully.

Chase smiled back, realizing that she was successful, once again, in diffusing a potentially explosive situation for him. But just as the effects of her charms had washed over him, they were just as quickly washed away when they approached the door they'd been searching for.

Standing beside the door were a man and a woman in plain clothes. Chase had pegged them for cops before he even saw a badge. They turned to Chase and Suzanne as they drew near. The man spoke first.

"Mr. and Mrs. Dempsey?"

Chase nodded to the affirmative.

"I'm Lt. Quinn. This is Detective McKue."

Chase mentally noted that Lt. Quinn did not reach out to shake his hand. He took that as a sign of distancing between themselves and the family of the suspect.

"My name's Chase Dempsey. This is my wife Suzanne. Where's Scott?"

"He's right through that door. You can see him in a moment. But first I'd like to talk to you."

Chase knew what was coming. He'd done it dozens of times before himself. He let Lt. Quinn continue.

"I'm not certain how much information has been shared with you yet."

"Very little," Suzanne responded. Chase turned his head slightly towards her. He hoped that he saw the gesture. He wanted to handle this his way.

"Well, then let me give you a brief summary. A student at South Cuthbert University was found murdered early this morning, very gruesomely, in the basement of the Kappa Chi Rho Fraternity House. He was a pledge brother of your son's. We have a very strong reason to believe that your son is responsible."

"What reason is that?" Chase asked calmly. As much as his anxiety had affected his life, he found that when he was discussing a case he had the innate ability to remain the calmest person in the room. He drew on that ability here.

"We found your son's student ID next to the body."

"That's circumstantial, at best," he retorted.

"Mr. Dempsey, your son's behavior surrounding the murder has us feeling different. Now we have always found that..."

And here it comes, Chase thought.

"...if a family member is present, a guilty party is much more likely to come clean. All we want is for this process to go as smoothly as possible for everyone. If your son is guilty, a confession is actually his best path forward. If this goes to trial and he's found guilty, the judge will string him up. Send him right to death row. Can you help us Mr. Dempsey?"

And there it is.

Chase glanced over at Suzanne for a moment. Her face was red with anger at the prospect of being expected to help them put her son away. Chase nodded slightly to her, signaling that he can do this on his own. He turned back to Lt. Quinn.

"Well, first of all, it's not Mr. Dempsey. It's Lt. Dempsey." Chase reached into his pocket and pulled out his badge, holding it out for the two of them to see.

Quinn's eyes went wide as Chase continued.

"I work Homicide in Philly and have been for fifteen years. So no, we will *not* be going in to talk our son into a confession. And yes, it does sound very circumstantial. And no, right now PA is *not* in the practice of executing its prisoners. So if you don't mind, we'd like to see our son. His lawyer will be here shortly. And then you can begin your interrogation."

Quinn's shoulders slumped, knowing that he'd be caught in a common practice among cops. "Philly, huh?"

"Yeah."

He glanced back at McKue before turning back to Chase and Suzanne. "Ok, sure, go ahead in. I'll give you ten minutes."

Chase and Suzanne glanced at each other, sharing their first win of the day, before moving past Quinn and McKue towards the door. INTERROGATION ROOM B was stenciled across the center.

"Are you ready?" Suzanne asked.

"Nope." Chase sighed, before reaching for the door handle. "Let's Go."

He opened the door to find Scott alone and handcuffed to the table.

"Mom! Dad!" Scott tried to stand, but was held back by the handcuffs.

"Oh my God, Scott, are you ok?!" Suzanne immediately embraced her son, despite the fact that he was unable to return the embrace.

"Mom, I didn't do any of this, I swear!" he said.

"I know sweetie! I know! I'm so sorry about your friend. Are you ok?"

"Yeah, I'm ok." It was the first lie he'd told today. He turned to Chase. "Dad, you have to believe me. I had nothing to do with this."

Chase wrapped his arms around Scott and squeezed as tightly as he could. "I know, son. You don't have to tell me that." He stepped back, and looked Scott in the eyes. "But listen, I need to know what you have told them. And I don't want you saying another word to them until Renato gets here."

"You called Mr. Brambilla? Oh wow!" Scott asked.

"Yeah, he'll be here shortly," Suzanne replied.

Scott recounted to his parents exactly what he had shared already in his earlier interview at 407, along with the fact that his student ID was somehow found next to Coleman's body.

"How the hell does that even happen?" Suzanne asked.

Chase didn't miss a beat. "I've seen some odd things happen before, Suz. Could be a number of ways. Maybe Coleman had found it and was going to return it to Scott later. Or, more maliciously, someone could have planted it there." He turned his attention to Scott. "When was the last time you remember having your student ID?"

Scott was quick to answer, as he'd been thinking about it for the past few hours. "Last night at the caf, when I was getting dinner."

"And do you remember anything odd from last night? Possibly somewhere you might've lost it or placed it down where someone else could've maybe taken it? Were you at 403 earlier in the night and just dropped it there? Then Coleman might've fallen near it?" Chase asked, searching for a way that could put Scott's involvement in question.

"No, nothing. I've been wracking my brain trying to figure out how it could've gotten there. I wasn't even at 403 last night. I couldn't have dropped it there."

"Well, we're going to need to figure out how that got there," Chase responded.

"Dad, Sully...Mike Sullivan – he's the head of Greek Life – he was in earlier to see me."

"Sully came in here to see you?" Chase's guard immediately went up at the thought of Sully implanting himself into the situation further. The last thing he wanted was him attacking Scott the same way he had attacked him so many years ago.

"Yeah," Scott replied, "and he said something weird."

Chase knew what was coming.

Scott continued. "He said, 'like father, like son.' Dad, why exactly would he say that?"

This was the moment Chase had dreaded since the day Scott was born. He knew Scott would find out someday. He tried to tell him before he left for school, but he let his emotions get the better of him and walked away from the opportunity. This, however, was not the way that he wanted to share it with him.

"Scott, there's something I need to tell you." He briefly recounted the events from twenty-eight years ago. He told him about the night of Chris Wilbanks' death. He told him about the investigation and the fact that he was a suspect. But most importantly that he was exonerated. He mentioned that Sully never accepted his exoneration. Although he stopped short of detailing the effect that the events, and Sully, had on his time at SCU. He left out the anxiety that he'd hidden from Scott for so many years. Chase knew that Scott saw him as someone who was strong and could handle anything. The last thing he wanted to do at this point was to give any more reason for Scott to be stressed. He had already had enough reasons as it were.

He did, however, need to warn Scott of one eventuality. "But, listen bud, at some point what's happening here is going to be tied to what happened to me by the news and the public. We need to get ahead of that. We need to find a way to make it clear you had nothing to do with this, and we need to do it quickly."

Scott let his head drop to his chest before flinging it back and thrusting himself back into his chair. "Yeah, well, I'm open to suggestions."

"You let your Mom and I worry about that stuff. Mr. Brambilla will be here soon and then the police are going to question you. You just answer truthfully and calmly. Don't offer any more information than is absolutely necessary to answer the specific question that they asked. Short and to the point. They will take anything that comes out of your mouth and try to twist it into a confession from you if they can. So short and specific. Do not offer anything that wasn't asked. Got it?"

"Yeah, I got it Dad," Scott replied. "I've already told them everything I know about last night. So there shouldn't be any more info available for them to drag out of me."

Chase hoped that that was the case. He knew from his experience on both sides of the interrogation table that anything can result from a poorly run interrogation. And truthfully, he was scared to death of how it would turn out for Scott.

CHAPTER 17

Sully's BMW made a hard right turn out of the police station and onto Stone Boulevard. The turn was faster and harder than Lynn Clowry had expected. "Whoa, a little worked up there?" Her biceps could be seen flexing through her tight sleeve as she gripped the handle above the passenger door.

Sully, unaware of how fast he was driving, glanced down at the dash and then let his foot off of the gas slightly. "Sorry, yeah probably. I seriously can't believe this is happening. Let me tell ya, that family is a mess!"

"Yeah, what was that all about back there, anyway?" she asked.

"That guy back there, Scott Dempsey's Dad, he and I went to school together here. I was in Sig Phi and he was a Crow"

"And his wife too?" she asked.

"Yeah and his wife. She was in D Phi E. How he landed her, I'll never know. Anyway, back in college his Pledge Brother died during a hazing incident."

"Oh my God, are you serious? That's terrible!" A genuine look of sorrow came across her face.

"Yeah, and he was always believed..." Sully corrected himself. "He was the last one to see the guy alive. So he was suspected to have had something to do with it. But the cops could never prove it."

"Holy shit, and did you know him? The guy I mean that died?"

"Yeah, I did. Well, sort of," he corrected himself. "I had met him once or twice. He was a good guy. But Chase Dempsey that fucking guy. Most people would just leave school after being involved in something like that, right? Not this guy. He friggin' stays in school. Stays in his Fraternity and goes through his life here at South Cuthbert like nothing ever happened. And he's actually a cop now! I hear he works on homicides, believe it or not."

"Seriously? What an asshole!"

"Right?!"

"Do you really think he did it?" she asked.

"Hell yeah! I mean, well probably," Sully responded. "Cops didn't have the evidence to charge him. But it had to be him. No one else was in the woods that night. It was just the two of them."

"The woods?"

"Yeah, KXP had drop-off night and..."

"So wait." Lynn interrupted him in a surprised tone. "KXP. It was the same Fraternity as the one from today?"

"Yep, can you believe that? Amazing right? Anyway they had drop-off night during their Hell Week. The Brothers dropped the two pledges in the woods off of campus, the idea being that they would have to find their way back home on their own. They were there all alone. But only one of them walked out of the woods. Chase Dempsey. The other was found dead at the bottom of an embankment the next morning."

"You sure seem to know a lot about it," Lynn poked at him with a wry smile.

"What?" He asked somewhat flustered by the question. "No, everyone knew. It was all common knowledge around campus."

"Relax I'm just fucking with you," she said with a small laugh. "So what does this mean for us anyway? From an SCU standpoint."

Sully pushed both hands forward on the steering, thrusting himself back into the seat. He let out a loud sigh as he relaxed into the leather of his seat. "Shit, I don't even know. Goddamn it! The last thing I need is the world looking at this school as having a hazing issue."

"Isn't there anything you can do to stop it from getting out of hand?"

"Well, the detectives said they'd be in touch. Gave me their cards. But, to be honest, I have no friggin' idea what to expect from all of this. This is not going to be good for the school. I can tell you that. I need somebody to offer me some guidance. That's what I need."

"Well..." Another smile came across Lynn's face, as she ran her hand over her mouth as though she were trying to keep the words inside. "...who do you know that knows anything about murder investigations?"

A confused look creeped onto Sully's face. He glanced over towards Lynn once before looking back at the road. A second later his chin dropped and his eyes opened wide. "Ohhh no! Nope. No way."

"Why not?" she protested.

"Because that's insane! That's why!"

"You said he works homicide, right? And he's clearly been through all of this firsthand. Seems like a natural next step to me."

The two sat in an uncomfortable silence for a moment before Sully finally spoke. "Why do I let you talk me into these things?

"Because you know I'm always right," she replied.

As they pulled up to the light at Stone and Roseland she pointed to the corner and undid her seatbelt. "Can you pull over here? I'm going to jog home from here."

Sully's head turned towards her in surprise as he quickly pulled over. "Jog? I never realized that you live that close."

"Well, it's not *that* close. It's about five miles off of campus," she smiled. "Just a light run for me."

"I could drive you," he offered.

She waved off the gesture. "Not a big deal. I can make it pretty quickly. Besides, I haven't finished my run yet today because of all of this. I was in the middle of it when I got your call and just ran to the office from there."

"Alright, sounds good. Thanks for offering to come today. I appreciate it."

"Of course," she responded as she got out of the car. "Anything I can do to help put the prick responsible behind bars. It's a damn shame, for sure."

She closed the door and started on her way. Sully watched her as she jogged away for longer than was probably acceptable, considering he was her boss. But he was definitely impressed with what he saw, with her being in street clothes for the first time. It was always clear to him that she kept herself in shape. But today's outfit left nothing to the imagination and it was abundantly clear that she worked much harder than he ever would have guessed. It was clear that she had regularly worked out on the weights as well, as he could see muscle definition through her tight clothes. But not so much that he would label her as muscular. More so, fit, than anything.

Lynn rounded the corner and left Sully's field of vision. He shook himself back to reality and turned his attention back to the road as he re-entered traffic. Just like an old specter had re-entered his life.

It had been nearly twenty-five years since he'd seen Chase Dempsey. But six weeks ago he was handed the list of Fall Pledges for Kappa Chi Rho. He had always made it a point to read through the names that were seeking to join the Greek Community. Certainly some of them would become just another Greek that fades into the background. But there would always be a handful of names that would eventually become a part of his everyday life as they move into leadership positions, both within their Fraternities and Sororities and within the Greek Community as a whole.

When he saw Scott Dempsey's name on the list of Kappa Chi Rho pledges, it immediately jumped off the page at him. The chances were high that there was no relation. Dempsey isn't exactly a rare name. But he instinctively was drawn to Scott's name and couldn't move past it without investigating further. The age made sense, after all. After a few clicks into the student directory, Sully had his answer.

Emergency Contact: Chase Dempsey.

At that point he knew it would only be a matter of time before he would cross paths with Chase once again. He had assumed, however, that it would be during move-in day or on some random day when Chase decided to visit his son. But with today's events, everything he had ever said about Chase would now automatically be projected onto Scott Dempsey.

CHAPTER 18

Chase and Suzanne were now wandering down the hallway after leaving the interrogation room. A few minutes ago, Renato Brambilla, the Father-in-Law of Suzanne's sister, and also a trial attorney, arrived at the station. Chase and Suzanne left the interrogation room to allow the official questioning to begin.

Chase rubbed his hands across his face and rested them over his mouth for a moment, as he tried to make sense of what was happening. But there seemed to be no earthly way to do that. He looked over at Suz, who returned his glance and echoed his worried look.

"Hey, just like you said," he told her. "He's gonna be alright." He tried to sound reassuring for her. Though he was saying it in an effort to convince himself, just as much as her.

"I know. I know," she said with a rapid nod. "He didn't do it. Renato is here. It's a misunderstanding that's all. It'll all shake out. We just need to be patient."

"Yep...you're absolutely ri...nope. No, I can't play the optimist here. This is bad, Suz. This is real bad. Shit, his student ID was there? I truly don't believe he did it. But seriously, what the fuck? How does that shake out for him? Even if he isn't charged today, once word gets out about that ID, he is effed. You can trust me on that! This is not a good situation for him to be in."

Suzanne wrapped her arms around him, burying herself into his chest. "Shit, I know this isn't easy for you. We *have* to be the optimists though. We need to be there for him. We can't fall apart. Either of us."

"Suz, I'm not going to fall apart," he said, defending himself. "I just...I just want to be prepared so that we can get out in front of this. He does not have an easy road ahead of him. That's for sure. And I can't be an optimist. I need to see the worst possible scenario and be ready to combat it."

"Well, that's the truth," she responded knowingly. She wasn't there with Chase during the majority of his college years, when he was going through his battles with the student propaganda machine. But she saw the results. She heard the rumors multiple times and from multiple people, long before she met him. She'd heard enough of the facts to make a rational decision for herself on what to believe. But she knew that often people didn't act rationally, and that the result of that was a large majority just following the path of least resistance and choosing to believe the rumors. They say that a lie can go around the world three times before the truth gets out of bed. Which means that it would get around South Cuthbert even faster. They had seen it before, and that was before the dawn of the Internet and social media. She knew that Chase was right to worry that they'd see it happen again.

"Come on," she said, giving him a light pat on the chest. "Let's go find a place to sit down. We aren't going to figure it out standing here."

"Yeah, good idea. He's probably going to be in there a while," Chase started walking down the hall. "If I remember correctly, I think there's a waiting area around the corner here."

"A waiting area?" Suzanne was surprised at the idea. "Well that's nice of them, I suppose."

"Yeah, well, it's where my parents sat waiting for me. So..."

The waiting area was smaller than Chase remembered, but just as plain and sterile. Tile flooring and uncomfortable chairs filled the space, and it had the same old white walls as the rest of the building. There was one person already seated there alone. A girl that looked to Chase to be in her late teens maybe twenty.

92

Brown hair. Pretty. As they entered the room, she turned to Chase and Suzanne and stood to face them nervously.

"Hi," she said, rubbing her hands together. "Are you Mr. and Mrs. Dempsey?"

Chase and Suzanne glanced at each other, each hoping that the other could offer some context to the situation

"Yeah, yes," Suzanne responded. "I'm sorry, and you are?"

"Oh sorry," she responded. "I'm Sydney. Sydney Moore. I'm Scott's girlfriend."

"Oh, right! Of course, Sydney!" Suzanne responded in surprise.

"Oh, okay, great, yeah!" Chase chimed in, not trying in any way to hide his impressed state. When Scott had mentioned he was at his girlfriend's house, he didn't really consider that Scott's girlfriend would be so attractive.

"Sorry, I wasn't sure if he told you about me," she said meekly.

Suzanne quickly moved towards her. "Well, we've been trying to give him some space to let him get used to school."

"Guess he got used to it pretty quickly," Chase quipped.

"Chase!" Suzanne sent an elbow into his side. "Can you please not?!"

"No, that's not what I meant!" he said apologetically, looking back and forth between the two. "Sorry, what I meant was that he clearly settled right in and found himself a nice girl."

He turned back towards Sydney. "I swear I'm not a dick. I promise."

Sydney laughed off the comment. "No it's fine, I get it. Scott has specifically told me that you are a really nice person that sometimes says..."

Suzanne interrupted to finish her sentence. "Stupid things?"

Sydney smiled and chuckled. "Something like that. Yeah."

"How you holding up, sweetie?" Suzanne asked, reaching out and wrapping an arm around her as they moved over towards the seats.

"As good as can be expected I suppose," she responded. "Whatever that means. I mean seriously. Coleman was a really good guy. I've known him since high school. We didn't know each other that well. But...I mean...no one deserves that."

Suzanne nodded as she immediately shifted into what Scott had always referred to as Mother Mode. "Aw, sweetie, I'm so sorry." She helped Sydney into her seat before sitting down next to her. Chase sat across from the two as Sydney continued, her head buried in her lap.

"He didn't really like that Scott and I were together, honestly. Scott thinks that Coleman liked me. But I think he was just being protective because of the hometown connection. But anyway, he was a really good guy and didn't deserve this. And Wilby, well, he's a real sweet guy. I hope he's ok."

Sydney perked her head up and looked at the two of them. "But, I know that Scott didn't do this. It's just not possible. I'm mostly worried about him right now."

"Not to be too forward," Suzanne said cautiously, "But, your house is where Scott spent the night last night?"

"Yeah, that's right," she said. She seemed slightly embarrassed by it.

"That's fine," Suzanne responded reticently. "He's an adult."

Sydney stood for a moment after an awkward pause, before interrupting the silence abruptly.

"That's why I know he didn't do it" she said it louder than after faster than she'd meant to. "He came right to my house from CJ's. And he showed no signs of being involved in anything like...," she paused, and motioned her hand towards the hallway leading towards the interrogation room, "...like this."

"We know," Chase chimed in. "Believe me, there's no way he could've done the things they're saying he did,"

"Right?" Sydney replied emphatically. "He's not that kind of person. I mean, I've only known him a couple of months. But we've been spending a lot of time together. You can get to know a lot about a person. And I have a good instinct about people. I *know* Scott Dempsey! He did *not* do this!"

Sydney was clearly on the verge of tears. Suzanne stood and pulled her in for a hug. Chase followed Suzanne over and awkwardly laid his hand on Sydney's back as she fell into Suzanne's arms.

"We know," Chase added. "And having known him his whole life, we can fill in the blanks for what you haven't learned about him yet. And believe us, it's all good. You're right, he couldn't have done this. It's not in his nature."

"Every pet we've ever had is a rescue animal that Scott found," Suzanne added. "He couldn't stand the idea of anyone leaving these animals without any care."

"Yep!" Chase agreed. "Remember when we wanted to go to that dog breeder in Lancaster? Scott was ten years old. He wouldn't let us go to a breeder."

"He called it a, what was it again?" Suzanne asked, trying to recall.

"A cruel bombasity!" Chase replied.

Sydney laughed. "But that doesn't even make any sense."

"Yeah, well, he was ten," Suzanne laughed. "He didn't really know what he was saying."

"But," Chase chimed in, "He knew what it meant to him. He knew how he felt. And we got the point. But yeah, you're right. He's not the type of person to hurt someone. He even gives money to the homeless."

"I've seen him do that too," Sydney said chuckling.

"He volunteers every year at FEAST. That's this organization at home that collects food donations for people."

"Yeah, he's told me that actually. He mentioned he was going to go home to do that. Because..."

"Thanksgiving's coming up." Suzanne finished her sentence.

"Yeah, he said it's an important time of year." Sydney was clearly taken by his generous nature.

"Yep, that sounds like Scott," Chase agreed.

"So, you see then, right? This doesn't make sense!" Sydney stated it as fact. "Someone who has a heart like that just doesn't do the things they're accusing him of. And I know what I know about last night. It just doesn't add up."

"Did they take a statement from you?" Chase asked.

"Yeah, I told them everything I know about the night. What time we spoke when he called me to say he was leaving. And then what time he got to my place."

"Did they ask about his appearance and demeanor when he got to your place?" Chase asked.

"Yep, and I told them. Nothing weird. He was a little buzzed. But not drunk. There was nothing odd about him. His clothes looked normal. He's even wearing the same clothes when he got here that he was wearing when he showed up at my house. They can see for themselves! If they ask the other guys that were at CJ's, then I imagine they'd hear that he had those clothes on there too." She was visibly upset.

From what Chase was hearing it was clear to him that they didn't have enough evidence to charge Scott with anything. At least not right now. There wouldn't be any evidence on his person that would place him at the scene of the crime, and Sydney's statement would give him an alibi that should exonerate him.

But it was the Student ID that was the sticking point. The ID itself doesn't place him at the scene. Anyone could have taken his ID and placed it there. But it did paint a target on Scott's back. If they can't charge him now, they'll be looking for every possible shred of evidence that would allow them to. Right now Scott Dempsey is their main suspect for the murder of Francis Coleman.

CHAPTER 19

Scott had no realistic parallels to draw from when it came to his expectations for a police interrogation. He'd seen them on television, of course, and he'd always joked that being questioned by his parents was akin to an interrogation. After all, his Dad is actually a real life Homicide Detective and would commonly use all of his trade tricks on Scott.

But in both of those cases, the interrogations would last just a matter of minutes, either minimized on TV to allow for time, or shortened in his own kitchen because the stakes were never high enough to warrant a major parental investigation.

At this point, however, he had now been in the interrogation room for two straight hours. This was not what he expected when he was carted away this morning in the back of a patrol car.

Lt. Quinn and Detective McKue had been asking him the same four questions, a thousand different ways, for the duration of this interrogation.

"Where were you last night?"

"Where did you go after you left CJ's apartment?"

"How did your student ID find its way next to Francis Coleman's body?"

and finally...

"Did you kill Francis Coleman?"

Each time and every time, for each and every variation of the same four questions, Scott had the same four answers.

"I hung out in Trout's dorm room. I left there and went to CJ's. I then left there and went to my girlfriend's house."

"I went straight to Sydney's house."

"I have no idea."

And finally...

"No! I didn't kill Coleman!"

He wasn't quite certain what their specific strategy was. But he knew there was one. And he knew enough to realize that they'd be employing various tactics to trip him up to try to get him to reveal what they believed to be the truth.

The problem with this, of course, was that the truth was that he didn't kill Francis Coleman. He didn't know any other way to approach them than with the truth. He did his best to answer truthfully and clearly and, per his Dad's instructions, offered no further information for them to twist. This became more of an issue when they would ask about his relationship with Coleman. They did indeed have an argument the night prior, which nearly escalated into an altercation. It was no secret that they didn't get along, and Chase didn't try to hide that fact. That would surely do nothing to help the situation.

Renato Brambilla, or Re as his friends called him, was the first person Chase and Suzanne called when they had heard the news about Scott. It was the phone call that he would always joke about with everyone at parties. His specific form of trial law was not one that anyone ever anticipated needing. But the obligatory "Well, if I ever find myself being investigated by the police, I'll be sure to call you first." Would invariably come up at any gathering. Today, the Dempsey's found themselves making that exact phone call.

As soon as he hung up the phone, he dropped what he was doing and was en route from South Plainfield, NJ to South Cuthbert, PA. He had arrived not long after Chase and Suzanne and sat with Scott for the duration of the interrogation to ensure that Scott was treated fairly and that nothing was done to put him in an unnecessary light. Police interrogations sometimes had a way of resulting in a "confession" that the accused had no intention of making, or reason to make. Renato had known Scott since he was just a baby. He was not about to let that happen to him.

"Lieutenant," he interrupted as Quinn was starting to ask another one of his repetitive questions. "You've been questioning my client for two hours and have received the same exact answers to every single question that you have repeatedly asked. I know that you expect that those answers will change. But clearly they will not. My client has done nothing wrong, and has no further information that he can share."

"Your client's Student ID was found at the scene of the crime, Mr. Brambilla." Detective McKue chimed in defensively.

"Well then perhaps you should question his student ID," Renato fired back sarcastically. "Because, as much as you like to pretend that it does, that does not put my client at the scene of the crime. He was not observed at the scene of the crime by anyone. We have witnesses placing him elsewhere in the very clothes that he was wearing when he came here – clothes that show no signs of him being at the scene and involved in the crime. He has already handed them over to you, willingly, for inspection. Your evidence is circumstantial at best and would not hold up in a court of law, and I suspect you know that. Which is why you're spending this much time trying to trip up my client. Now unless you have any new questions, or unless you're charging my client with a crime, then I'd say that this interview is over and that he should be free to go."

Scott sat quietly while he watched Quinn and McKue exchange angry looks. He was impressed with the way Mr. Brambilla had handled them. He had never seen him in a professional environment prior to today and had no idea that the man he knew to always have a smile on his face could adopt such a terse tone with the police in the way that he had just witnessed. He only hoped that it would help, and not make things worse.

"Fine," Quinn said with a passive wave of his hand, to Scott's relief.

"I can go?" Scott asked, glancing up at Mr. Brambilla.

"Yes," McKue chimed in. "But don't go far. You need to stay in the area because I expect that we'll have more questions for you."

"I would also like to state for the record," Renato added, "That my client is pledging the Fraternity whose house the crime took place at. He has spent a high volume of his time at this house. You can expect that when examining the shoes and clothes that he has provided you, you are highly likely to find a connection to that house and basement floor. And when you examine that basement floor, you are highly likely to find foot prints that match my client's shoes. This does not equate to my client being at the scene of the crime, at the time of the crime. Now, I thank you both for your time. Please enjoy the rest of your day."

Mr. Brambilla turned to Scott and motioned towards the door. "Scott, it's time to leave."

Scott looked at Quinn and McKue, partially waiting for them to object, but mostly awaiting them to unlock his handcuffs. Quinn looked over at McKue, who reluctantly leaned forward and unlocked his restraints. Scott slowly stood and walked towards the door. Passing through the doorway felt akin to an escape. Walking down the hallway, he was sure that this wouldn't be the end of it.

CHAPTER 20

Quinn and McKue stood alone in the interrogation room. Their interview with Scott Dempsey had yielded nothing of value and they were no closer to a point where they could press charges than they were this morning.

"Well that was a waste of time," McKue said as she threw a pad of paper down on the table in frustration.

"Do you think he did it?" Quinn asked. He seemed unsure, himself.

"Well his ID being at the scene certainly points to him doing it," she fired back.

"But based on his behavior here," he clarified.

McKue let out a sigh and fell backwards against the whiteboard. "I don't know," she said. "He's consistent in his answers. I'll give him that. Right now, given his rocky relationship and his ID being at the scene, he is our main suspect."

Quinn nodded in agreement as McKue continued.

"And yes, what we have is circumstantial. But this kid, Francis Coleman, he was slaughtered in that basement. You saw him. Whoever did this, has serious issues. Whoever did this has a lot of baggage that they need to unpack. Like serious baggage. I mean like walking around with a giant griefcase on wheels."

"Do you think Scott Dempsey has those kind of issues, though? That large of a...griefcase? I love that by the way," he asked without a hint of a smile. He wanted McKue's input. She's a young detective, but a talented one. He's been impressed with her ability to profile a perp with incredible accuracy.

"Quite honestly, I don't know. I would have to lean towards no. But right now everything points to him. And I'm concerned that if we don't move quickly on it and get a confession out of him, it'll end up a cold case."

"Agreed," Quinn responded. "Alright, let's get out of here. We've got work to do."

The two exited the interrogation room and began walking down the hallway when they heard a voice call out from down the hall.

"Excuse me! Lieutenant? Detective?"

They turned around to see Chase Dempsey walking briskly in their direction.

The two turned their heads in unison. "Mr. Dempsey," Quinn said. "What can we do for you?"

"It's Lieutenant," Chase corrected them. "Thank you. But, anyway, I was hoping to get a moment of your time."

Quinn glanced slowly over at McKue before unceremoniously replying to Chase. "Ok."

"Yeah, so I just wanted to connect with you. I was hoping to get a professional courtesy from you two." He saw their body language immediately change. Backs were now up. Arms were now crossed. He knew what they were thinking right now. *Ok, here we go? Who does this guy think he is?* He admitted to himself that he would have thought the same thing. He decided to push forward anyway.

"What can you tell me? My son's life is on the line here. I'd like to know what you guys are looking at."

"Mr. Dem..."

"Lieutenant," He corrected McKue. "Lieutenant Dempsey."

"Heh, not here you're not...Mr. Dempsey," Quinn interjected. "Here you're the Father of a murder suspect who happens to be thirty miles outside of his jurisdiction."

Chase expected this type of reaction. He ignored Quinn's tone and instead decided to focus on the words he was saying. "So you're looking at him as a suspect...officially?"

"Well officially right now, we have to call him just a person of interest. But, yeah, it's certainly looking like it may move in the direction towards suspect. Here's what I can tell you. We've got a dead body. Your son got in a tussle with him last night and your son's ID was found at the crime scene. That's about as much as we're willing to share right now."

"Is there anything else linking Scott to the scene?" he asked.

"No, right now it's just his ID. But you know the drill. We'll be testing for DNA. Questioning other witnesses. The truth," he paused for effect, "whatever it happens to be, it'll come out."

McKue took a step closer and leaned in. "But don't think that, just because you've got a badge, you can walk in here swinging your dick around and get whatever you want. You're the Father of our suspect. So, you're not exactly on the top of our list as someone we'll be offering a...How did you put it?...professional courtesy."

Quinn lightly motioned McKue back with his hand and addressed Chase. "Alright, well Mr. Dempsey, you get the picture. Like I said, you know the drill and you know what to expect here. This isn't going to be any different because you happened to be a cop."

"Yeah, I do know the drill. And you know as well as I that none of this is enough to secure a guilty verdict. So don't go getting all cocky with me about this. You aren't exactly stationed in the murder capitol of the world. But I think you'd be wise enough to avoid judgment before all of the facts come in. I realize that I'm his Father and I'm going to be biased. But my son is innocent, and I'm going to prove it. You'll be seeing more of me."

Chase turned abruptly and stormed down the hall.

"Oh, I'm counting on it," McKue said to herself as Chase turned the corner towards the exit.

CHAPTER 21

Scott, Sydney and Suzanne walked out of the South Cuthbert Police Station feeling drained, but also mildly triumphant. Scott had been genuinely concerned that he might not see the sun for the foreseeable future. Feeling the cool air hit his face as he stepped through the door was the best he'd felt since he woke up this morning. The fresh clothes of his that Sydney had retrieved from her house were a welcomed feeling compared to the rough feel of the orange shirt and top that he'd been given by the South Cuthbert Police. He stopped at the top of the steps, took a deep breath, and then promptly slumped his shoulders. He felt selfish, and a strong sense of guilt, for being happy right now. Coleman, whom he still considered a friend despite their differences, was dead and he'd barely had a chance to even process it.

"Scott?" Sydney turned to him with a look of concern. The edges of his lips were angling downwards and his cheeks began to quiver. She reached out and pulled him in for a strong embrace. "Scott, it's ok."

Scott returned her embrace and collapsed into her arms in tears. The full stress of the day's events that had been piled on top of him like a weight he'd never experienced before. He tried to speak as he sobbed over her shoulder. "He's dead, Syd! He's dead and I couldn't do anything about it. We may not have been the best of friends. But I would have done anything to stop that from happening."

"I'm so sorry, Scott! I'm so sorry!"

Suzanne looked on as the two held each other. She could tell that they had developed a close bond. One that would be able to help him through this difficult time. It was something she knew that Chase was missing during the bulk of his time here at SCU. She was happy to see that at least Scott would have that benefit.

Scott became keenly aware that he was standing out in public sobbing like a child. He reluctantly pulled away from Sydney. "I'm sorry," he said, wiping the tears from his eyes.

"Oh my God, Scott, don't be sorry!" Suzanne said, forcing herself to stop short of hugging him. "Please, with all that you've been through today, you have the right to cry all you want."

"I just...I should've been able to help him," he continued.

"Stop. Don't say that," Sydney commanded. "This is not your responsibility. Do you understand? Whoever did this. This is their fault. Not yours! It's not on you. There is nothing that you could have done to stop this. Can you agree with me right now on that?"

Scott nodded slightly and Sydney reached up, placing her hands on his cheeks and turning his face towards hers."

"Are you with me?" she asked quietly.

Scott looked her in the eyes and focused on her intently. "Yeah," he said softly, "I'm with you."

Chase interrupted the moment as he came bursting through the door.

"Ok, we all set?" He looked at the group and could see that he had missed something. "Everything OK?"

"Yeah, it's fine," Suzanne replied. "Scott's just decompressing. What were you doing in there?"

"Me? Oh, I just wanted to go talk to the detectives and see if I could get any more information that we might not already know."

"Chase," she paused, reluctant to ask what she was about to ask, "You didn't make things worse did you?"

"What? No!" Chase replied. His voice had a higher pitch than normal. "Why would you think that? No not at all, it's totally cool. Just three professionals having a conversation. Totally cool."

"Why do you keep saying it's totally cool?" Scott asked in a worried tone.

"Because it is," he said, brushing it off. "It's totally cool. Alright, we ready to go?"

"Yeah, I guess...Oh God, Will!" Scott suddenly exclaimed. "Will! I need to find out how he is."

"I've actually been texting with Archie about it," Sydney told him. "He's in critical condition over at Cuthbert County Hospital."

"I need to get over to see him," Scott told the three of them.

"Wait, Scott, don't you think it'd be best if you came home?" Suzanne pleaded.

"To Warrington?" Chase asked in surprise. "No. Not a good idea. That'll make him look guilty. Trust me."

"He can't stay here, Chase. This is not a good place for him right now. I think you know that!"

"Suz, he needs to ride this out here. I'm sorry, but that's how..."

"Guys!" Scott yelled at them. "I'm not even worried about that now. My friend's in the hospital. I've already lost one today. I'm worried about the other." He looked at the two defiantly. "I'm going to go see Will."

Turning to Sydney he asked, "Do you have your car?"

Sydney looked nervously at Chase and Suzanne, clearly unsure about crossing Scott's parents so soon after meeting them.

"Well, yeah, I..."

"That won't be necessary, Sydney," Suzanne interrupted. "I'm not about to make you decide on who to side with when we just met you today. And Scott's right. He deserves to be able to go see how his friend is doing. We can drive. Let's get moving."

CHAPTER 22

Unlike your quintessential inner city hospitals, which were required to build up, instead of out, due simply to a lack of land, Cuthbert County Hospital has never been faced with an issue of space. CCH was a typical suburban hospital. Which is to say that it took up more acreage than airspace. It sprawled out wide over what once was an area of open fields, and in most sections it only stretched three stories into the air.

It was on that third floor where Will Bonnetti lay unconscious in the Critical Care Unit. He'd been stabbed in the abdomen and had lost a great deal of blood. He was rushed into surgery immediately upon arrival. It was fortunate that he was found as quickly as he was. Otherwise, he likely wouldn't have made it to the hospital alive.

Mick Perry, a KXP Brother that had graduated a year prior, had come back for the weekend to see his Fraternity Brothers. Mick was at Jake's Bar until well after closing before stumbling his way along the two block stretch to 403 in hopes of finding a couch to crash on. Entering the house, however, he was met with the sight of a blood-soaked Will Bonnetti lying in a clump on the kitchen floor. He had immediately begun yelling out for help while simultaneously pulling out his cell phone to dial 911.

Brian Green was the first to hear Mick's cries for help. Jumping out of his bed, he raced down the stairs and was in the kitchen within moments. Brian, who happened to be working towards his Nursing degree, quickly checked Wilby for signs of life. Finding a faint pulse, he pulled his own shirt over his head and used it to place pressure on the wound.

A visibly drunk Mick attempted to communicate with the 911 Operator and was eventually directed by Brian to hand him the phone. Brian put the phone on speaker while he described Wilby's injuries and vitals so that the 911 Operator could get word to the already en route paramedics. He held the now blood soaked shirt on the wound until they arrived to find Wilby clinging to life.

Less than sixteen hours later, Wilby was in no better shape, aside from his proximity to medical care. His heart rate was sitting at a dangerously low level. The blood transfusion he'd received earlier made a difference. But he was still far from in the clear.

Two hundred feet down the hall, thirty Crow Brothers and Pledges held vigil in the surgical waiting room. They had ridden over en masse once they had all completed their statements with the police at 403, and were immediately directed to the waiting area by the Charge Nurse. She had cringed at the thought of having thirty college students roaming the halls and demanded they remain within the waiting area. A select few were granted a few moments to see Wilby.

The waiting room at Cuthbert County was large enough to hold up to seventy-five people. Although, it was broken up into several smaller sections to allow for privacy and a more comfortable environment. The Crows took up nearly half of the space. Most of the initiated brothers sat in two of the larger areas. They sat and stared at each other in silence, trying to make sense of what had just happened.

The Pledge Class instinctively separated themselves from the Brothers, choosing instead to take up one of the smaller available spaces. They sat quietly while Fox News played in the background on the wall-mounted TV. They'd been there for hours now and have said all they could think to say. Many of these eighteen and nineteen year old men, just in the past twelve hours, had now been met with the most intense situation that they would ever encounter.

A full twenty-five percent of their Pledge Class sat embroiled in a story that none of them could ever even begin to think up on their own. One of them is dead – murdered. Another teetering on the brink between life and death. And a third, it seemed, could be the one responsible.

None of them wanted to raise the one question that was on each and every one of their minds – could Scott have really done this? 407 is not that large of a house. They were only one room away and could clearly hear Lt. Quinn and Detective McKue tell Scott that his student ID was found by Coleman's body.

It was Wick that first let the heaviness of the moment get the best of him and felt the overwhelming need to break the silence. As he opened his mouth to speak he was interrupted by the ding of his phone.

He stared down at the text message that crossed his screen.

"It's Demps," he announced to the group. "He's done at the Police Station. He's coming here."

Everyone sat at attention upon hearing this.

"Are you serious?" Trout asked with disgust.

"Well that's what his text says," Wick responded matter of factly.

"He's got balls, that's for sure." Casey added. "We all heard what they told him. Sounds to me like he's their number one suspect. And he thinks coming here is a good idea? He's lucky if he makes it out of here in one piece. Shit, do you remember what he said this morning? He was the first to bring up the idea that Coleman and Wilby might be at the house already. He was probably laying cover for himself before we even knew there was something to lay cover for."

"Hey!" Archie came over and interrupted them. "What is this shit I'm hearing?"

"It's Scott," Wick told him. "He's coming here."

"And you guys are blaming him. Judge and Jury over here, I guess?" Archie snapped back, deriding them for where they were allowing their minds to go.

"Brother Arch, what do you expect? You heard the same thing we all heard!"

"Yeah, and I also know Demps just as well as you do. Do you think he'd do this?" He looked around at the group as they lowered their heads, refusing to look at him. He didn't know if it was in shame or in an attempt to avoid showing their disagreement.

He continued, "If he's on his way here, that means that the cops didn't find it necessary to charge him. So if they didn't have a reason, then neither do you. He's your Pledge Brother. He's your friend. This could've been any one of you, and if it was, well then you can bet that the last thing you'd want and need is for the people you trust the most to turn on you. This is when he needs you most. I hope you realize that."

He stood in front of the group for another moment and scanned their faces before turning to leave. Once he did, Wick addressed the group.

"He's right. We don't know enough right now to have a valid opinion. We need to let this play out. And until then we need to be there for Demps and give him the benefit of the doubt. He deserves that much."

"Wick, I don't give a shit what anybody says," Robbie shot back in a loud whisper. "Coleman is dead and Wilby is lucky to be alive. Man, right now it seems pretty cut and dry right to me. I'm pissed. I want answers, and the most logical answer is that Scott did it. If something comes out to change that, great. But right now that's the direction I'm looking in."

"Wick, I hate to say it, but I'm inclined to side with Robbie on this," Trout interjected. Wick turned to the two of them with a surprised look on his face. "It just seems logical," Trout added.

"Does everyone feel like this?" Wick asked the group. He looked at each of them and was met with some light nods. Others avoided his gaze altogether.

Woody sat in the corner and seemed to be the only remaining voice of reason.

"Guys, Arch is absolutely right. We cannot be Judge and Jury. Look, I'm no idiot. What we know right now doesn't look good for Demps. But, I have known him for years and I know enough to say that he would never do this. Most of you have only known him for less than two months. But as a group we've been through more together than we've been through with some of our closest life long friends. Scott has shown his loyalty to us in more ways than I can count during that time. And that includes towards Coleman and Wilby. We owe it to him to return that same loyalty that he's afforded us. Because if I know one thing right now, it's that Scott Dempsey is not a killer. I've known him long enough to know that his character would not allow for it. Scott Dempsey is our friend. He is our Pledge Brother. One day he's going to be our Brother. It's time for us to treat him like it."

Everyone in the group looked back at Woody, mostly with nods of approval. Trout and Robbie, however, sat next to each other in the opposite corner. They exchanged a look of exasperation at the fact that they were even being made to choose, followed by a look of surrender. They both nodded in obvious reluctant agreement.

"Ok good," Wick said to the group. "Then let's show him what we know Brotherhood to be all about. When he gets here, he's got our support."

CHAPTER 23

Scott felt as if his heart would punch a hole straight through the center of his chest as his parents' car pulled into the parking lot at Cuthbert County Hospital. He had no idea what type of reception he could expect from the Brothers and his Pledge Brothers that were waiting inside. He knew that they had heard the line of questioning that the police put him through this morning. Their eyes told him as much as he was being led out in handcuffs. His main question was whether or not they believed that he could commit such a horrible act.

Sydney gripped Scott's hand as Chase put the car into park. He looked at her and gave a half smile and a nod.

"You ready for this, bud?" Chase turned and asked him. "You don't have to do this, ya' know."

"I wish that were true," Scott responded, realizing how despondent he sounded. He continued with more enthusiasm, "I need to talk to these guys now. I can't put it off. If I put it off it'll just make things worse. Besides, I need to know if any of these guys can think of any place where I might've lost my student ID."

"Ok, I hear ya'. And I don't blame you. It's good that you're taking this head on," Chase said approvingly. "Let's do it then."

The group exited the car and made their way into the hospital. While the hospital itself was founded in late 1892, at the time it was only a small building with enough beds for five patients. What was currently the main building of the hospital was constructed in 1918, but you couldn't tell by looking at it. The I and the interior had been continuously refurbished in order to maintain a modern appearance. Patients coming in today would have no idea that the facilities they were entering were over a hundred years old.

As they reached the third floor and exited the elevator, Scott could see the large glass windows offering people a view into the waiting area, through which he could see a large group of Crows assembled. He took a deep breath and started down the hall. The weight of their stares made each step forward more difficult for him. Opening the door, Woody and Wick were the first to greet him. Scott reached his hand out, hoping simply for a handshake from one of them. "Come here," Wick said to him, pulling Scott in for a tight hug. Woody wrapped his arms around both of them. Scott did his best to fight back the tears. He was mostly successful.

"You doing OK?" Woody asked, as the others began to gather around them.

"Hey guys," Scott said to the group, then returning his attention to Wick. "Yeah, not really doing great. But I...I don't even know what to say."

"What did the cops say?" Robbie asked bluntly.

Scott looked at him, surprised to be getting the question so quickly. It answered one of his main questions for him – what did they think? At least some of them were clearly wondering whether or not he was guilty.

"Alright, let's do this now," Scott surrendered to the reality of the situation. "Guys, I want you all to know that I had nothing to do with this. But, unfortunately, the cops don't necessarily believe that. It's definitely going to look like I did. And I know how that sounds." He glanced around the room and it was clear to see that some of them at least had serious opinions on it already. The stern looks on the faces of Trout and Robbie made that clear to him.

"I'm guessing you heard from the other room this morning that the cops apparently found my student ID by Coleman's body. So yeah, they're probably looking at me as a suspect. But, I swear to each and every one of you...and you can believe me if you want or not...but I have no idea how it got there. I left CJ's apartment last night and I went straight to Syd's house and spent the night there. I found out about all of this at the same time as you guys. I've spent hours being questioned by the cops and I told them nothing but the truth. And they found no reason to hold me any longer."

He paused for a moment in order to offer the others a chance to respond if they felt the need. He was met with silence. *How does one even respond to that?* He thought to himself before continuing. "But listen, I'm trying to figure out what exactly happened to my student ID. Somewhere along the line, I lost it, or it was taken. I don't know...and it wound up there. So I'm hoping that you guys can think back to last night and see if you can remember anything at all that might help explain what happened to it. It got there somehow and it wasn't from me. I had it at dinner and that's the last time I even had a reason to have it out. So if anyone remembers anything, even the smallest thing. Please, let me know."

He looked at the group as they continued to stare in silence. He wasn't sure how they'd respond, and wouldn't blame them if they didn't believe him. He recognized that it did not come off as an ironclad story on the surface.

"Demps," Wick began, "I can't speak for everyone. But I know I'm behind you on this. I know you, and if you say you didn't do it, that's all I need to hear."

Wick turned to the group. "Guys, I believe him. And Scott lost a friend today too. He needs, and has, my support." He then turned back and wrapped his arms around Scott in a hug. The rest of the group slowly joined in. Soon Scott was surrounded by a sea of Brothers and his Pledge Brothers.

Trout and Robbie stood looking on. Their arms crossed in defiance.

The love fest eventually broke up and Scott introduced his parents to some of the group. Many of them were in awe to learn that Chase was a Crow from the same Chapter. None of them were even born yet when he was gracing the grounds of SCU. They had no idea that their experience was far from the experience that he endured, or that they were witnessing the beginnings of history repeating itself.

"How's Will?" Scott asked. "Are they letting people in to see him?"

"There's not a lot that we know right now," Arch replied. "It sounds like he's barely hanging on. You might be able to go down to see him. Earlier they let a handful of us in just so that he could hear familiar voices. We can walk down to the Nurses station and ask."

Wick turned to Chase and Suzanne. "Mr. and Mrs. Dempsey do you guys want something to eat? There's some donuts and brownies over on the table."

"Lynn, from Sully's office, brought them in earlier," Danny G. said with a smile.

"Aw, dude she looked friggin' hot," Phatty added, stretching out the word 'hot' with a high voice.

Sydney rolled her eyes at them. "Serious question, does your immaturity have a pause button?"

She looked over at Scott, who had a wide smile in response to Phatty's comment, and promptly elbowed him in the stomach.

"It doesn't stop after college, sweetie," Suzanne warned her, while shooting a sideways glance at Chase who was following the conversation and chuckling with a smile across his own face.

Mid-chuckle, Chase looked towards Suzanne and caught her staring him down, prompting him to steer the conversation back on course. He cleared his throat and changed the subject.

"So Scott, do you want me to head down with you?"

"No, actually if Brother Archie could go with me that'd be good. They said one at a time. He knows the way and who to speak to. I don't want to have us appear as this large group of people and make them want to push us away."

Chase nodded in agreement, impressed at Scott's ability to read the room and look ahead at what he might be faced with.

"Ok, yeah that works," Archie agreed. "Come on, follow me."

115

The two made their way down the hall towards the CCU. Scott had no doubt he could've found it by himself. It's not that large of a hospital and the CCU is literally right down the hall. But he wanted to have a few moments alone with Archie to get a realistic assessment of what people were actually thinking about him.

"Well," he began as he turned to ensure the waiting room door was closed, "what's the verdict from back there? Am I innocent until proven guilty or am I guilty until proven innocent?"

Archie seemed to be surprised by the question and paused a moment as he walked, seeming to choose his words carefully. The longer he waited the more nervous it made Scott.

"I think it's a mix, to be honest," he replied. "Leaning heavily on innocent until proven guilty I'd say. I'm sure that speech you made back there helped. But, Brotherhood or no Brotherhood, these guys are human. Some of them are definitely going to rush to judgement."

"Yeah, I'm already starting to spot some of them," Scott acknowledged.

"Don't mind them. They've got zero impact on your situation right now. Their opinions change nothing for you. Ok?!" he said forcefully. "Just focus on yourself. I know you want them to believe you. But their beliefs don't impact the truth. They aren't the ones that you need to convince."

Scott's face showed his surprise at the deep thoughts coming out of his Pledge Master. "Yeah, I suppose you're right.," he told him. "I'm just trying to get a grip on who I've got on my side."

"Well, you can count on me being there. That's for sure." Archie threw his arm around Scott's back as they walked and gave his shoulder a squeeze. "Anything you need, you let me know."

It heartened Scott to know that he had support from at least one initiated Brother within the Fraternity. He knew that there would be dissenters. But he couldn't stomach the idea of everyone he knew turning on him. It was important to him that he had people in his corner.

As the two reached the Nurse's station, Archie stepped ahead of him and approached the Nurse sitting behind the desk.

"Excuse me? Hi, me again," he greeted him. Scott got the impression that Archie had been there quite a bit this afternoon.

"We've got another Pledge Brother of Will Bonnetti's here," he said, throwing his head back in the direction of Scott. "He would like to have a moment with him. Is it possible for him to go in?"

The man took a long look at Scott, seeming to examine his face. Scott didn't know if it was typical or if there was a reason for it. He shook it off and told himself he was being paranoid.

"Yeah, sure," the Nurse responded. "But just for a moment, ok?"

"Yep, absolutely," Scott confirmed.

"Ok go ahead down," the Nurse told them. "Room 2034."

As they walked into Wilby's room, Scott saw a form lying in the bed that he barely recognized. At 5'8" and 160 lbs, Wilby was never exactly an imposing force among men. His runner's frame didn't have an ounce of fat on him. There were muscles there. Although not enough for him to be mistaken for someone that might be considered as being well-built. But Wilby carried with him a confidence that few others in their group could hope to muster. It served to give him a perceived extra inch or two, and ten-plus pounds in stature.

However, the Wilby that Scott was staring at now looked frail and weak. Scott had always seen him as someone that would enforce his will on the world around him. But, now, Wilby's body seemed to sink into the bed. The amount of wires and hoses connected to him made him seem to be more reliant on the world around him than Scott could have ever imagined. Gone, it seemed, was the man whose power came from within.

Scott knew better than that though. He knew that it was likely that power from within that was the only thing keeping Will Bonnetti alive right now.

"Hey Will, it's Demps," he said quietly as he leaned in towards his Pledge Brother. "Listen, I'm guessing you can hear me. I need you to hear me. You need to stay strong, got it? We can't lose you man. You're too important to this world. And, listen, I only have a minute. So I'm sorry but I need to be selfish with that time. You're also too important to me. You probably don't know this. But...well listen, I just need you to get better, ok?" He stopped short of mentioning Coleman. Scott was sure that Wilby could hear him and he didn't want to put any further stress on him.

He continued, "I need you to pull through so that you can..." he paused. "What I mean is that you're my only way to get through this. So come on man, stay strong, ok? Will Power! Right! You got this."

"Excuse me, that's all the time I can give you," the Nurse said from just inside the door.

Scott turned back towards him and nodded. "Got it, thanks," he replied before turning back to Wilby.

"Alright buddy. Stay strong! This is just a detour, not a roadblock. You'll get past this. Stay strong!"

Archie patted Scott on the back as the two walked out the door and began the walk back to the waiting room.

"You ok?" he asked Scott.

"Yeah man, I'll be good. Thanks," Scott replied.

"It just occurred to me when you said that to him," he said. "We realized already that he's a potential witness. But he's also your potential vindication," Archie stated. "Isn't he?"

"Yep," Scott replied matter of factly. "He sure is."

CHAPTER 24

Cuthbert County Hospital was, oddly enough, somewhat of an escape for Chase Dempsey. Throughout all of his time at SCU, he never once had a need to visit the hospital. Arriving there today allowed him to separate himself from the constant flashbacks that he had been experiencing during the past few hours of wandering through the Police Station.

Sitting in the waiting room, amongst the Kappa Chi Rho Brotherhood, gave him a reason to relive his college days without the need to tie it to every memory he had of his time at the University. That is, until the sight of Sully crossed his field of vision.

"Hey Demps," Sully called out from the waiting room door as their eyes met. "Can I talk to you for a minute?"

Chase let out an audible groan. "Christ, Sully, what are you doing here?"

"No, no this is serious," Sully said, waving his hands in front of him. "I'm not here to argue with you."

"Why don't I believe you?" Chase asked dismissively.

"Come on man, two minutes." He motioned over to the doorway, implying he'd like to speak to him in the hallway. "Just two minutes?"

Chase had been spending much of today balancing the line between father and detective. He had a feeling that he was about to be asked to add another title to that list and weighed whether or not he wanted to give Sully the opportunity to do so.

"Alright, fine." He relented. He slowly rose to his feet and followed Sully into the hallway.

"Ok, so what do you need?"

"Alright, I know that we may have gotten off on the wrong foot earlier," Sully began. "That's probably my fault."

"Well yeah, probably" Chase said with obvious sarcasm.

"Ok, so that was my fault. But, listen, I need your help. I hear you're a cop. That true?" Chase made a mental note that Sully was speaking fast, as though asking the question was an inconvenience for him.

"Yeah, I work Homicide in Philly," he replied. "What's that matter?"

"That's perfect. Listen, I've never had to deal with anything like this before, and I need to know what we can expect from the SCPD. I've never had anything like this happen in my time as head of Greek Life, and truthfully, I don't want to fuck it up. I was hoping you could offer some," Sully paused as he searched for the right word, "some knowledge of this type of thing to help me anticipate what I'll need to be doing in my role. Plus, you've had...you know...personal experience."

"Jesus Christ, Sully, really?!" Chase replied incredulously.

"I don't mean it like that! I swear!"

"You were doing well there for a minute. And then..."

"I meant that your point of view in this situation, since there are young men involved, could be valuable." Sully did his best to recover.

Chase thought for a moment before responding. "Sully, the main 'young man' that's involved, in case you haven't noticed, is my son. That's where my focus is going to be. I didn't drive out here to be your sounding board and offer you advice to make your job easier."

"Demps, I get that, I do," Sully replied, attempting to deescalate the situation.

"Well you didn't seem to get it back at the station." Chase fired back.

"You're right, and I'm sorry. I shouldn't have reacted that way. I let my emotions get the best of me. I just need a little bit of your time. Just sit down with me and walk me through...I don't know...what's next even. I'm so far out of my element here."

Chase looked at Sully with contempt. A dozen different thoughts ran through his mind all at once. How could this man who treated him so horribly during his own time of need, have the gaul to ask him for help while the same thing was happening to his son? Chase wanted to tell him no. He wanted to tell him to screw off and go find someone else to make him look good. He wanted to finally take advantage of the moment he's been waiting on for over twenty years.

But it wasn't the right time. There were simply too many reasons to say yes. Paramount of which was that it would help Scott. Certainly, Sully was right. Chase could be valuable to him. But that would, in turn, make him valuable to the room full of young men standing on the other side of the door. They had just lost their friend and Pledge Brother and were worried that they'd soon be losing another. Sully is tasked with guiding these young men through this horrific experience. Turning away Sully would be akin to turning them away as well. He'd be turning away his own Fraternity Brothers. Sure, he was not in school and active in Fraternity today. But he went through the same experiences as them and took the same oath that they took. He was still a Brother of Kappa Chi Rho – their Brother. He couldn't abandon them.

Twenty years ago he would've absolutely told Sully to go to hell. But that was twenty years ago. Chase had grown as a person since then. He's learned things about life through his marriage and his life on the Police force that he just didn't understand back then. Namely that sometimes you have to put your differences aside for the greater good, and that forgiveness is a real thing that can make a person's world better. But most importantly, family means everything.

Right now, Chase was being handed an opportunity to help his KXP family. Sully would be in fairly close contact with the police, as the University's main point of contact for the investigation. It was clear that Quinn and McKue weren't going to be any more forthcoming with information than they were legally required to be. At least not when it pertained to Scott. But the Police are prone to share more information with people in a position of authority at institutions that are involved in an investigation. They need to play well with each other in order to maintain a strong relationship. He anticipated that they'd be keeping Sully updated with a limited amount of information at the very least. The closer he could remain to Sully during this, the better chance he had of staying informed of how the investigation would impact Scott. He couldn't let his feelings get in the way of that.

"Ok fine, I'll help you," he told Sully. "But on one condition."

"Anything at all," Sully quickly replied. Chase had a quick thought that he could literally ask for anything right now and Sully would agree. But he only wanted one thing.

"You have to give my son a fair shake."

"Sure of course, why wouldn't I?" Sully responded, seemingly offended.

Chase titled his head and grimaced in a look that said, *Really?*

"Dude, that episode back at the station? You were immediately attaching my past to Scott's present. That is not the reality of things. I didn't kill Chris Wilbanks. But most of this University probably still thinks I did. And that had a lot to do with you. From the beginning you were spreading lies about me. I have no idea why. I don't know if you didn't like me. If you were just young and immature. Or if you were just plain being a dick. Maybe all three! Who knows! But we both know that I had nothing to do with Chris' death. And I can tell you that Scott didn't have anything to do with this one. I need you to promise me that you will not let how you treated me glob onto how you treat him. He is a student in your care as the Director of Greek Life. In your eyes, and actions, Scott Dempsey needs to be innocent until proven guilty."

122

Sully thought through what Chase said, and then straightened his posture. "Ok you're absolutely right, he deserves a fair shake."

Sully extended his hand to Chase. "It's a deal? Innocent until proven guilty."

Chase paused for a moment before doing what he once thought was the unthinkable. He returned the gesture and the two shook on it. "Yeah, it's a deal."

"And for what it's worth," Sully continued, "I'm sorry."

"Well, OK, thank you," Chase said, unsure how to reply. "That's a conversation for another time I guess. That's in the past. For now, we need to be focused on the present."

"Agreed, ok so where can we talk?" He asked, unsure what the next step should be.

"Well not here. I don't want to be talking about things around these kids and Scott. Can we meet somewhere in about an hour?"

"Sure, will my office work?" Sully was eager to begin.

"Yeah, that's cool. You in Barness?" Chase asked, referring to the Barness Student Union Center.

"Yeah 231."

Chase paused and thought for a moment. "Is that...Charlie's old office?"

"Yeah," Sully said with a laugh. "Nice memory. He was nice enough to pass it on to me after he retired."

Chase nodded, thinking to himself that Sully had a long way to go before he could consider himself as having filled the large shoes of his predecessor.

"Ok I'll see you there in an hour."

CHAPTER 25

Barness Union Hall was built in 1992, not long before Chase had started attending South Cuthbert University. He spent a good deal of his time there, as KXP would often utilize their meeting spaces for their weekly meetings. He was surprised to see that the years hadn't had much of a detrimental effect on the building. It still looked as good as new.

Chase had an Uber pick him up and drive him over to campus. He requested that he be dropped off near Scott's dorm, the opposite side of campus from Sully's office, in an attempt to avoid any trail tying his involvement to the campus. He quickly made his way along the uphill stretch that led him toward Barness. Arriving at Roseland Avenue, he was transported back twenty-five years as though he was just on his way to the fitness center.

A rush of memories came back to him as he walked into the large, open lobby. Centrally placed in the three story building, you could see most of the areas of the building from that one space. He scanned the room and mentally called out everything he'd had occasion to frequent – the meeting spaces, the fitness center, and the Greek Life office.

Walking up the stairs was like stepping back in time for Chase. As he walked down the hall towards Charlie Bateman's *old* office, now Sully's, he heard voices coming through the doorway. He recognized one as belonging to Sully. The other sounded familiar, but he wasn't sure why. Glancing his head around the corner and seeing a pair of fit legs inside a pair of black leggings, he realized immediately that it was Lynn Clowry. Chase stood outside the door and listened for a moment.

"All I'm asking is whether or not you think you can trust him," he heard her ask.

"Well I have to," Sully shot back. "I have no choice."

"Sure you do!" she quickly responded. "Look, I know this was my idea. But I've been thinking about it. You gave this guy a really hard time in college. That right there would give me reason to wonder about his intentions. And what if he actually *was* involved in that guy's death, what was his name? Chris...?"

"Wilbanks."

"Chris Wilbanks, right. What if he was actually involved in his death? And they just never caught him. And now you'd be siding with him in a case where his son is the main suspect? Look, I'm no Perry Mason. But I know that doesn't sound like something that works out well for someone in your position."

Sully dismissed her viewpoint without a second thought. "Lynn, listen. First of all, like you said, this was your idea. And second, I know what I'm doing. I'm going to be fine. And I appreciate your concern. But you don't have to worry."

Chase recognized that he'd been hovering a bit too long and didn't want Lynn to walk out and find him standing there. He quietly made his way back down the hall about twenty feet before walking back towards the office, this time being certain to make enough noise to be heard.

"Hi, everyone. Sully, how it's going? Lynn," he paused. "good to see you again."

"Good to see you too," she replied with a surprising smile. She seemed to quickly turn on the charm in a complete one-eighty from the exchange he had heard just a moment ago.

"Ok, so what'd I miss?" he asked, partially for his own amusement.

"Oh, nothing, nothing at all." Sully said, searching for the words. "We were just discussing how we don't really know anything more than we did this morning. But hopefully you can help us figure out a normal timeline for what we can expect."

"Ok yeah, sounds good. Let's get started then," Chase replied as he sat down in a chair across from Sully. He'd been there five seconds and already had his question answered. No new info. Time to offer whatever he could to them and then get out of there. He had his work to do.

"Lynn, there's no need for you to stick around. Thanks for your help again. But it's a Sunday. I don't want to keep you here. I was surprised to even find you here, actually."

"Oh, OK." Lynn said, a bit surprised and seemingly hurt a little. "Well, I just decided to take care of a few things to get ready for tomorrow. It's probably going to be a bit crazy here. I've got a few things to get together at my desk first for the morning. Then I'll get out of here." She stood to leave. Chase couldn't help but notice her figure as she left and saw exactly what was causing the KXP Brothers 'immature behavior', as Sydney had put it earlier at the hospital.

He turned back and saw Sully flash a knowing smile and a small chuckle. Chase returned the sentiment and Sully threw his hands up in a "Hey, I get it." Motion.

"Ok so where do we start?" he asked Chase.

"Alright, so here's what we know. Or at least what I know. You tell me if I'm missing anything. And all of this should be the same information that we know the Police to have. There was a late-night at this guy CJ's apartment. He's a Crow. The full KXP Pledge Class was there."

Sully nodded in agreement.

"Around 1:30am, Coleman and Wilby leave. They decide to go by 403. Reason unknown at this point. Not long after, Scott leaves CJ's. He says he goes straight to Sydney's... his girlfriend... place."

"You say 'says' as though you don't believe him," Sully interjected.

"Oh no, definitely not the case. But I need to lay this out exactly the way SCPD is viewing it."

"Gotcha. Sorry."

"No worries. Anyway, at 403, I'm unclear on what happened there. I haven't been told much about the scene. From what I gather though Coleman was found dead in the basement. Scott's ID was found by the body. Will Bonnetti was found injured in the kitchen."

"Correct," Sully replied. "The feeling, I'm told, is that Francis Coleman was killed in the basement and then the killer encountered Will Bonnetti when coming up the stairs and had to go through him to get out."

Chase made a quick mental note that Sully was using their full names. He has a couple of dozen Greek organizations under his purview. He clearly never met either Coleman or Wilby. Two pledges that haven't even completed their pledge period yet are basically numbers to him. Chase had never met them either. But he's had enough exposure to their friends, Brothers and Pledge Brothers in the past few hours for them to be humanized in his eyes. It was a small detail. But it gave Chase a sense of Sully's view on the situation. He continued with the conversation.

"Got it, that's what I was missing," Chase added, nodding his head. "But it's also the direction I was going in myself, given what I knew. It makes sense given that Wilby," he was sure to use his nickname, "was left alive. The killer was shaken. So, tell me. What do we know about how and when they were found?"

"Mick Perry," Sully quickly answered. "He's a Crow Alumni, good guy. He found Will Bonnetti around 2:30 am. He came into the house and found him in the kitchen. He called 911."

"Got it, ok. What time was that?"

"Around 3am, I'm told. And that's all we really know. That kicked off the chain of events that took us through today. Cops showed up and it's been a circus ever since."

"It usually is," Chase offered with raised eyebrows.

"So what happens next?" Sully asked. "What can we expect?"

"Well, they don't have enough evidence to charge Scott. And they won't because they won't find anything more than his ID at the scene. And even that is only circumstantial. They know that if they charge him based on that they won't get a conviction. So they need more. And they'll keep looking. They'll be testing everything they've gathered from the scene. They'll test his clothes. My understanding from his girlfriend is that they showed no signs of blood or any involvement in a struggle. So I expect they'll find nothing there. Who knows when the last time he did wash was. So they may find traces of the 403 basement. But since he would likely spend a good deal of time at the house, that's circumstantial. They'll probably bring more people in for questioning. And finally, there will likely be a press conference. They may even ask you or someone else from the University to attend. Maybe even speak."

Sully's eyes widened at the concept of him speaking to the press about this.

Chase continued. "My concern is that they'll feel a rush to wrap it up quickly and charge Scott with only the information they have."

"Well if they won't get a conviction then he'll still be OK, though, right?"

Chase again looked at him sarcastically. "After what I went through in college, you think that *not* being convicted matters?"

The words weren't needed. Sully realized his gaffe quickly. "Right, sorry. I need to work on that."

"So what I need to do," Chase continued, "is to start talking to people. I need to talk to all of the Crow Brothers and Pledges that were there."

"Got it, what then?"

"Well from there I'll just go where the information takes me. I really can't know at this point."

"What can I do?" Sully asked.

"Do you have access to student addresses and schedules?"

"I do. But I'm definitely not supposed to be sharing that with you."

"Sully, come on. This isn't a hazing violation that I'm investigating. I'm trying to clear my son for murder. You, of all people, owe me this."

Sully sat quietly for a moment. Typically Chase was exceptional when it came to staying quiet and waiting for the other person to speak. But he let his emotions get the best of him.

"Ok, listen, tomorrow I'll get a short list of kids I want to speak to. I'm not asking to get the entire KXP member list."

Sully sighed. "We didn't have this conversation, ok?"

"What conversation?" Chase asked in obvious agreement.

"Exactly," he responded with a heavy nod.

The two exchanged cell phone numbers and agreed to stay in touch before Chase left Sully's office. He walked quickly down the hall towards the lobby and exited Barness Union Hall. His exit was clearly absent the nostalgic feeling that he had walked in with. Instead, he now felt like he was in his element and ready to go do his job. It would be the most important investigation that he has ever worked on in his entire life.

CHAPTER 26

"How in the hell did we even get here?"

Scott was perplexed by the route that his Mom had taken he and Sydney in order to make their way up to Cleer Street.

Suzanne sat behind the wheel, with a smug smile on her face, as she turned onto Cleer, directly at the spot they wanted to be. "If you listened once in a while you might learn something from your mother," she told Scott with a laugh. "I spent four years here. You've been here for like four minutes."

While Chase was meeting with Sully, Suzanne thought it would be a good idea to take advantage of the time and let everyone decompress a bit. She invited Scott and Sydney to grab some dinner with her in downtown South Cuthbert. Although, in this case, the word 'downtown' is relative. South Cuthbert is not exactly a sprawling metropolis. It only covers 1.8 square miles of land. But the town uses that 1.8 square miles to its fullest and squeezes as much as they can into the space.

The main focus of the town is the University. Without it, the population would be barely a quarter of what it is now. There is a radius of a few blocks surrounding the campus that consists of privately owned houses and apartments that are primarily rented out by students. This is generally the loudest area of South Cuthbert and generally where all of the parties are held. There are also more quiet sections that are populated by families, or even alumni, along with a lower income section, affectionately known as South Cuthbert's ghetto.

But then there is Downtown South Cuthbert, which is technically the Northernmost part of Borough. It has everything that a normal downtown area would have – restaurants, bars, shops, lodging, as it should. South Cuthbert is home to a population of over 18,000 residents. This is just shy of the population of Warrington, PA, where Chase and Suzanne currently live. The difference is that it's only a quarter of Warrington's geographical size.

Scott had originally suggested they just grab some slices of pizza, instead of a sit down meal.

"Oh, is Little Man's still open?" Suzanne asked with her eyes wide in anticipation.

Scott and Sydney looked at her like she had two heads.

"Little Man's?" she continued. "Pizza place? Corner of Elm and Bradford?"

"Oh you mean Double Decker?" Sydney asked.

Suzanne's heart sank. Little Man's was a late night staple for South Cuthbert students. A slice after leaving The Rat or Jake's to soak up all of the cheap beer you've had was a rite of passage here. Even entertaining the idea of going to this...Double Decker...seemed blasphemous.

"Tell you what," she said. "You two look like you could use a good meal. You've probably been eating that cafeteria crap for every meal for the past two months. Let's get something proper in you."

The two of them agreed and off they went through South Cuthbert's back roads.

Downtown South Cuthbert was nothing like Suzanne had remembered. It had been built up a great deal and there was a great deal more available to them from the standpoint of finding a meal. The town had definitely embraced its reputation as a college town and was now catering to the students. The number of bars and affordable restaurants on Market Street seemed to have quadrupled since she was last here. The Iron Hill Brewery jumped out at her as a name that she recognized. They had a handful of locations throughout Southeastern PA.

Being an hour outside of Philly, on a Sunday, she assumed that a large contingent of South Cuthbert's Philadelphia Eagles fanbase would be gathered there to catch the Birds game. So, she knew that it would be crowded. But she knew what their food options would be here – quality bar food. In addition, she knew that despite it being a bar crowd, they'd be able to get a table with restaurant service.

"Mom, you're taking us to a bar for dinner?" Scott half joked.

"No, I'm taking you to a bar and restaurant. Some bars do sell food, ya' know!" she said with a smile.

She opened the door and approached the Host. "Table for three, please."

"Right this way," the Host quickly replied as he grabbed three menus from a stack behind him.

They walked past the bar area and, as expected, were met with a gaggle of Eagles jerseys filling the room with a mix of Kelly Green and Midnight Green colored jerseys, the two colors that the Eagles had adopted throughout their history. The dining area, however, was populated mainly by families and couples. They stopped next to a booth as the Host waved his hand in a welcoming manner.

"Here you are," he said with a smile.

The three of them quietly slid into the booth, barely acknowledging his presence. He placed the menus on the edge of the table and glanced at each of them, noticing their lack of energy.

"Ok," he said, "your waitress will be with you in a moment" He waited a brief moment, with no response, before turning to walk back to the front of the restaurant. Scott collapsed into a heap as he leaned back into his seat. His hands covered his face and slowly slid down into his lap.

"What the hell happened today?" he asked absently. "I feel like I just got steamrolled by JJ Watt."

"I'm so sorry this is happening, Scott." Sydney leaned in and wrapped her arm around him. "It's going to be ok."

Suzanne couldn't help but let a smile creep across her face as she watched Scott lean back into Sydney's embrace. She was happy that he had someone to turn to during this, and found herself wishing that she was able to be there for Chase.

"She's right, Scott," she told her son. "This is going to pass by. We'll make sure you're cleared and soon this will be a distant memory."

"It's not just a distant memory though, Mom. I almost don't even care what happens to me. I just want Wilby to be ok. And Coleman...I...just..."

"She knows that, Scott," Sydney said, leaning in closer. "We just want to do whatever we can to help."

"I know. I know. I'm sorry. I just..."

Scott was interrupted by the waitresses arriving at the table. She spoke in a high pitch tone that was exponentially more chipper than all three of their moods combined.

"Hi, everyone! Welcome to Iron Hill! How *is* everyone tonight?" she asked cheerily.

The three of them looked up at her with blank expressions. Nearly in unison, they replied with as much energy as they could muster.

"Fine."

"Fine."

"Ok, I suppose."

"Ooookay," she replied after a slight pause. "Well, my name is Jennifer. Have we dined at Iron Hill before?"

"Nope," Scott replied.

"Can I start you guys off with something to drink?"

"I'll have a Lager," Scott fired back quickly.

"He'll have a water!" Suzanne quickly interrupted. The waitress was startled at the sudden burst of energy. "They'll both have waters," Suzanne then added, "and *I'll* have a Lager!"

"Got it, a Lager," she replied, before looking over at Scott and Sydney. "And, two waters." The previously uber-happy Jennifer shied quietly away from the table with her drink order in hand.

"Why do you get to drink and we don't?" Scott pleaded.

"Because I'm legally allowed to drink. You're not."

"I just want to calm myself down a bit, Mom."

"Well, I'm sure you've got beer back at one of your places," she replied, knowing full well what college life is like. "Drink all you want when I'm not there to be blamed for it."

A few moments later, Jennifer returned with a tray full of drinks.

"Two waters," she said, placing them in front of Scott and Sydney. "And one Lager."

She placed a pint glass filled with Yuengling Lager in front of Suzanne. Despite the fact that a lager is technically a *type* of beer – just like ales, porters or stouts are types of beer – when you're in Pennsylvania and you order a lager, it's understood that the brand of beer doesn't need to be requested. You are ordering a Yuengling Lager. Located just an hour and a half North of South Cuthbert, Yuengling is the oldest brewery in the country, having stayed operational during Prohibition by selling ice cream instead of alcohol. As a result, it is the most well-known beer in the area and doesn't even require that you ask for it by name. In PA, they have a monopoly on lagers.

Suzanne took a long drink from the glass and relaxed her shoulders.

"Are we ready to order?" the waitress asked.

The three all nodded in unison without ever even opening their menus. They each ordered a burger and fries, and Jennifer was on her way.

She returned a short time later with their food. The three of them sat and ate without a word, unsure of what more they could say. An occasional roar from the Eagles fans at the bar would break the silence.

Ordinarily Scott would have his eyes peeled on the game, just like everyone else. But today, he looked around at the crowd and was suddenly overcome with a feeling of dread.

"I feel like everyone in this place is looking at me," he said as he crouched down low against the table.

"No one is looking at you, Scott," Sydney told him. "These people have no idea who you are."

"You don't think some of them are students?" he asked argumentatively.

"I'm sure a lot of them are actually," she replied. "In fact, I recognize some of them. But the chances that they know who you are or that you're connected to anything from today are nill. It just happened this morning. They might not ever know that it happened yet."

"I'd just like to get out of here," he said, lowering his head into his hands.

Suzanne couldn't bear to see him like this. "Scott, if I've learned anything from your Father it's that you can't run from this."

"Yeah, and what the hell is *that* all about?" Scott demanded. "This same thing happened to him in college? How is that even possible? And how could you guys not tell me about that before?"

"It wasn't something that we felt was necessary to share," she told him. "It was in the past."

"Well it sure seems necessary now, doesn't it?" Scott was visibly angry.

Sydney put her arm around him. "Easy, hun. I'm sure they were just trying to protect you from having to worry about that."

"Well it's too late for that now. I'm officially worried. Can we please get out of here now? Actually we don't even need to wait. Aren't we close to the Police Station? We can walk to Syd's car."

"Uh yeah," Sydney responded with a hesitant look towards Suzanne.

Suzanne gave a reluctant nod to Sydney.

"Yeah," Sydney continued. "We can walk over from here. Thank you for dinner, Mrs. Dempsey."

"Please," she told Sydney, "call me Suzanne. Or just Suz. And it's my pleasure. You two get going and I'll hang around to pay the bill."

"Well thank you for dinner, *Suz*," Sydney responded with a light smile. She turned to Scott, "You ready?"

"You know I am."

Suzanne took Scott by the hands before he was able to get up out of the booth. She looked him in the eyes and spoke. "Scott, I love you. Please be careful. Everything is going to be alright. Trust me."

Scott stared back for a moment and then sighed and let his body relax. "I know Mom. I just need to be alone to process this." He looked up to Sydney, who was already standing. "Can we go to your place?"

"Yeah of course," she responded.

"Ok well, do me a favor," Suzanne said looking at the two of them. "Just stay there, ok? Don't go out to any parties or anything. You need to stay out of sight and remove yourself from everything right now. At least until we get this figured out. Got it?"

They both nodded in agreement and walked off. Suzanne motioned to a now frightened waitress for the check and looked down at her phone to see a text from Chase.

Done with Sully... Jake's?

It took only a single breath to decide on her reply. She would love to see if that hole-in-the-wall of a bar has changed even a single bit since the days that they were frequent patrons. Plus she needed something stronger than the Lager that she had just patiently sipped down despite her desire to drink it down in one gulp. *It sucks being the adult sometimes,* she thought to herself. She sent a text back immediately.

Absolutely. We'll be the only ones in there with a mortgage. But whatever 😊

Chase's response came back within a few seconds.

Good...cause I'm already here 😊

She smiled and began typing.

Order me an Old Fashioned.

On it. See u in a bit.

Suzanne paid the bill and was on her way. For what seemed like the first time today, she exhaled and gave herself permission to relax.

CHAPTER 27

On the surface, Jake's is nothing more than your ordinary dive bar. Located on Martin St., just one door in from the corner of Martin and Mockingbird, it probably holds fifty people comfortably, at least according to the Fire Marshal. But on any given night, while school is in session, it's standing room only. On the weekend, you're lucky if you can even find any friends that you might be looking for. It's essentially a house party with a full length bar, a quoits table and a jukebox.

You can't even turn a corner in South Cuthbert without seeing someone wearing the requisite dark blue t-shirt with Jake's Bar, a beer mug and a year emblazoned across the front in white. For at least thirty years, that Chase knew of, they've been selling the same exact t-shirt. Each year a new version of the same shirt is released with only one small change – the year. Chase and Suzanne each had a number of different versions of the shirt sitting in their drawers at home, all with different years listed on them..

During the days that Chase and Suzanne were gracing the grounds of SCU, draft beers were fifty cents each. They'd heard that prior to that, they were only a Quarter. Today, however, Chase was shocked to find that draft beers were now up to $1.25 each.

Highway robbery, he thought to himself.

The bar was relatively crowded, mainly due to the Eagles game. The game was nearly over, and the Eagles were, to no one's surprise, losing. So Chase had no trouble finding a seat at the bar.

"What can I get ya'?" he heard a voice call from behind the bar as he walked up. "Oh, man, would you *look* at this!"

"Hey Duane, how've ya' been?!" Chase leaned across the bar and shook the bartender's hand. Duane had been a fixture behind the bar at Jake's since long before Chase was a student at SCU. He had seen the faces of more students than the Registrar's Office. Chase definitely spent his fair share of time here, as well. Once he had turned 21, this was where he turned to find solace from the world that seemed to be falling down around him. He'd often come in during the day when it was empty. Crowds didn't show up typically until night time. So he and Duane had some long conversations about Chase's situation. Duane was a good ear. But also became a good friend to Chase during a hard time in his life. At a time when Chase needed it most, Duane was the closest thing to a therapist that he could find.

"I'm good, man, how are you?" Duane responded. "How've you been? It's good to see you!"

"Eh...I've been...uh...better. Could use a beer. Can I get a Lager?" Chase felt as if the record would scratch and the place would fall silent at the sound of someone ordering a bottled beer instead of the cheap draft.

"Sure thing, be right back," Duane quickly responded, pushing himself backward from the bar.

"Oh and an Old Fashioned!" Chase called out as Duane walked towards the mini-fridge under the bar. Duane turned and nodded. He returned a moment later with the drinks in hand and placed them in front of Chase.

"Been a long time since I've seen you around here? What've you been up to?" he asked him.

"Well, let's see," Chase answered pensively. He was unsure how much he was ready to share. "I'm a cop in Philly. I work on Homicide. Married. Our son actually goes here now." There it was. The door has been opened.

"Oh no way, that's great!" Duane replied with a smile.

"Well, not so much."

Duane responded with a puzzled look.

Chase looked over his shoulders before leaning in towards Duane and speaking as quietly as he could. Duane mirrored his pose in order to hear better.

"It's happening again," Chase told him.

"What do you mean? What's happening?" he asked him.

"Remember all of the shit I went through? Chris Wilbanks?"

"Yeah of course. You mean? No! That kid that I heard about today?" Duane's eyes were now wide. "You mean...your son?"

Chase just nodded and leaned back in his stool.

"Fuckin' A, that's insane!" Duane said.

"Yep." Chase nodded his head and then leaned forward again. "He didn't do it, of course," he whispered and waved his hands.

"Well, yeah, of course. But holy shit!" Duane exclaimed quietly.

"Anyway, that's why I'm here. I can't let this happen to him the same way it happened to me. I'll be working with Sully. He's the Director of Greek Life at the school now."

Duane nodded his head. "Yeah, of course, I know Sully. You two weren't exactly simpatico, if I remember correctly."

"Yeah, well not my ideal situation. But it's something I've got to do."

"Dude, you've had your share of shit. No need for your son to go through it too. You do what you gotta do. Hey, what about that pretty girl you used to come in here with? She still around?"

As the words were leaving Duane's lips, Suzanne strode through the front door. Every head in the bar was on a swivel as she made her way towards Chase.

"Speak of the devil," Chase said. "Duane, you remember Suz?"

"How could I forget? Great to see ya' sweetie!" Duane leaned across the bar and gave Suzanne a kiss on her cheek. Chase chuckled, knowing full well that he was showing off in front of every person that had just been checking her out as she walked in.

"You too, Duane! Been a long time!" she replied with a smile.

"I just heard the good news," Duane said sarcastically. "Chase was just telling me about why you two are here and that he's going to be working with Sully."

Suzanne swung a wide-eyed stare at Chase. "You're *working* with him?" she asked incredulously.

Chase immediately downplayed it. "Well, I wouldn't call it working with him, per se."

"Well then what would you call it?" she asked. Her face had a look of muted expectation.

"More like...working alongside him."

Duane, read Suzanne's face and took the hint. "Tell ya' what, I'm gonna leave you two alone for a moment. "

Chase flashed a faint smile at Duane. "Thanks buddy."

Duane held up his hands and mouthed the word "Sorry!" to Chase and walked off to help some other patrons.

Suzanne waited a moment until Duane was out of earshot before turning back to Chase. "What are you thinking? How is this helping us at all? How does this help Scott?"

"I have to, Suz. It's totally going to help us. I'm getting access to information that I need. We need to have someone on our side." He held up her drink to her as a peace offering. "Old Fashioned?"

Suzanne's face contorted. "What? He's not on our side. He's on his side. No one else's." She then snagged the drink from his hand and took a sip.

"Suz, believe me, I know that better than anyone. I don't trust him any longer than this beer is going to last." As he finished the sentence, the beer was already raised to his lips and pouring down his throat. He placed the empty bottle down on the bar. He raised his hand towards Duane who quickly brought him another Lager and placed it in front of him.

"I just don't love the idea." Suzanne said to Chase after Duane walked away. "He was such a dick to you."

"Yeah, he was. And he's still a dick. He's only working with me because he knows I'm a cop. He wants to get an idea of what to expect from SCPD during this so that he doesn't look like an idiot handling his end of it. He'll stop talking with me as soon as he thinks he doesn't need me anymore. So I need to use him to get as much info as possible, and as quickly as possible."

"Well, I suppose that's a good thing then." She tilted her head from side to side in agreement before looking around and finally taking a moment to take in her surroundings. "God, so many memories of this place!"

"Right?!" Chase said with a smile. "I spent way too much time in here," he answered with a laugh. "I played 'Unskinny Bop' an obscene number of times on that jukebox. People would get so annoyed from hearing that song over and over."

"Oh my God, I remember that. It *was* totally annoying. I hate that song now, thanks to you," she laughed. "You know a lot of people turned twenty-one right here too."

"Oh I definitely did! I puked on Potsy's shoe right over there that night. Right after I did a shot of tequila!"

"Oh my God, no you did not! Really?!" Suz asked with a giant smile on her face.

"All over his foot! I tried to make it to the bathroom. Didn't work out so well."

The two sat quietly for a moment and stared at themselves in the mirror behind the bar.

"I just hope that Scott gets the chance to make his own memories here," Chase lamented.

"He will," Suzanne said, wrapping her arm around his shoulder. "He's got us. Things are going to be different this time."

"You think he'll make it to the bathroom in time?" Chase said with a laugh.

"Well I'm sure he'll be able to hold his liquor better than you," she chuckled back at him.

Chase reached his hand up towards hers and nodded in agreement. "I just hope he gets the chance to figure that one out for himself."

CHAPTER 28

Not long after arriving at her house with Scott, Sydney had pulled out her laptop and started doing the only thing she knew how to do that might help - Internet Research. Hearing that Scott's Dad had gone through something similar had stuck with her. She decided to see what he had gone through in hopes of determining what Scott may have ahead of him.

"Wow, this shit with your Dad is insane!" Sydney sat on her bed with her eyes fixated on her laptop screen. "It looks like he had a seriously tough time."

"That's what it sounds like," Scott replied blankly as he laid back at the foot of the bed. "I just wish I knew about it sooner."

"He wasn't fully cleared of the charges until more than seven weeks after it happened."

"Seven weeks? Are you shittin' me? Seriously, how is this something they never shared with me?"

"Yeah, this article about him being cleared came out in early June of '93. It says that Chris Wilbanks died in early April."

Scott sat up and ran both of his hands into his hair in an obvious sign of desperation. "Shit, it's only been like twelve hours so far and this has been hell. If this goes on for six more *days*, let alone six weeks," he paused and turned to Sydney, "I don't think I could handle it, Syd."

Sydney slid herself down next to him and pulled him close. "C'mere. It's going to be ok. I'm here for you. I'll be by your side the entire time. No matter how long it takes."

Scott strained his neck to see her screen. "Did they ever even find out who did kill him?" What was the guy's name again? Chris..."

"Chris Wilbanks."

"Yeah, did they ever find out who killed him?" He had now pulled the laptop over onto his own lap.

"Not that I have found anywhere," she responded. "I haven't gotten that far into it though. But I was just wondering that myself. Might still be a cold case."

"Shit, I hope not. History tends to repeat itself. The last thing I need is for Coleman and Wilby's case to go unsolved. We really, really need to find out who took my ID."

"How the hell are we even gonna do that?" Sydney was becoming frustrated as well. "Do we just walk around campus and just start asking people?"

Scott heard his phone ding and looked down at a text message that had just appeared on his screen. "Actually, I have a feeling my Dad might end up doing just that. He wants to meet us for breakfast tomorrow at the cafeteria so that we can talk about how to find it. He wants to start at the last place I remember having it."

CHAPTER 29

Monday, October 25. 2021

It had been twenty-four hours since Scott had found out that Coleman had been murdered. Twenty-four hours since he learned that Wilby was clinging to life at Cuthbert County Hospital. Twenty-four hours since Scott began experiencing life as a potential murder suspect.

Three lives. Three families. All changed forever by one act of violence.

Scott had spent the night at Sydney's house. They agreed that they'd meet his parents for breakfast at 8am in the cafeteria, which was adjacent to Oreland Hall, where Scott's dorm room was located. Scott and Sydney walked hand in hand across the parking lot. They were early, which was typical for both of them. It was chilly outside. A typical Fall morning in South Cuthbert. Scott glanced over and took notice that the chill didn't seem to bother Sydney. He liked that she wasn't bothered by much. "It's just a little cold" he remembered her telling him the first cold morning they encountered when he had asked if she needed a coat. He smiled inwardly at how lucky he considered himself to be. He was even more aware of that now.

Shaking himself out of his trance, he remembered part of why he had wanted to leave early. "Hey, if you don't mind, I'dlike to check in with Woody," he said to her, pointing over to his Oreland Hall. "He doesn't have class until 10. So I'm sure he's around. Probably still asleep actually."

"Yeah sure, of course," Sydney responded. "Have you spoken to him since you left the hospital?"

"Just to text him last night that I was staying at your place last night. Also told him about what we learned about my Dad and how he had gone through this too," Scott responded. "He just replied 'thanks' and to let him know if I need anything. Not sure what I could need though. Other than if someone's got their hands on a Delorean that can go back in time and connect a tracker to my Student ID."

Scott turned his head to look behind him as he spoke. Sydney could tell that he was scanning the parking lot as they walked along. He seemed to be eying every car and trying to determine if it belonged to an undercover cop.

"They're not going to follow you everywhere, Scott," she reassured him.

"Well, they apparently knew enough to sit outside of your house all night. Why wouldn't they follow me across campus?"

A few minutes earlier, as they left Sydney's apartment, Scott's attention was immediately drawn to the unmarked police car parked halfway down the block. It didn't surprise him as much as it had acted as a reminder of how he was being viewed. It seemed clear to him that he could expect the police to watch his every move for the foreseeable future. But for the time being they would have to work hard at it. Scott and Sydney took their normal shortcut through the breezeway next to the Phi Sig house, exiting on the other side in a parking lot that feeds into Stone Boulevard. The car that was shadowing him would have had a difficult time fitting through there. Though he doubted he would evade them for long, it had seemed that for the time being, he and Sydney were relatively alone. He didn't expect that to last.

The two changed course slightly towards Oreland Hall. As the dorm came into view, Scott immediately could see a number of news vans parked along Wilkes Avenue. The Action News van was the first that he saw, and he instinctively thought of the tagline from their commercials and repeated it to Sydney. "There's that news van again." He stopped and motioned over to her. She looked over and saw the media circus beginning to take shape.

"Come on, let's go in the side door," she said to him. She took him by the arm and led him towards the other end of the building. Scott didn't object. He not only wasn't ready to be confronted by any reporters. He also dreaded the idea of being stuck in the elevator with anyone who might've heard the news about his Pledge Brothers. Let alone the news that he was the main suspect.

He also had no desire to walk down the hall past a dozen dorm rooms, opening himself up to a myriad of conversations that he didn't want to have right now. With his room being two doors away from the stairs, entering from the stairwell allowed him to avoid all of those situations. The only room he'd have to walk past was Archie's, and he had no issue with that.

When Scott and Sydney arrived at the top of the stairs, she slowly opened the door to the hallway and checked to see who was there before passing through. The hall was empty, so she moved through and motioned for him to follow. As it were, Archie's door was closed. His own door, on the other hand, was wide open. He and Sydney wandered in to find Woody at his desk hunched over his laptop. He turned, surprised to see them.

"Oh hey! What's up guys," he asked, quickly rising from his seat, seemingly to greet them. Instead he walked past them both and quickly closed the door behind them.

"How ya' doing? Any word on anything?" Woody asked pensively.

Scott shook his head from side to side. "Nope, nothing. There was a cop parked outside of Syd's all night. They probably followed us here too. There's also a shitload of news vans outside of here. But aside from that, nope, nothing at all." He offered a light-hearted smile.

"Are you effin' kidding me? They're staking you out?"

"Yeah, apparently," Sydney chimed in. She felt bad that Scott had reached what he had expected to be the safe confines of his room and was instead met with more discussions about the one topic he wants to avoid. So she sought to use Woody as a chance to change the subject.

"So, Woodman, you've got an empty room all to yourself again and you still can't find someone to share it with?"

"Ha ha, very funny," he responded sarcastically. "How do you know someone didn't already leave before you got here? Door was already open, wasn't it?"

"Oh come on, you know that's not true," she joked. "But, seriously, I could think of a half a dozen girls in my Sorority that would love to spend the night here," she said. Woody was a good looking guy and she had definitely heard her Sorority Sisters speak more than kindly of him when discussing this semester's pledge classes.

Scott recognized, and appreciated, Sydney's attempt to move the spotlight off of him. But he still had a schedule to keep. He didn't want to leave his parents standing in the lobby of the cafeteria looking like a pair of obvious and awkward parents waiting for their child.

"Yeah, well despite your inability to close the deal, Wppd, we're heading down to the caf to meet my parents for breakfast. You want to come?"

"Sure. I'm game. But," Woody pointed over towards his laptop, "I need to show you something first."

"Wood, we don't have much time, man," Scott replied dismissively.

"Dude, you'll want to see this." Woody stepped over and sat down at his laptop without even looking back to see if Scott and Sydney had followed him. "Dude, your Dad had a seriously fucked up existence here at South Cuthbert."

"Yeah, we know that, dude," Scott said, appeasing him by walking over to the desk. "We researched it a bit last night."

"A bit?" Woody looked up at Scott, "I didn't even sleep last night. I've been sitting at this desk since you and I texted last night. I've done more than 'a bit' of research." Woody made air quotes with his fingers to emphasize the extent he's gone to.

He continued. "Scott, seriously, there is a lot to unpack here with your Dad."

"Wood, I know. Syd researched it last night too." Scott was moving towards the door. "We have to go though. My folks are waiting for us."

"Scott..."

"Woody, we gotta go. Are you coming or not?"

Woody looked at Scott and Sydney. It was clear that Scott just needed to keep his day moving forward and not entertain conspiracy theories right now. He relaxed his shoulders and stood up. "Okay, yeah, let's get moving. But we need to talk about this later. Deal?"

Scott capitulated and nodded to the affirmative. "Yeah, deal."

"By the way, it's Monday, don't forget your paddle!" Woody said, handing a wooden paddle to Scott. The front of which was decorated thoughtfully with the Greek letters KXP. Also present on the front of the paddle were the Kappa Chi Rho Coat of Arms, and the words "POSTULANT SCOTT". 'Postulant' was a more formal way to say 'Pledge'.

Pledge conduct typically called for Pledges to carry their paddles Monday through Friday. from 8am to 8pm. For a moment Scott thought about whether or not he should bring his with him. He thought about the events of the past twenty-four hours and if it may have given him enough reason to bypass the typical Pledge rules. But then he thought about his Pledge Brothers that had stepped up in his defense. He then thought of Coleman, who would never be able to carry the paddle again, and Wilby, whose future was uncertain.

Scott reached out confidently for the wooden symbol that he had so readily grasped in the weeks prior. He wondered to himself if this was quite as important to him as it was two days ago. Given the gravity of the situation, it was a valid question. But he took it nonetheless.

"Thanks, totally forgot about that," he said as he took it. He turned and made his way to the door. Sydney and Woody followed in line and the three made their way down the stairwell, ready to face whatever lay before them.

CHAPTER 30

The cafeteria was located in Kellenberger Hall, no more than one hundred yards from Scott's dorm. Scott wished it was longer. He was finding these "in between" moments - walks and car rides taking him from here to there - to be welcome escapes. Every destination seemed to be one that required him to face a reality that he wished did not exist.

However, he was also finding that these escapes would be short lived. As they crested the hill into the parking lot, his parents immediately came into view. They stood waiting at the top of the stairs leading down into the cafeteria. Twenty yards away from them, alongside the curb in the parking lot, the site of an unmarked police car was immediately noticeable.

"Oh man, just as expected. These friggin' guys don't give up," he said, causing Woody and Sydney to glance in the same direction.

"I guess that's the cops that you said were staking out Sydney's place last night?" Woody asked.

"Yep, looks like it," Sydney confirmed.

Scott called out to his parents as the group approached the steps. "You invite these guys?"

Chase glanced over at the car. "Don't pay any attention to them. You'll be seeing a lot of them until we get you cleared."

"Is it really necessary?" Scott asked, clearly annoyed.

"Well they seem to think it is. Probably wouldn't happen much in Philly. But you won't need to worry about them. I'm not surprised by this. They're going to follow you around. But you've got nothing to hide. So it really doesn't matter."

Chase looked back over towards the car and waved. "Hiiiii! We see you!" he said softly.

"Don't provoke them, Chase," Suzanne said as she tried to nudge him along. "You look like one of the mobsters in Goodfellas, getting all cocky with the Feds."

"Yeah, yeah, you're probably right," he reluctantly agreed. "Which one? DeNiro?"

"Dad, can we get on with this?" Scott asked, clearly impatient and uncomfortable.

"Alright, well before we go in," he continued, turning to Scott, "I want to start by getting a bearing on your actions on Friday night here at dinner. That was the last time you had your Student ID, correct?"

Scott nodded in agreement. "Yep, I was here for dinner. I would've needed it here to get in. After that I don't recall if I put it in my pocket or maybe down on the table."

"We'll have to assume on the table," Chase added. "Less likely that someone pickpocketed you."

"You don't need it to get into the dorms?" Suzanne asked.

"Well we're supposed to. But typically we can just walk in without having to show it. And, besides, we would've gone in the side of the building, not through the lobby."

Chase pointed towards Kellenberger Hall while looking at Scott. "Ok, so somewhere in that building is likely where you would've parted ways with it. The question is how. Do you carry it loose or on a lanyard?"

"Loose, just like you taught me. My key is on my lanyard and..."

Chase completed Scott's sentence for him. "...and if you lose it and both are on there, then whoever finds it knows exactly whose room they can now get into. Good, glad you listened."

Scott tilted his head and grimaced. "Yeah, well unfortunately in this case that probably could've stopped this before it started."

Chase thought about it for a second. "Yeah, well sorry about that. I guess there's good and bad to every security tactic. Well, no sense in reliving it," Chase reassured him. "Let's head in. I want you to take your time. Think back to that night as we move through here and try to think of anything out of the ordinary that might have happened."

Scott shook his head, dismissing what his Dad said. "Dad, I've racked my brain about what could've happened to it. I don't remember anything"

"You have to remember!" Chase demanded with his voice raised slightly, before turning away and relaxing his shoulders. He then turned back and spoke in a calmer tone. "Listen, nine times out of ten, people don't remember important details when they're just sitting there trying to recall a situation. But if they're thrown back into the situation, their memory gets triggered. We need to do whatever we can to trigger your memory. Can you work with me on this?"

Scott dipped his head and nodded in agreement as he began walking. The others followed suit and Scott began recounting his actions from the last time he was there.

"Me and Woody walked over here from the dorm. So the same route you just saw us come from." He turned to Woody. "Wood, keep me honest here if I remember anything incorrectly."

Woody nodded in agreement. "It all sounds right so far."

Chase pointed in Woody's direction. "Yeah, Woody, definitely chime in if you remember anything that Scott doesn't mention." He turned his attention back to Scott. "So, around what time was this?"

"It was about 6:30, right Wood?" Scott replied, looking over at Woody for confirmation.

"Yep, around that time."

Scott nodded and turned back to his Dad. "We came in through the doors here and the woman scanned our ID's."

"Ok so that was probably the last time you would've needed to use it, right?" Suzanne confirmed as they entered the lobby.

"Yep," Scott replied. "After that I would *not* have had a need to use it for the rest of the night." He continued. "Like I said before, I usually keep it loose in my pocket. But, I'm not sure if I placed it in my pocket right away though or if I continued to carry it. And Dad, you don't think it could've been pickpocketed?"

"Well if it was someone with skills it's possible," Chase replied pensively. "But, I feel like it's less likely that there is a skilled pickpocket here. Anything is possible though."

"Yeah, I suppose so," Scott agreed. "That doesn't help us much, though."

"Well maybe it does," Suzanne said. "Do you remember who you saw there that night?"

Scott looked over at Woody as the two thought back. "Well, we sat with a few of the other guys. Archie, Trout, Robbie."

Woody nodded in agreement. "Right, and Phatty showed up too."

"Fatty?" Suz said with a surprised look. "You have a friend named Fatty? That's a bit mean isn't it?"

"Phat with a Ph, Mom," Scott clarified. "It's a compliment, not a dig." He left off the part about Phatty being the biggest pothead of the group, which was more than likely the origin of his nickname.

"We saw Lynn too," Woody added with a smile.

"Ha, yeah we did," Scott replied with a smile of his own before catching another look of disapproval from Sydney.

"Let's get back to the guys. These are all Crows?" Chase asked, dismissing the comments and tired of hearing their juvenile comments.

"Yeah," Scott replied. "Well, some were initiated Brothers and some are our Pledge Brothers."

"Got it. So did you go to your table first? Or did you get your food first?"

Scott thought for a moment before answering. "Table first. We went to the table and got our seats, and then went and picked up our food."

Chase pressed further. "So it's possible that you put down your ID on the table and left it there while you were getting your food?"

Scott shrugged his shoulders. "Yeah I suppose. I don't recall if I did that. But it's possible."

"And were the guys you mentioned..." Chase paused for a moment to recall their names. "Archie, Robbie, Trout, right? And..."

"Phatty," Scott finished his thought.

"Phatty, right. So are they the only ones that would've been with you at dinner?"

Scott looked at Woody for some help. "There were probably some other people that we would've seen there, right?"

"Yeah I'd say so," Woody agreed. "It's Saturday night. Gets to be a bit social as people chat about what's happening that night."

"Can you do me a favor?" Chase asked Scott. "Can you do your best to remember as many people that you either ate with you that night or that might've come to your table and text it to me?" Chase asked as he slowly backed away from the group towards the door.

"Yeah sure, where are you going?" Scott asked with a confused look on his face.

"I need to go see Sully."

"Chase, tell me you're not going to question everyone in the Fraternity," Suzanne chimed in.

"No, that'd be ridiculous," he responded. "Only the ones that had access to your ID. So the people that Scott ate dinner with that night."

"Dad, you can't interrogate them. You aren't a cop here. This isn't Philly."

"I know it's not Philly, Scott. But we can't leave the detective work to the detectives here. They have a predetermined outcome in their mind and it involves you being behind bars. If you want to be cleared, then send me that list."

Scott watched as his Father walked through the lobby doors and made his way up the stairs towards the parking lot. Glancing first at Sydney, Woody and his Mother, he found no sense that they were on his side. He reached in his pocket, took out his phone and began typing out the list for his Dad.

CHAPTER 31

Chase didn't even slow down as he pushed through the door leading into Barness Union Hall. He hurried through the lobby, reaching into his pocket for his phone as he made his way up the stairs towards Sully's office. Reaching the top of the stairs he finally saw the notification indicating a text had arrived from Scott. He tapped on his screen to display the list.

"Perfect," he muttered to himself.

Making his way down the hall, he saw Lynn Clowry step out of Sully's office. Her face looked surprised as her gaze met his.

"Oh good morning, Chase!" She called out in a cheery voice. Chase had the impression it was meant to be more of a warning for Sully than a warm salutation for him. He had an initial impression of her from the day prior. But, this morning's interaction cemented it. He definitely felt that she didn't like or trust him.

"Good morning, Lynn," he responded with a smile. He knew from experience that a smile can be an excellent tool and often resulted in better treatment. "Sully around?" he asked as he drew nearer to her, although he already knew the answer.

"Yep, he's right in there. Go ahead in."

Sully was already walking with his hand outstretched when Chase walked through the office doorway.

"Mornin' Chase! Manage to get any sleep?"

"Few hours maybe. Suz and I also popped over to Jake's for a bit to decompress."

"Oh yeah? Duane behind the bar?" he asked with a smile.

"Yeah he was back there. Nothing has changed there. Except the reflection when I look in the mirror," He chuckled.

"Ha, yeah that's for sure," Sully responded with a chuckle of his own. "We definitely aren't the target audience there anymore. Alright, so what are we looking at today?"

Sully led Chase back into his office, seating himself at his desk.

Chase sat down across from him and sank into the chair. "Well SCPD is wasting no time. They already have what looks like a 24-hour surveillance set up on Scott."

"Oh wow, really?"

"Yeah, I may or may not have let them know this morning that I noticed them outside of the cafeteria."

Sully leaned forward in his chair. "Wait, they're on campus?"

Chase nodded in response.

"Ok, well first of all Demps. I can't have you running around campus here getting into it with the cops."

Chase dismissed it with a wave of his hand. "We didn't get into it. It was just a quick 'hey how ya' doin'.'"

"That doesn't matter! If we're going to be working together, then I need you to be on your best behavior."

"Yeah, yeah I know. Well, anyway, I felt like you should know that you've got cops trolling around campus. They probably didn't make it a point to notify you of that fact, did they?"

"No they most certainly did not," Sully confirmed.

"Right, well you may want to call Quinn and McKue and ask them to put a stop to it, if you don't want that. I know I would appreciate it, for sure. But it's clear that Scott isn't going anywhere."

"I can make a call and ask. But no promises," Sully said with a shrug.

"I get it, anyway, so what's happening right now is that they're likely running through their lab tests and the autopsy results. Unless they find something pointing them to the real killer, then they'll continue to be stuck with what they have and will be left with just Scott as a person of interest and no further evidence to charge him. It's a small town and my gut tells me they'll want to get this closed quickly. I worry that they could hold a press conference announcing that. I don't expect that would be any time extremely soon. But, once that happens, well I don't have to tell you that puts Scott in a bad place."

Sully paused and gave an understanding nod to Chase, indicating that he caught the underlying implication that he was to blame for much of the hard times that Chase went through in college. "How soon until you think they'd have that press conference?"

"Couple days maybe? Maybe longer. Hard to say." Chase replied.

"Ok, well, what can I do?" Sully asked with his arms outstretched and his hands pointing back in towards himself.

"I'm going to text you a list of names. Crow Brothers and Pledges. They had access to Scott's ID that night."

"You think it was one of them that took it?"

"I don't know who it was. But I know it wasn't my son. I'd like to get any information I can on those guys. Where they live, class schedules, a photo of them if possible."

"Demps, I'm about to ask the SCPD to get their cops off the campus. I can't have you going around just interrogating students."

"Why does everyone keep saying that?" he asked, exasperated. "Listen, I need this! I can't let this happen to him. He doesn't deserve this. No one does. You owe it to me, Sully. You owe it to those two kids. Scott didn't do this and we need to figure out who did."

Sully looked for a moment at Chase and then nodded in agreement.

"Fine, send me the list. But just keep it low key. Like I said before, we never had this conversation. We can't make a big deal out of this. I don't want students getting freaked out about some rogue cop walking around questioning people."

"Hey," he said in his best Harrison Ford impersonation, "it's me!"

CHAPTER 32

The Quad, as it is commonly referred to among students, is a one-hundred yard wide courtyard on the Southeast corner of campus. It's flanked on the Northeast by Main Hall, the Library to the Southeast, Coruscation Hall to the Southwest, and Robbins Hall to the Northwest. Williams Auditorium sits in the North corner and appears as if it had politely added itself to the group, even though it was the oldest of the five buildings. McGovern Hall, while not officially part of the Quad, sits directly behind Coruscation and, being only a few steps away, is typically included in the Quad conversation.

Prior to bringing Scott to visit the campus last year, Chase hadn't set foot on these grounds in over twenty years. Much of the campus had been built up, rebuilt and expanded over time. But as he walked up the steps that lead past Robbins, where many of his Criminal Justice classes were held, he could see the Quad begin to come into view and he found himself feeling a sense of relief and nostalgia. The Quad had remained untouched and the view was exactly as he remembered it. He felt as though he was a student again on his way to his first class.

Today, though, his goal wasn't to work towards a diploma. It was to instead work towards an exoneration. Much like Main Hall was the location of his very first class so many years before, it was also where the first step needed to be taken for him to save his son. It was where Phil Trout's first class of the day was scheduled to take place.

Scott had sent him a list of people that were present at dinner that night that included Trout, Robbie, Archie, Casey, Woody and Phatty. Trout, however, stood out to Chase early on during the hour or so that he had spent at the hospital the night prior. It was clear that he wasn't a fan of Scott. His dissent amongst the group when it came to Scott's innocence made him the first person that Chase wanted to speak to.

The schedules that Sully provided for Chase told him that Trout's first class was at 9am in Main Hall. He positioned himself outside of the door facing the Quad. Trout lived in the dorms, which meant this was the most logical door that he'd be entering from.

He didn't have to wait long before Trout came into view. He was walking up the path alongside a girl in a Delta Phi Epsilon sweatshirt. Chase could see the two sharing a laugh as they drew nearer. The smile left Trout's face, though, when he looked up and saw Chase.

"Trout, right?" Chase asked, extending his hand to greet him.

"That's right," he responded, shaking Chase's hand. Chase noted that his handshake was limp and weak. "Good morning, Mr. Dempsey."

"Call me Chase," he responded. He wanted Trout to feel as relaxed as possible when answering his questions.

Trout turned to the girl he'd been walking with. "You can go ahead. I'll see you in class."

The girl eyed Chase suspiciously before looking back to Trout. "You sure?"

"Yeah, it's all good. I'll see you in a few."

Trout watched as she walked off. Chase noticed him checking out her ass, and making no attempts to hide it, before he turned back to address him again. "What can I do for you? Everything good with Scott?"

"D Phi E, huh? Scott's Mom was D Phi E. Good to see they're still around."

"Oh she was?" Trout asked. "And you were Crow too, weren't you?"

"Still am," Chase responded flatly. "Once a Brother, always a Brother." He wondered if Trout would look at him as Scott's Dad or as an Alumni Brother. Either way, he noted that he didn't feel that he was getting the respect he deserved. He noted to himself, too, that his first instinct was to think that the Alumni Brother should demand more respect from a Pledge than a parent. He was tempted to address Trout as a Pledge, but stopped short. He felt it was better to be viewed as a concerned parent in this instance.

"Yeah, I suppose so. So is there something I can help you with? I've got to get into class."

"Oh right, of course. I won't keep you long. I just have a couple of questions. I'm trying to find out any information possible that might help to clear Scott."

"Yeah, anything I can do to help. Sure. Just ask."

Chase could sense his uneasiness.

"Well, I'm mainly trying to account for Scott's whereabouts in the hours leading up to, and including, that night. As you know his ID was found near Coleman's body. And by the way, I'm sorry for your loss. I don't want to gloss over that. But I'm trying to find a point where Scott's ID might have been accessible to someone else."

"So you think that maybe someone is framing him?" Trout asked.

"Well I definitely don't think he did it. So unless there is some reason that Coleman had Scott's ID already on him, which could be possible, he may have found it and planned on returning it to Scott. But otherwise, then someone must've planted it there."

"Yeah, I suppose there are a number of ways it could've gotten there," Trout replied, seemingly thinking out loud. Although Chase wasn't quite convinced that he believed what he was saying.

"I have to admit, Trout, you sound like you've got a different view than you did when I saw you yesterday."

Trout appeared embarrassed. "Yeah, well...it was not my best moment, Mr. Dempsey. I actually plan on reaching out to Demps. I thought about it later and I think I was just reacting out of anger. I had just lost a friend, and another one is in the hospital. I wanted to blame someone. He deserved better from me."

"I'm glad to hear you say that," Chase replied. Perhaps he was wrong about Trout. "Well he went to your room that night, right? Before CJ's place? You guys were drinking in your dorm room."

"Yeah, Scott and a few other guys."

"Were you at the caf with him for dinner before that?" Chase already knew that he was. But he was interested in his answer.

"Yeah, that's actually when we decided to pick up some beers and hang in my room. It was going to be a boring night otherwise."

"Yeah, I would imagine," Chase said with a chuckle. "Do you remember anything weird or out of the ordinary happening at dinner that night? Did you see anything or see anyone take Scott's ID?"

Trout glanced off in the distance as though he was reflecting back on the night.

"No, nothing that I can remember. It was just a normal meal. We just sat and shot the shit like any other night. Only thing that was out of the ordinary was Lynn Clowry bumping into some guy in front of our table. Food went everywhere."

"Really?" Chase asked. "Who'd she bump into?"

"I don't know. Some dude. Never saw him before. I mean, people drop trays all the time. Nothing out of the ordinary there. But it was right in front of our table, and she's hot. That's the only thing that made it notable."

"Do you know of anyone that would want anything to happen to Coleman or Wilby?"

"No, no one at all," Trout answered quickly. "Those guys are about as on the level as you could ask for."

"And Scott? Anyone who would..."

"Nope," Trout cut off Chase. "Look, Demps and I don't always see eye to eye. I'll be the first to admit that. But he's a good guy, there's no doubt about that. And I consider him to be a friend, KXP or not. And I don't know of anyone that doesn't think that about him."

"Even Robbie?"

"Well, Robbie's a bit of a special case, I guess. He doesn't get on with many people at all as it is."

"Got it," Chase answered with a nod. "Well I appreciate your time. I'll let you get moving and get to your class."

"Sure thing. Let me know if there's anything else I can do. I hope they find the guy that did it."

"Yep, me too."

Trout turned and headed into Main Hall. Chase watched and thought for a moment about following him in to see if the inside was just as he remembered it. But he had more important things to do. He turned to make his way towards Schmucker Science Center. His conversation with Trout seems to have given him one less person to consider. He hoped that a conversation with Robbie Goldberg, the other suspiciously vocal detractor, would yield better results.

CHAPTER 33

"Your mother would kill me if she knew that I was letting you skip class, Woody" Suzanne said as they walked across campus along with Scott and Sydney.

"Mrs. Demps, I'm *pretty* sure this is a reason that she'd approve of," Woody joked. "I'm not gonna go sit in class when I could be doing something to help Scott."

"Yeah well, maybe so. but I still feel like I'll owe her an expensive bottle of wine or something."

"Well then, in that case, I *know* she won't mind," he said with a laugh.

With Chase suddenly running off to solve this crime all by himself, Suzanne was left to figure out some other way to help. She decided to do the one thing she knows how to do best - research.

"Are we really going to the library though?" Scott asked.

"Do you have a better suggestion?" Sydney chimed in.

"Thank you, Sydney," Suzanne said with an approving nod. "As good as your Dad is at his job, Scott, I can't sit still while he goes off and does his thing. You'd probably be going crazy trying to do the same. I'm an academic."

"You mean nerd?" he joked.

"Noooo..." she replied, "...an academic. When I'm faced with a problem, I tend to dive into books to find the answer. So I'm going where the books are."

"And why are you bringing us?" Woody asked.

"Sydney, you want to field this one?" Suzanne asked with a smile, and a strong suspicion that Sydney was smart enough to understand what she was thinking.

Sydney smiled and turned to Woody and Scott. "Because there's more than one way to pass information, and she needs our youthful expertise to find the things that she might not find as quickly."

"Well said, and thank you for not calling me old," she said with a wink. "I like her, Scott. Keep this one around. By the way, do you know why the library here is named after Kathleen P. Ormond?"

"No but I'm sure you're going to tell us." Scott said in a flat tone.

"Oh you can count on it. South Cuthbert first opened in 1871. It was actually known as the South Cuthbert Normal School then, whatever the hell that means," she said with a wave of her hand. "Even back then, it had a focus on educating students interested in becoming teachers just like it's known for now. In 1882 Kathleen P. Ormond graduated and later became head of the English Department. She had that job for thirty years! I used to look at the name on the front of the library and think that maybe one day I'd do something long enough for people to just decide that, well, I guess she deserves to have a building named after her."

"There's still time Mrs. Demps," Woody offered.

"Thanks, Wood, I'm sure you're right," she said with a smile.

"Yeah, you're not *that* old!" he continued.

Suzanne shot a death stare in Woody's direction.

"I mean, you know...compared to other women your age. I mean...I'll just stop talking now. Oh, look, we're here!" He pointed anxiously towards the library to draw attention away from himself.

Once inside the library they found a free table that they could all fit at.

"Alright," Scott said, "we're here. Now what?"

"Well, truthfully I was hoping that I'd figure it out when we got here," Suzanne responded. "So let's figure out what exactly what it is that we need to figure out. What don't we know?"

"Who actually did it," Scott replied matter of factly.

"Yeah, well I'll just walk down to the "Whodunnit" section and pick up some Hardy Boys books then," Sydney responded with a laugh.

"Well that is really the main question though. One of them at least," Suzanne said.

"I suppose the next logical question is who would want people to think you did it? Who here has something against you?"

Scott leaned back in his chair and shrugged. "No one that I'm aware of. And really it's not necessarily about me. What if they just wanted Coleman and Wilby dead and needed someone to pin it on?"

"Yeah but they still would've had to have the forethought to pin it on you. They had your Student ID. Why yours?"

"No wait, Scott's right!" Woody chimed in.

"I am?"

Woody smiled at Scott. "Maybe you should've let me finish talking back at the room this morning, huh? So, as I was trying to say before, what if it's not about you? What if they're using you to get to someone else?"

Suzanne's face told Woody that she knew exactly what he was thinking.

"Um...why are you two looking at each other like that?" Woody asked.

"Chris Wilbanks," Suzanne said while lowering her head.

"Chris Wilbanks," Sydney echoed with enthusiasm.

"You kids spent your night doing some of your own research, it seems." Suzanne said.

Woody replied with feigned smugness. "You're not the only academic around here, ya know."

"Wait, what are you saying?" Scott asked. "You think someone is trying to get at Dad by pinning a murder on me?"

"It's possible," Sydney chimed in. "It's awfully convenient that things are working out the way that they are, isn't it? And from what I've seen, even though your Dad was cleared, they never figured out who actually did it"

Suzanne didn't seem completely sold on the idea. "But who? That part doesn't make any sense to me."

Scott echoed the thought. "Well, none of it makes any sense. But especially that part."

Suzanne lightly slapped her hands down on the table. "Well, I suppose *that* is why we're here. It's as good a thought as any. And since it's the only thought right now, by default, it's the best one. We need to research every possible connection that this University, and anyone that is currently here at this University, could possibly have to Chris Wilbanks."

"You mean aside from Dad?" Scott asked.

"Well that's the obvious connection. Sully's definitely another one."

"Director Sully?" Woody asked. That was the last name he'd expect to hear in this conversation.

Suzanne nodded. "He was a student here at the time. And he actually gave Scott's Dad a really hard time during all of it. He fully blamed him for Chris Wilbanks' death."

Scott, Woody and Sydney sat stunned for a moment. That is not the Sully that they've come to know. The Sully that they knew always had a smile on his face, a good joke, and a solid word of advice. Painting him in that light didn't seem right to them.

Suzanne continued, "There are probably other employees here that were students at the time. And kids here whose parents were students here then. Possibly even a family member of his that goes here right now."

"How do we get all of that info though?" Scott asked.

Suzanne slumped her shoulders. "Well that might be a bit harder. But let's start by just researching everything we can about Chris Wilbanks. And we'll go from there. Let's get moving. We don't have much time."

CHAPTER 34

Forty-eight hours ago Chase was packing for a trip to visit his favorite mouse. He never dreamed that today, rather than sitting by the pool and enjoying a Jai Alai IPA, he'd instead be walking across University Avenue to track down Robbie Goldberg in hopes of clearing his son for murder.

Robbie was the other one that stood out to Chase at the hospital. By virtue of his outward enthusiasm for Scott's guilt, he was another one that he wanted at the top of his list of people to talk to. Chase wondered how he hadn't picked up the nickname "Rocky" instead of "Robbie". He bore a slight resemblance to the famed silver screen pugilist, Rocky Balboa. But it was his physical stature that reminded Chase more of a scrappy fighter than anything. Robbie was five and a half feet tall, at best. But his one-hundred and seventy pound frame was all muscle, and he carried himself with what seemed to be an ever-present stance that said he was ready to mix it up at a moment's notice.

Chase assumed that most people likely found themselves afraid of pissing off Robbie, for fear of the potential repercussions. For him though, Robbie's outward appearance was only something he wanted to mentally note as reason to look at him as a possible suspect. He'd seen enough tough guys to know that they rarely did anything more than act tough. He expected nothing more from Robbie today. He also noted, though, that his physical size would have made it easy for him to overpower Coleman and Wilby, with neither of them being what you might see as a scrapper.

170

Robbie's class ended at 9:15am. So Chase didn't need to wait for very long once he arrived at Schmucker. As he expected, Robbie was one of the first ones to leave the building. He definitely struck Chase as someone who didn't enjoy learning and would be one of the first ones making his way for the door at the end of the class.

As expected, Robbie was one of the first people Chase saw exit the building. He watched him turn left and begin briskly walking down University Avenue. Chase sidled up alongside him and began to keep pace.

"Robbie, right?" he asked while attempting to veer in and out of the foot traffic that Robbie was quickly making his way through. "Chase Dempsey. Scott's Dad."

Robbie was clearly surprised by the sudden conversation and began to slow down, but only slightly.

"Oh," he said before pausing and then continuing his normal pace. "Yeah, how ya' doin'?"

"Been better, as I'm sure you can imagine."

"Yeah, I'm sure you have been," he replied.

Chase was quite surprised when he sensed a tone of annoyance in Robbie's voice. "Have I done something to upset you, Robbie?"

"Me? No, you didn't do anything to me."

Chase paused for a moment, partially to choose his words carefully and partially to keep his eyes on the people he needed to dodge on the sidewalk as they hurried along. He reminded himself that this conversation wasn't about him.

"Robbie I just have a few questions that I'm hoping you can answer."

"Sure, man, go ahead."

Chase got right to the point. "Saturday night, we believe sometime between arriving at the cafeteria for dinner and when Scott left CJ's apartment, someone took Scott's Student ID. Did you see anyone take it?"

Robbie never took his eyes off the sidewalk ahead of him, and never slowed his pace. "Nope."

"Did you notice anyone acting suspicious around Scott? Anyone out of place?"

"Not at all."

"Nothing? No one?" Chase was growing tired of these short answers and whatever this act was.

"Isn't that what I just said?" Robbie replied with obvious annoyance.

Chase was done with this. He decided that he needed to play his Alumni Brother card.

"You do know that I'm a Crow Brother right? You're supposed to address me as Brother when you speak to me."

Robbie turned to him with slight surprise as he continued to walk. "Really? No, didn't know that. Ok, well, no I didn't notice anything, *Brother Chase*." He put an obvious sarcastic emphasis on the last part.

"Robbie, I need you to understand that this is a serious situation. More than just with regards to Coleman and Wilby. Scott's future is on the line here."

Robbie quickly responded. "Yeah, well maybe he should've thought of that. He's not going to get away with it like you did."

"Excuse me?" Chase's head swung towards Robbie, shocked at what he had just heard. He forcefully placed his hand on Robbie's shoulder and turned Robbie in his direction as he brought the two of them to a stop in the center of the sidewalk. "Did I just hear you correctly?"

"I know your history," Robbie responded with obvious contempt. "I know about Chris Wilbanks."

"I don't think you know as much as you think you do."

"Yeah well I know enough to know that the apple doesn't fall far from the tree. I can't imagine it's a coincidence that he's repeating your history."

"Robbie, I suggest you do a little more research before you go accusing people of things. Because what you'll find is that I was found to be innocent of all allegations. So I'm actually hoping that history does repeat itself here. You're wasting a lot of time on conspiracy theories that just aren't true." Chase was now in Robbie's face.

Robbie refused to stand down. "Yeah, well, I guess we'll find out soon enough, won't we?"

Chase fought with every fiber of his being against the urge to teach Robbie Goldberg a lesson right in the center of campus. He knew that it would do nothing except make himself feel better for a brief moment, and cause more trouble for Scott and himself. He relaxed his shoulders and took a step back before replying. "You enjoy your day now, ok?" he said. "Thanks for your time."

Chase turned and walked away, his heart was pounding and his head reeling. Robbie Goldberg's words echoed in his head.

I know about Chris Wilbanks.

Why would an eighteen year-old college student know anything about his past? This can't be something he just learned about within the past day, he thought to himself. How could he have possibly come into that information? Scott just learned about it himself yesterday. Whatever the reason, one thing was clear. These past five minutes have shined a giant spotlight onto Robbie Goldberg.

CHAPTER 35

When Suzanne first met Chase Dempsey, he was three years removed from the events of Chris Wilbanks' death. She knew the general story, having had limited exposure to it through the newspapers and the rumors that were circulating at the time when it happened. But once the two of them started dating, her focus was surprisingly on damage control. She was faced with taking this man, seemingly strong and fierce on the outside, who was in reality embattled and weak on the inside. Chase spoke very little about the time he spent suspected of Chris' murder, and even less so about the events of that night. But the effects were clearly visible.

At the beginning of their relationship, the Internet was in its infancy. Avoiding the urge to dig into Chase's reported involvement in Chris Wilbanks' death simply required not asking him about it. As their relationship grew, technology certainly made it simpler for her to learn more, if she had the desire. But she had decided early on that the past was the past. She believed Chase, and she felt no need to prove it to herself by digging any deeper.

Sitting at the computer in the Kathleen P. Ormond Library, she was learning more about her husband's sordid past than she ever wanted to know. Unfortunately, this meant that so was their son and his friends. Scott, Sydney and Woody each sat side by side at the same row of computers. They all worked towards a common goal - find out how Chris Wilbanks was connected to modern day SCU.

There was no shortage of articles on the incident. There were few mentions in the Philadelphia Inquirer immediately after it happened. After a week or two, however, the Inquirer mentions trailed off and most of the stories were found in the South Cuthbert Daily Local, and The Forum, South Cuthbert University's Student newspaper. A dead student with an ongoing murder investigation was exactly the type of story that the editor of a local newspaper in an area of this size would latch onto and bleed dry. And from the looks of it, The Forum didn't exactly try to protect one of its own students from ridicule. The majority of the early results listed in the search actually came from The Forum.

Suzanne scanned through the titles, silently thankful that South Cuthbert had transferred most of their articles from microfiche to digital as she flashed back to her late nights here at the library. Her heart screamed out as she read the headlines. She wanted to reach back in time and hug the Chase Dempsey that she hadn't even met yet. Comfort him. Save him from the pain. The titles of the stories were too much for her to bear.

South Cuthbert Student Found Dead. Pledge Brother Suspected.

Greek Tragedy at South Cuthbert University

Police Question KXP Pledge In Wake of Student's Death

The only thing that was, thankfully, missing from the headlines was Chase's name. Otherwise, it was an all-encompassing view of the hell that he had gone through so long ago.

Suzanne scanned through the articles looking for any information that seemed even remotely relevant. Most of it she found to be repetitive. Journalists often needed to find ways to fill inches in the paper. Sometimes that meant finding different ways to say things that they've already reported.

Scott sat just a few feet from his Mother, finding much of the same information. Eventually, he had had enough. "This is ridiculous," he protested. "I can't sit here and just read about all of these people who thought that Dad was a murderer. Was it a rule to include a recap of this guy's death, and Dad's connection to it, in every single article?"

"Demps, what're you just gonna give up?" Woody asked. "Come on, man be real. I know this sucks. But we need to do this."

Scott turned to his long-time friend, offering a look that they both knew meant to kindly back off.

"Scott, he's just trying to help," Sydney chimed in.

"No, Scott's right," Suzanne interrupted.

"Again?" Scott asked in surprise.

"Yeah, this is ridiculous. There's just too much repetitive information here and not enough..."

She stopped speaking mid-sentence and sat, her mouth agape, staring at her screen.

"Not enough what?" Woody asked. "Clarity?"

"No. Well yeah, but...wait." She responded, turning to the others for a moment before turning back to her computer and scanning the screen with her finger. "They're here."

"Excuse me?" Sydney asked.

"His family. Shit, why didn't I think of this?"

"His family?" Sydney asked. "Chris Wilbanks has family that goes here?"

Suzanne shook her head, realizing that she wasn't really being clear. "No, sorry. His family still lives around her. Or at least they probably do. This article says that Chris Wilbanks went to Henderson High School. That's just a few minutes away from campus. The family probably still lives around here. And wait..." She said as she examined the contents on her screen. "...well this is interesting."

"What's that?" Scott asked.

"The author of all of these articles. I know her. Well, *knew* her."

"You knew her? Who?" Sydney asked.

Suzanne leaned back in her chair, keeping her eyes on the screen. She spoke in a low voice. "Donna Kopecki."

"Donna Kopecki?"

"Yeah," Suzanne replied, "She was a year older than me. But I remember her. She wrote for The Forum. She wrote all of the articles that I'm seeing here." She clicked the mouse a few more times, leaned forward once more and scanned her screen. "And it looks like she went to work for the Daily Local after that. I see a lot of articles by her from there as well."

"So she may still be around here too," Woody said.

"Well, most likely, I imagine. And we may not need to scour articles to try to find a connection," Sydney said with a smile. "We can just find the Wilbanks address and go talk to them in order to find out what connections there might be. Or maybe we should go see this Donna Kopecki woman."

"Or maybe both!" Woody added.

"So we just wasted how much time then?" Scott asked.

"Jesus Christ, Scott," Suzanne pleaded. "I know this is tough. But just see the bright side, ok?"

Scott sighed and bowed his head for a moment. "You're right. I'm just...a little bit..."

"Yeah...I know hun," Suzanne responded softly.

Sydney could see that Scott and Suzanne clearly needed a moment to be Mother and Son. "Tell ya' what, Woody and I will head over and talk to the head librarian about how we might go about locating an address."

Woody chimed in as though the answer was plain and simple "Well, we can just grab it from..."

Sydney cut him off before he could finish. "Woody, why don't you come with me. Mmmkay?"

Suzanne glanced up at Sydney and gave her a look of thanks and a nod. She tilted her head slightly to watch as they walked off, then turned back to make eye contact with Scott. "We haven't had a moment to really sit down and talk since your Dad and I got here, have we?'

"No," Scott said, exhaling and leaning back in his chair, "no, I guess we haven't."

Suzanne thought back to the early days of her relationship with Chase, thinking that the same tone could help with her son. "Listen, I know that you're..."

Scott quickly leaned forward and interrupted. "No, Mom, I don't think you do!"

"Hey! You just stop right there, okay?" Suzanne was having none of it and invoked what Scott had always referred to as the "dreaded Mother's tone".

As if he'd been transported back to sitting at their kitchen table in Warrington, Scott stopped himself from saying another word. He immediately glanced around to see if anyone had seen him being 'mothered' in the middle of the library.

Suzanne continued. "Now please let me finish. We're sitting here in front of four computers full of search results about the death that your Father was suspected of being responsible for. I may not have been there right at the time when it happened. But I witnessed the aftermath."

"Mom, I know."

"No, Scott, you really don't. I saw the hell that your Father went through! I saw the shit that he's still dealing with. Don't sit and tell me I don't know. Because I know! I know so much of it that I hope you will never even have a need to experience what I know, and what your Father knows. Do you understand me?"

Scott sat silently and took in the enormity of the truth that his Mother had just shared. It was just one day prior that he had learned that his Father had even experienced anything like this, and he hadn't even had a moment to consider anything beyond what he himself was going through. In that moment, he had realized that this was much larger than he ever could have imagined. He now realized that this struggle was not just his own.

"Now I know this sucks," Suzanne continued. "It friggin' blows. But you need to allow yourself to take some comfort in the fact that you have something your Father did not have."

"What's that?" he asked.

"All...of...us," she said with a faint smile. "Me, your Dad, Sydney, Woody. All of us. The knowledge that we have available to us from the fact that your Father already went through this. Scott, you know I've never lied to you."

"Never? Santa? The Easter Bunny?' he joked.

Suzanne smiled, wishing they could be transported back to a moment when he still had that innocence. "Last I checked, you still believe in the Elf on the Shelf."

"You mean Sean?" he replied, referencing the name he'd given the elf that has sat on their mantle at Christmas since he was a toddler. "He's totally reporting back to Santa."

"I still can't believe you named him Sean. Who the hell names their elf Sean?"

"Sean's a great name!" he said with a laugh. Suzanne laughed along with him.

"Well anyway, you get the point. There's a million reasons for you to be confident in the fact that we're going to get this worked out. I know it sucks. I know it's not a great situation. But I've spent more than twenty years wishing that I could've been there for your Dad. I never would've dreamed that we'd be in this position for you. But now that we're here, I'm not about to leave a single stone unturned if there's a chance that underneath one of those stones is the key to your freedom. Let me help you."

Scott relaxed his shoulders. "Ok, Mom. I get it. Whatever you need."

"No, whatever *you* need. Understand?"

Scott nodded his head. "Yeah, I get it."

Suzanne smiled. With Scott mentally on board, she was now feeling better about their chances. "Good, let's do this. We've got some people to go see."

CHAPTER 36

Sydney Moore had been with Scott for only two months. But that was long enough to know his emotional tells when she saw them. She could clearly see that this was a moment where, as cliche as it sounded, Scott needed his Mom. Since the moment his parents had arrived, nearly every moment Scott has spent with them was shared by her. If there was a chance that he was holding back in an effort to not break down in front of her, she didn't want to prolong the inevitable. A few moments to talk things out in private with his Mom could be what he needed to continue pushing forward. So when she saw the chance to give Scott that opportunity, she decided to remove herself and Woody from the situation so that Scott and his Mom could speak.

This would also give her a chance to go find the address that they now knew that they needed. Sydney had spent her fair share of time at SCU doing research in the library. So much so that she had found herself on a first name basis with some of the staff, and she often knew exactly who to go to with different questions regarding where to find certain items. When it came to the quest she currently found herself on, she knew exactly who to ask.

"I have a feeling that Barb is going to be able to help us," she told Woody as he followed her blindly through the building.

"Barb?"

"Yeah, Barb. You don't know, Barb?"

The blank look on Woody's face answered the question for her.

"About yay high?" she said, holding her hand up in the air. "Short brown hair?"

A complete lack of recognition occupied Woody's face.

"Glasses?" Sydney continued, hoping to jog his memory. "At the Reference Desk?"

"Reference Desk?" he asked, seemingly unfamiliar with the term.

"Are you sure that you were actually accepted here? Or did you just show up at the dorms and they felt bad telling you to go home?"

"Hey I do just fine," he said in his defense.

"Yeah, sure. You do know there's a minimum GPA that's required to be an active Fraternity Brother, right?"

"I'm sorry, what?"

Sydney was already ignoring him before he even finished his short sentence, and was instead greeting her Librarian friend. "Hey Barb!"

"Hey there, Mizz Moore!" Barb called out as the two approached. "How you doing today? And who's your friend?"

"Barb, this is Woody. Woody...Barb. Woody is Scott's roommate."

"Oh well, it is a pleasure to meet you then. A friend of Demps' is a friend of mine. How have I not seen you in here before?" she asked.

Sydney smiled at Woody before turning back to Barb. "Barb, I was hoping you could help us out with something. Something pretty important."

Barb was more than accommodating. "Well absolutely, my dear. Tell me, what exactly is it that you and this newbie here need?"

Sydney explained as quickly as possible what they were looking for. A few minutes and a few keystrokes later, Barb had exactly what they needed. A few extra keystrokes and suddenly the printer behind her roared to life. She reached back, grabbed the sheet and flung her arm back towards Sydney and Woody.

"Here ya' go. I hope this helps."

Sydney reached out and took the paper from her. "Thank you so much, Barb. You have no idea what this means to us...and to Scott."

"Anything for Demps," she replied with a smile. "That boy is sweet as pie."

Sydney and Woody were now on their way. Woody reached over and took the sheet from Sydney and glanced down at it. "This is perfect."

"Absolutely," Sydney responded. "And I'd say we've given Scott and his Mom enough time at this point."

"Enough time for what?" Woody asked.

Sydney just smiled and shook her head. "You know, if you could learn to be observant of what's right in front of your face, you would probably be amazed at what you saw throughout the day."

Turning the corner, Sydney could see Scott and Suzanne come into view.

"Hey, there, how's things here?" she asked with a light tilt of her head.

"We're all good now," Scott replied with a slight nod. "Thank you."

"Good," Sydney responded. The pace of her speech increased tenfold. "Because we have everything we need. We need to get moving now."

"Everything?" Suzanne asked.

"The Wilbanks family is definitely still in the area. Their house is only a few minutes down Rt. 3. by car"

"Oh that's perfect!" Suzanne's eyes were wide with excitement.

"Right?! And Donna Kopecki is still working at the Daily Local. So we can hit her up too."

"Where's the Daily Local even located at?" Suzanne asked while checking her phone.

"That's in Exton. About twenty minutes from here," Woody replied.

"Exton, Hmmm..." she said looking down at her screen and texting.

"You thinking we should split up?" Sydney asked.

Suzanne glanced down at her phone before replying. "Well, yes." she said as she began walking, motioning for the others to follow. "But not for the reason I think that you're thinking of."

Sydney continued, slightly confused, as the group struggled to keep pace with Suzanne. "Ok, well you said that you know this Donna Kopecki, right? Why don't you go see her and we'll..."

In the middle of Sydney's sentence, she realized that Suzanne had led them to the doors and they were exiting the library.

Sydney, clearly miffed by the sudden movement, continued following along while she spoke. "Wait, why are we going outside now? Can we stop and talk first?"

"In just a second."

"Mom, where are you going?"

Suzanne squinted as she stepped through the doors and into the sunlight. Turning her head in all directions, she finally saw the reason she'd led everyone outside. Chase was making his way up the walkway towards them.

She turned back to the group and began speaking again. "Ok, so yes, we're going to split up. But not as in some of us go to the Wilbanks house and the others go to the Daily Local."

"Then as in what?" Scott asked.

"As in, I go to the Daily Local with Sydney and Woody, and then to the Wilbanks house, and you go with your Dad."

"Go with Dad? And do what? He's got his own..." Scott waved his hand absently, "...detective work...that he's got to do."

"You can't go to the Daily Local with us," Suzanne explained. "Do you have any idea what would happen if you walked into the offices of the South Cuthbert Daily Local right now and asked to speak to a journalist? You're a person of interest in a murder. Probably the biggest news to hit this school since..."

She glanced towards Chase and nodded in his direction as he drew near. Scott understood her meaning without further explanation.

"We can't march you into a den of reporters right now. They'd suddenly forget that the phrase 'off the record' even exists. You need to go hang out with your Dad while I speak with Donna Kopecki."

"Well, why can't I go to see the Wilbanks family? And why wouldn't Dad go?"

"You can't go because we don't want you going around getting involved in questioning people. And your Dad can't go because they would never want to speak to him if he showed up. For all we know they still blame him for Chris' death."

Chase was now stepping into the group fold. "Hey Guys! How'd you make out? Suz tells me we've got something hot to check out?"

Suzanne, Sydney and Woody stood silent, waiting for Scott's reaction to what he'd just been told. A few seconds passed before he responded to his Dad.

"We found some good info. A couple of things actually. Mom's got a solid plan for checking it out. They're going to head over to the Daily Local and talk to..."

"Wait," Chase interrupted, "The Daily Local? As in the *newspaper*? Are you crazy?"

"Chase," Suzanne interjected, ignoring his questions, "do you remember Donna Kopecki?"

Chase's heart dropped at the mention of the name. It was a name he'd seen far too often during his time here at South Cuthbert. She'd hounded him relentlessly during the weeks following Chris Wilbanks' death, hoping for a comment for one of the myriad of stories she'd run villainizing him. Her work amounted to one of the biggest reasons for the difficulties he'd faced ever since.

"Donna Kopecki still works at the Daily Local?"

"Yeah, it looks like she's been writing for them since college. I want to go talk to her and pick her brain. Maybe get her to help us out."

"Suz, she is going to eat this up. We can't trust her to help. She hates me. She wouldn't want to help us anyway. I mean, why would she?"

"Well, I'd planned on offering her some..." Suzanne paused for a moment, seemingly unsure of how it would be received. "...incentive."

Chase was growing more cynical. "Incentive? What kind of incentive?"

Suzanne straightened her back and answered confidently. "An exclusive."

The entire group all turned to her in shock

"Are you shitting me?! Suz!" Chase was incensed.

"Mom, why would you even think of considering that?" Scott was equally upset at the notion.

"If we have her on our side, then we can control the narrative. This is a good move. Trust me." She turned to Chase. "If we were dating while you went through this, I would've suggested the same thing. We have a chance to drive this thing. We need to take it."

Chase thought it through before reluctantly offering an approving nod. He turned to Scott. "She's right, bud. We do need to be able to control this. Now is our chance to do it. If we pass it up, we may never recover. Trust me, I know."

Scott looked back and forth at the two of them before relenting.

"Fine. We'll do it. I'm putting my trust in you two." He turned to his Dad. "How did you make out so far this morning?"

Chase gave an understanding nod before continuing. "Well, I was able to speak to everyone on your list. No one really offered any more pertinent info. Trout actually was able to change my mind about how I viewed him. He seems to have come around on you since yesterday. But Robbie, well he's a different case altogether. We may need to keep an eye on him. I was a bit surprised when he suddenly brought up my past. He knows about Chris Wilbanks."

The other four slowly turned and looked at each other.

"What? What don't I know guys?"

Suzanne turned back to Chase. "That's the other thing we found. Well, not found, necessarily. More like thought of. We're wondering if there's a chance that whoever is framing Scott is doing it in an effort to get revenge on you for Chris Wilbanks. Chris still has family near here. We're going to go over there and ask them some questions."

Chase slumped his shoulders and looked up towards the sky. He then looked over at Scott with sadness in his eyes. "Buddy, I'm so sorry."

"Dad, there's nothing to be sorry about," Scott replied.

"If this turns out to have anything to do with me, I don't know how I could forgive myself."

"There's nothing to forgive, Dad," he reiterated. "This isn't your fault. Now let's you and I get moving and let them get on their way."

Suzanne nodded as the two spoke. She was happy to see her plan accepted and decided to move it forward before anyone objected any further. "Perfect. Sydney, can we take your car? That way we leave Chase and Scott with a car in case they need to get anywhere."

"Yep, sure can," Sydney replied. "I'm parked over on Elm."

"Sweet," Chase added. "We'll just head back to Scott's dorm room then, and think about next steps for us."

"Ok great, let's all get moving!"

The group split up once again and headed in separate directions as their investigation took a new turn.

CHAPTER 37

A lone figure sat out of sight behind the tinted windows of a 1996 Mustang GT parked on Roseland Avenue. The engine gently rolled under the hood, as though it had just come off of the manufacturing line. It'd only been driven a few thousand miles over the years and had always been garage-kept. No one even really knew that the driver owned it.

Roughly one hundred yards away, the Dempsey family, along with their two loyal helpers, were clearly visible standing outside of the entrance to the library. It wasn't the most recent Chase Dempsey sighting. Still, memories of Chris Wilbanks came rushing back. Seeing Suzanne also served to invoke some long forgotten feelings.

You're just as pretty as I remember you to be. And every little bit the helper.

Suzanne came into Chase Dempsey's life long after his involvement with Chris' death. But once she was there, it was clear that she was going to be a permanent fixture in his life and that she was willing to do whatever she needed to do in order to help him through his "issues".

If she only knew the truth, she would never go near him again. At least this time she's justified, being that her son is innocent. Everyone will soon believe that Scott killed Fran Coleman, and that he nearly killed Will Bonnetti. I made sure that would be the case. At first, planting his student ID at the scene seemed too simplistic. But the simplest explanation is usually the correct one, right? No one would ever suspect that I, a respected member of the South Cuthbert University community, could ever perform such a gruesome act. Chase won't be successful in proving anyone's innocence this time though. I won't allow it. This time the entire family is going to pay for what he did to Chris.

The Mustang pulled out into traffic and slowly cruised down the block past the group. They had no idea what kind of danger they would find themselves in if they dug too deep.

CHAPTER 38

Chase and Scott were making their way across campus in the direction of Oreland Hall when Sully had called Chase on his cell phone to let him know that he had spoken to Lt. Quinn. He said that they seemed very confident in being able to have charges filed soon against Scott. It was not the news that Chase was hoping to hear. They seemed to be moving quicker than he had expected.

"Thanks, Sully. I appreciate the update. Yeah, some of our work this morning has produced some potential paths for us to follow."

"What type of paths?" Sully asked.

"Well nothing concrete unfortunately. But we're wondering if this has anything to do with me, honestly."

Sully was confused. "With you? What would you have to do with this?"

Chase was unsure about even mentioning the name. Against his better Judgment, he blurted out the name. "Chris Wilbanks. We're wondering if this is somehow connected to Chris Wilbanks."

"Chase, I don't know if digging up the past is the best way for you to save your son's future."

"Do you have a better idea?" Chase asked.

Sully was silent for a moment before responding. "No. I don't."

"Well then until you do, then just leave me to it, ok? I'll call you later." Chase hung up on Sully without waiting for a response.

The events of the morning played back through Chase's head as he tried to unravel the mystery of why his son is being investigated for murder. For his Pledge Brother's Murder! He felt bad for having to remind himself of that. A young man was dead, and another in the hospital, clinging to life. Both of them were young men that were working towards a goal that would give them a Fraternal bond. Both of them had a lifetime of potential in front of them. Now they would never have the opportunity to realize that potential.

And now Chase had the newfound worry of whether or not Donna Kopecki would be working towards a goal of stopping Scott in his journey to do the same. She certainly seemed to make it her goal in life to take Chase down so many years ago. It wasn't out of the question that, given the chance to extend that vendetta to his son, she would be more than enticed by the thought.

He looked over at Scott as they continued down University Avenue. He recognized the look on his face. Overly steely-eyed. Clenched jaw. A look of resolve. Only it wasn't resolve. Chase knew well that it was the mask that Scott wore to hide his concern. It was a trait Scott had picked up from him.

Scott turned to his Father. "So what did Sully have to say?"

"Well, Sully got SCPD to lift the surveillance. He didn't need that kind of thing on his campus. So you won't have to worry about them following you around. At least not on campus."

"Well that's good!" Scott said, thankful that he could now have some sense of privacy back. "Anything else?" he asked.

Chase paused for a moment before answering. He had always been a believer in telling Scott the truth in any instance. He decided that today should be no different. "He said that the police feel like they're getting closer to being able to charge you."

"That's not even possible," Scott shot back. "There is zero evidence placing me there!"

"I know. I know. I think it's a load of shit. I think that they're just telling Sully that to keep the school from having a negative view of the investigation. But, just in case, we have to move quick on this."

Scott took a moment to change the scope of the conversation, if for nothing else other than to feel normal for a moment. "Hey, when we get back to my dorm room, I can show you my Pledge book. Probably been a while since you've seen one of those. I'd love to get your signature actually."

Chase thought back to his own pledge period and the weekly ritual of obtaining the signature of every active Brother. It was an exercise meant to help Pledges get to know the Brothers, and vice versa. Obtaining the signature of a visiting Alumni was always highly sought after. A hint of a smile started in the corner of Chase's mouth as he thought about how rare the signature of your alumni Father must be. But, as enticing as the idea might have been, he needed to table the idea.

"Tell you what, let's make it a point to do that when all of this is over. But right now we aren't actually going back to your dorm room."

"We're not?' Scott asked.

"No, we've got something more important to do right now."

CHAPTER 39

The South Cuthbert Daily Local was first published in 1872. One of the many local newspapers covering the suburbs of Philadelphia, the Daily Local over time came to be known as one of the most trusted news sources within the area immediately West and Southwest of Philadelphia. On the campus of South Cuthbert University though, the news from The Forum often took precedence. Every student read their free copy of The Forum before even considering purchasing The Daily Local. While they were in school, it was The Forum that ran the majority of the stories about Chris Wilbanks, and they were all written by Donna Kopecki. Once she graduated, however, she went to work for the Daily Local and continued writing about her favorite subject. This was a fact that Suzanne quickly realized when she and Chase began dating in college. The bulk of the news stories about Chase appeared in print long before she knew him. But, she was able to see the effects of those stories once the two of them began dating. The last thing she ever expected that she'd be doing twenty-five years later was walking into the Daily Local to speak to the same reporter that vilified her husband so many years ago.

The Daily Local is headquartered in Exton, PA. It's in a relatively large building, compared to the other businesses around it. Suzanne was surprised at the size of it when she turned into the small parking lot. Her best guess was that much of the building was taken up by the machines used for printing the actual newspapers. She wondered how many copies of the paper were actually in circulation these days. Online content began overtaking the print medium years ago, and the trend has never slowed.

But it was the speed at which online content moved in this day and age that brought Suzanne here. If Donna Kopecki gets her information from the South Cuthbert Police Department, which she highly suspected she already had, there will be no catching up with her once she decides to run with it. She likely already has a story queued up and ready to publish on their web site. Suzanne knew that she needed to appeal to Donna's good nature, assuming she had any, and convince her to print only the facts. She needs to give Scott a chance to clear himself before the public has a chance to convict him themselves.

Sydney pulled her 2011 Honda Civic into a spot near the front of the lot. Woody exited from the front passenger seat, followed by Suzanne, who had some difficulty squeezing out of the back of the two-door coupe. After offering to give Woody the front seat in order to give him more room for his much longer legs, she quickly regretted it. She hadn't considered that it had been over two decades since she needed to ride in the back of such a small car.

"Not too tight back there for ya', was it Mrs. Demps?" Woody asked.

Suzanne smiled politely. "No, not at all. I'm pretty small, so...ya' know..."

"Sorry," Sydney said with a wince. "Maybe we should've let Scott take this car and driven yours?"

"Next time," Suzanne said with a slight laugh as she stretched to crack her back. "Ok, so here's the deal. You two stay quiet in here, got it? Let me do the talking."

Both Sydney and Woody nodded in agreement without saying a word. They both appeared to be unable to grasp how they could've found themselves spending their day this way.

Suzanne began walking towards the front door of the building, Sydney and Woody in tow, when she suddenly stopped in her tracks. Her eyes grew wide at the sight of a woman walking along the walkway towards the front door with a messenger bag thrown over her shoulder.

"Oh my God, that's her."

"That's Donna Kopecki?" Sydney asked, louder than she meant to. The woman turned her head towards them for a brief moment, just as quickly returning her attention towards the path ahead of her and entering the building.

"Ok, well we know she's here, at least," Woody quipped.

"Let's do this then. Come on," Suzanne said as she began walking.

Suzanne opened the door to the lobby, turning back slightly to hold the door for Sydney and Woody. Turning her attention back to the lobby as she entered, she saw that only the receptionist was visible. Donna Kopecki was nowhere to be found.

"Good morning," the man, whose head was visible from behind the tall desk, said cheerfully. "What can I help you with?"

"Hi there," she responded with a pleasant smile. "We're here to see Donna Kopecki."

"Of course, do you have an appointment?" he asked.

"No we do not," she answered plainly.

"Well, Donna sees people by appointment only. I can ring her line though to see if she's here. Can I ask your name?"

Suzanne smiled and nodded, knowing full well that Donna had just walked right past this man's field of view. She may not have cared enough to say hello to him. But there's no way he didn't see her.

"Sure, can you let her know that Suzanne Dempsey is here to see her?"

"Of course," he responded. "One moment."

He picked up the phone and dialed a three-digit extension. "Hi Donna? It's Steven from the front desk. I have a Suzanne Dempsey here in the lobby that is requesting to see you?"

Suzanne watched him carefully as his eyes turned back to meet her's.

"Yes Dempsey," he reaffirmed

Ok so she recognizes the name, she thought.

He shifted his eyes to look at Woody and Sydney. "Yes, a young man and a young woman...mmm hmmm."

The receptionist hung up the phone and looked back up at Suzanne.

"Ms. Kopecki will be out in a moment."

"Great, thank you," Suzanne responded with a smile before turning to wait in the corner of the lobby with Woody and Sydney. It was clear from what she heard that Donna is expecting that Scott may be with her. For a moment she toyed with the idea that she could pass Woody off as him in order to keep her interest longer. But she didn't want to put Woody in a position where he might say something that gets attributed to Scott in the newspaper. That wouldn't be fair to him.

It was less than a minute before Donna Kopecki came speed walking into the lobby. It was quicker than Suzanne had ever been greeted for a meeting. This reaffirmed her thought that Donna expected to see Scott standing there when she turned the corner.

"Suzanne?" she asked with a surprised face, one eye glancing quickly at what she hoped was Scott Dempsey. "Gosh, it really is you!"

"Yep, it's me." Suzanne responded in a deadpan tone. "How are you?"

"Well, just living day to day, you know? So tell me...what brings you here?"

Suzanne was less than impressed with Donna's attempt to hide her hope that a story was falling into her lap.

"Can we actually go somewhere private to speak?" Suzanne asked.

"Private? Sure, of course. Just follow me." Donna led the three of them past the reception desk and into the office space.

"There's probably an open conference room..." she scanned the perimeter of the space. "Yep, right over there. Follow me."

The three of them, two of which Donna hadn't even tried to be introduced to ye,t despite the fact that she was clearly aching to be, followed her into the conference room as Donna closed the door behind them.

They each sat themselves down at the large table as Donna sat herself across from Suzanne.

"So what can I do for you? And actually, I'm sorry," she said, turning to Woody and Sydney, and focusing mainly on Woody. "We haven't been introduced. I'm Donna. You must be..."

Suzanne interjected "This is my son's roommate, Woody,"

"Oh..." Donna responded, attempting to hide her disappointment with a smile. "...of course. Nice to meet you."

Sydney allowed the pregnant pause to stretch out before inserting herself. "I'm Sydney...her son's girlfriend."

"Girlfriend?" she asked. "Well, that's nice. So what brings everyone here today."

"Donna, I imagine you're well aware of the murder that occurred on campus this past weekend."

"I am, yes. Such a terrible tragedy."

"And I imagine, since you're an experienced reporter, that you know my son...Chase Dempsey's son..." she paused for effect, "...is being questioned about it."

Donna's demeanor quickly changed. "Well, Suz, as I hear it, he's being more than just questioned. He's a suspect."

Suzanne's heart dropped. If that's what Donna is hearing then that cements how the police are now looking at him. Leaks like that don't happen by accident. She worked to maintain her composure.

"That's actually why I'm here, Donna. The evidence against Scott is circumstantial at best. There is nothing linking his physical person to being there at the scene of the crime."

"So only his ID then?" Donna asked.

Suzanne paused for a moment. Not wanting to say anything that might be misconstrued or can be quoted.

"Let's back up. I want to make sure that this entire conversation is off the record. Can you agree to that?"

Donna paused for a moment and took in a deep breath. "Sure, I can agree to that."

"Good, listen, Scott didn't do this. Aside from the fact that he's just not that kind of person, nothing lines up. Timelines. Evidence. Nothing. He didn't do it. We both know you've been in this position before. Your writing nearly ruined an innocent man because you were young and made assumptions that you shouldn't have. And I don't want that to happen to Scott. He needs to be given a chance. I'm here to ask you to find it in your heart to keep that in mind when you're covering this story. Please see him as innocent until proven guilty. I don't want him to go through what his Father was forced to endure. Can you please do that for me?"

Donna sat patiently while Suzanne made her plea. She held her lips close together and looked away as if she was giving thought to what she'd just heard. She inhaled deeply and slowly released the breath, then relaxed her shoulders and turned back to Suzanne.

"No."

"What?!" Woody and Sydney both yelled out in unison as they both began spewing hate at the reporter.

"Guys, guys, calm down!" Suzanne pleaded. The two of them eventually fell back into their chairs, allowing Suzanne to take the floor again.

Suzanne turned back to Donna and in her most professional voice asked, "What the fuck do you mean, no?"

"It's simple. I think he did it. The cops think he did it. His friggin' Student ID was sitting underneath this kid's body. It's an open shut case. There's not a jury in this land gonna' find him Not Guilty."

"He didn't do it, Donna!"

"I don't give a shit what you say. I believe he did. My son and his other pledge brother's think he did. It's going to be a thing. I'm getting out in front of it."

"Your son?" asked quizzically.

"Yeah, my son is just broken up over it. He was really close to poor Coleman. I've met the boy a couple of times. He was very nice."

"Your son goes to SCU?" Suzanne asked.

"Oh you didn't know? Our sons are both pledging KXP together this semester."

"Who is your son?" Woody asked.

"Robert Goldberg," she responded, as if it were common knowledge.

Woody stammered for a moment as he put the pieces together "Robert...Robbie? You're Robbie's Mom?"

She stiffened her back before replying to Woody. "I never did like people calling him that. But yes. I'm his Mother."

Suzanne, recognizing that they were no longer in charge of this conversation, stood to leave. "Come on guys, we need to get going. It's clear that she doesn't want an Exclusive on this story."

Donna, surprised to hear the word, tilted her head. "Did you say Exclusive?"

Suzanne, feeling that she had regained the upper hand, turned back to Donna. "Well, yeah, I was thinking about offering you an exclusive interview with Scott in exchange for giving him a fair representation in your stories."

Donna leaned back in her chair and let out a hearty belly laugh. "Oh sweetie, that's nice and all. But I don't need your exclusive. I'm already close enough to this story to know that it's going to sell enough papers all on it's own. Pandering to your murderer son isn't going to do anything to improve the bottom line of this paper. Or the story, for that matter."

Anger filled Suzanne's face as she clenched her fists. It took every ounce of willpower that she had to keep from launching herself across the table at Donna.

"You friggin' bitch," she said angrily.

Donna took that as a cue to remove herself and stood up. "Actually I need to leave as well. Please see yourself out."

She walked past the group and through the doorway, turning to face Suzanne before exiting. "Please give my best to Chase," she said with a smile.

CHAPTER 40

"That friggin' bitch doesn't know what the hell she's talking about." Suzanne was livid as she flung open the lobby door on her way out to the parking lot. "How the hell does she succeed as a reporter if she's not going to report the actual news instead of nothing but opinion pieces and fluff."

Sydney's face mirrored that of Suzanne's. "This is in our hands now. We need to find evidence to clear Scott. Because it's clear that no one else is trying to."

"And can we also talk for a moment about how she's Robbie's Mom?" Woody added.

"Oh God, right?!" Sydney responded.

"Oh I know! What the hell is that all about? Woody, have you spoken with anyone else in the pledge class that might feel the same way?"

"Well, Robbie definitely is no fan of Scott's. And I haven't really seen what she's describing about everyone feeling that way. There have been moments of doubt. But right now most people seem to be in Scott's corner. But that doesn't really mean anything I suppose for us right now. If Robbie is feeding her information...real or made up...that's what's going to get printed."

Suzanne was livid at the idea that they've lost the ability to drive this narrative. Clearing Scott as quickly as possible was now more important than ever. "We need to get this done before she can get something published."

CHAPTER 41

"So why, exactly, are we following Mom again?" Scott asked from the passenger seat of his Dad's car. Instead of hanging back and patiently sitting in Scott's dorm room, Chase and Scott hopped in the car and followed Suzanne, Sydney and Woody to the South Cuthbert Daily Local.

"To keep them safe," Chase responded.

Scott seemed confused. "Safe from a reporter? By the way, this car is really spacious. Did you just buy this?"

Chase quickly latched onto the chance to have a brief, normal conversation. "Oh, yeah we did just buy it! Do you like it? And yeah, your Mom loves how spacious it is. Lots of legroom. In the front *and* the back!"

Scott nodded and took in the interior. "I bet she does. Seems comfy."

"Anyway," Chase said, reluctantly bringing them back into reality, "no not safe from the reporter. But I will say that this bitch could be just as dangerous with her words as anyone could with their fists. But, no, I have concerns about the three of them going off on their own. More specifically about them going to the Wilbanks house."

"Which you don't have the address to. So, you need to follow them in order to get there yourself."

"Exactly. And actually..."

Chase's thought was interrupted when he pulled into the parking lot of the South Cuthbert Daily Local and saw a hauntingly familiar face come storming out of the front door.

201

"Actually what?" Scott asked in confusion.

"Holy shit, that's her. That's Donna Kopecki!" Chase couldn't take his eyes off of the woman. Visions from his past flashed before his eyes. "Scott, that is the woman whose name I hope you never have to be haunted by. Man, she is going somewhere in a hurry."

"Should we follow her instead?" Scott asked.

"No, we don't want to get into a situation where the off-duty cop, slash father of a murder suspect, was found out to be tailing a reporter. That's not a good look. Let's just wait for the girls and Woody to come out."

Scott pointed to the front entrance. "And there they are! Man, they don't look happy, do they?"

"Guess it didn't go too well," Chase quipped. "Looks like we may have our work cut out for us."

The two watched as Suzanne, Sydney and Woody got into their car and sped out of the lot. Chase followed suit, taking care to remain far enough behind to avoid being noticed. They turned left onto Rt. 3 and headed towards Rt. 202 South. The next step, it appeared, would be the Wilbanks house.

CHAPTER 42

"I always knew that Scott's Dad had good reason to hate her. But I'd never really spoken much to her myself. Now I completely understand," Suzanne mused. "What a friggin' bitch!"

Sydney floored the gas pedal and attempted to summon any power that the engine in her Civic might have in an effort to get them to the Wilbanks house as quickly as possible. "How can she just play with people's lives like that?" she asked.

"She thinks she's judge and jury," Woody added. "I see now where Robbie gets it."

"Ya' know, I never did like Robbie." Sydney was gripping the wheel tightly as she hunched over the steering column. "Why did they let him pledge anyway?"

"Got me. He's the only one in the pledge class that I don't really like. He gets along with a few people but he's clearly the odd man out in the group."

"Well, maybe that's good for us then," Suzanne responded from the back seat. "If he's not that well-liked, then maybe he won't be able to sway too many opinions in the group."

"Yeah but that doesn't help us if his Mom is publishing stories in the paper calling Scott a murderer." Woody was now showing more emotion than he'd shown all day.

"That's the truth." Suzanne was now resting her arm on the edge of the side window with her head buried in hand. "God, I still can't believe we're even saying those words. How did we even get here? Jesus Christ, she is going to have people ready to execute him right there in the center of campus."

Woody turned back to look at Suzanne. His voice now carried a determined tone. "We won't let that happen, Mrs. Demps. We'll fix this. I promise."

She looked back at him and sighed. It occurred to her that she should be the one being the adult and keeping the kid's emotions in check. But it seems that they weren't quite kids anymore. "Thanks Woody. I know. It's just tough. I need to change my focus though. I can't let that woman take me away from what we need to do. How much further to the Wilbanks house?"

Sydney looked at the GPS mounted on her dashboard. "Not long. Two minutes."

Suzanne allowed herself to relax back into the seat. "Ok so hopefully we can find some answers there."

"What are you going to say?" Woody asked.

"I honestly have no idea. I'll figure it out...I don't know...when it comes out of my mouth, I guess."

Sydney looked at Suzanne in the rearview mirror "It is possible that one thing doesn't have anything to do with the other. I mean it was really so long ago."

"Yeah well it's the only idea that we've got right now. We are literally working from square one right, grasping at straws, and any of a dozen other figures of speech."

"Right," Woody added. "and the police are already much closer to what they think happened. So even if we're just trying to figure it out with nothing to go on. We have to start somewhere. Won't know anything until we try."

Suzanne nodded her head in agreement. "Exactly. I just hope that we get something. Because I don't know what the hell the next step would be if we don't."

"Well, we're about to find out," Sydney said matter of factly. "We're here."

The three of them all turned their attention toward an old home along the left side of the road. It looked to be about fifty years old and consisted of mostly original finishings on the outside. The driveway was long and lined with gravel covered grooves for drivers to line up their tires as they traversed through the tree-lined path that led to the wide expanse outside of the old exterior garage.

"Well, it's certainly...well-lived-in?" Woody said only half-jokingly.

"Doesn't look like it's been...lived in...very recently, does it?" Sydney responded.

Sydney pulled the car into the driveway and parked alongside the house. The three exited the car and stood for a moment as they took in the surroundings. Suzanne peered around the back of the house and made note of an black Mustang parked there.

"Well, someone's here I guess. Odd place to park it. I wonder if they even want anyone to know they're here."

"Am I blocking it in? Should I move my car?" Sydney asked.

Woody walked over and checked the clearance. "No, looks good. Should be able to get by without any problem. I'd say you're fine."

Suzanne motioned to a door on the side of the house. It was slightly ajar with only an aluminum screen door keeping out the rest of the world. "Well, let's knock and see if anyone's home."

"Shouldn't we go around front?" Sydney asked.

"Not sure it really matters. Besides, this one's open." She walked over and knocked on the old metal door. She could hear the sound of the aluminum echoing inside of the house.

The three glanced at each other, stretching their ears for any sign of life. There was no response. Suzanne banged on the door once again.

"Hello?" she yelled. "Anyone home?"

They were met once more with no response. Suzanne slowly reached for the door handle.

"Are you crazy?" Sydney whispered. "We can't just go in!"

"I don't have the luxury of time right now, Syd. I can't wait around for people to come to the door today."

She pulled the door open slowly and stepped into the house.

CHAPTER 43

"So what do you plan on doing when we get there?" Scott asked his Dad. He had noticed that his Dad had been silent for much of the drive after leaving the Daily Local. Seeing that woman seemed to have an effect on him.

Chase turned to Scott, a bit startled. "Hmmm? Oh, well not sure I guess. I suppose just drive by and assess the situation from there."

"Just drive by? You don't even have a plan?" Scott asked.

"A plan? What kind of plan would I have? This isn't your garden variety type of situation here." Chase let out a light chuckle, attempting to make light of the situation. But his frustration was visibly growing.

"Well they're turning in up ahead," Scott pointed out. "So I guess we'll have to figure it out."

Chase looked up just in time to see the rear of Sydney's car disappearing down a driveway. "Ok, let's pull over on that shoulder." He pointed to the right side of the road in the stretch just past the driveway and catty corner from the house. "This should do nicely."

"Won't they see us when they come out?" Scott asked.

"Well by that point it won't matter so much," Chase said as he inched the car up just enough so that he could still see down the drive. Twisting himself around, he could see Suz, Sydney and Woody get out of their car.

"Can you see them?" Scott asked.

"Yep, I see 'em," Chase responded.

"What are they doing?"

"Looks like they're being let in," Chase said. "I just saw them go in the side door. I guess someone's home."

"Ok, so now we just wait?" Scott asked.

"Yep, we just wait."

CHAPTER 44

Suzanne found the kitchen of the Wilbanks house to be just as dated as the outside of the house. It was filled with appliances that appeared to be from the 80's, a laminate-top kitchen table with metal chairs that appeared to be from the 70's, and even curtains that appeared to be made from the same material and pattern as the flower-print wallpaper. "Hello?" she called out as she inched her way in. "Is anyone home?" she yelled louder. "Hello?"

Sydney and Woody glanced at each other as they reluctantly followed behind.

"Hello?" Woody called out. His deeper voice reverberated through the kitchen and startled Suzanne slightly. There was no way that anyone that might be in the house didn't hear that.

"My name is Suzanne Dempsey," Suzanne yelled, in a feeble attempt to match Woody's volume. "Is anyone here? I have some questions about my son."

"This place is creepy," Sydney whispered.

"Yeah, you're not kidding," Suzanne replied quietly. She glanced around for any sign of life, noting to herself that there were dirty dishes in the sink. Someone had been here recently.

"Do you think anyone's even home?" Woody asked.

"Maybe not," Sydney shrugged. "Although there is that car in the drive."

"Well, I suppose they could have more than one car," Suzanne considered. "Possibly left in a hurry and forgot to lock up?"

"My guess is no one is here," Woody chimed in. His voice now at a normal volume, unafraid of who might hear him. "I'm going to go look around."

Before Suzanne could object, Woody had already passed through the swinging door and left the kitchen. She glanced at Sydney and the two shared a disapproving look. But, their disapproval was soon overtaken by alarm when a loud crash was heard from the room that Woody had just entered

The two ran through the door to find Woody face down and motionless on the dining room floor. Broken dishes and glasses from the china cabinet were scattered all around him.

Suzanne quickly looked around, expecting to see a nearby attacker. But no one could be seen. Suddenly a figure appeared through the corner of her eye. Turning her head towards the window, she saw the faint form of someone running behind the house.

"Stay here and help Woody," she yelled to Sydney as she bolted for the door.

Running back through the kitchen, Suzanne burst through the storm door and out into the driveway. She quickly swung herself around, expecting the attacker to appear at any moment. Seeing no one in the direct vicinity, she looked towards the nearby woods, thinking that perhaps the person ran in that direction. At that moment, she remembered the car that was sitting behind the house, and as if on cue, the roar of the Mustang's engine came to life. With barely a second of time passing, she heard the wheels spinning and the sound of a car quickly moving closer. She looked up just in time to see the muscle car turning the corner and racing towards her. As she dove to her right and tumbled to the ground, the car sped past her and raced up the driveway. Suzanne lifted her head in time to see it skidding onto the roadway and speeding away.

Watching it speed away, she caught sight of the front of a Honda Pilot that she recognized as her own car.

"Chase?"

CHAPTER 45

Chase looked around, as the silence grew. "How ya doing anyway? I haven't really had a chance to talk with you about what's been going on."

"Eh, I'm getting by," he responded solemnly.

"Scott, I've been through this myself. You can't tell me you're getting by and expect me to believe it."

"Well, yeah, I mean. I'm not all hunky dory over here. But I'm managing. This sucks for sure. I have no idea what's going to happen." Scott was beginning to show signs of wear.

Chase's voice grew stern. "I'll tell you what's going to happen. We're going to find out who did this and get you cleared." He allowed his head to sink for a moment before looking back towards Scott. "I won't allow what happened to me to happen to you. This will not define your life."

"How did you manage to get through it?" Scott asked.

"It wasn't easy. The longer it dragged on, the harder it became. And even after I was cleared, some people wouldn't forget."

"Some people...meaning Sully," Scott interjected.

"Well, yeah, I mean I felt like nobody would forget it. But definitely him for one. And I don't trust him one bit today. That's why I'm keeping him so close to me right now."

"Do you think he has something to do with it?" Scott asked, surprised at the implication.

Chase looked away for a moment, and then brought his attention back to Scott. "I don't know. Let's just say I'm not convinced that he doesn't."

"Wait, are you trying to tell me that..." Before Scott could finish his sentence, he was interrupted by the loud roar of an engine. The two looked up to see a black Mustang barreling out of the Wilbanks driveway. Its tires screeched as it skidded around the corner and turned onto the road. It came within inches of Chase's car before speeding off.

"Holy shit, who the hell was that?" Scott screamed.

"Couldn't see. The windows were tinted. So was the plate. But we need to get in there," Chase yelled. His door was already open with one leg out before he had even finished his sentence. "Let's go!"

The two raced across the street and ran down the driveway towards the house. The sight of Suzanne laying on the ground quickly came into view.

"Suz!"

"Mom!"

"What the hell are you two doing here?" she yelled at them as they neared.

"Are you ok? Did you get hit?" Scott asked.

"I'm ok! It didn't hit me." she yelled. "But get inside! Woody's hurt!"

"Woody? What happened?" Chase yelled as he raced inside. Entering the dining room he found Woody and Sydney sitting on the floor. Woody was holding his hand to his head while Sydney did her best to comfort him.

"Mr. Dempsey?" Sydney was clearly surprised to see him. "What are you doing here?"

"Scott and I followed you here. And looks like with good reason. What happened?" Chase crouched down next to the two of them. "Who did this?"

"No idea," Woody responded, wincing in pain. "I never got a look at him."

"Is anyone else here?" Chase asked.

Sydney shook her head. "I don't think so. We knocked a few times. But no one answered. The door was wide open. So we came in and started calling out for someone. Woody came into the dining room here, and next thing we know we hear a loud crash. Come in here and find him on the ground. Then Mrs. Dempsey saw someone running outside and ran after. Where is she? And where's Scott?"

"They're both outside. It looks like whoever did this also tried to run Suz down with their car."

"We need to get Woody to a hospital," Sydney pleaded.

"A hospital? Are you serious?" Woody asked. "We can't go to the hospital. They'll ask how this happened. And what we just did basically amounted to breaking and entering."

Sydney quickly turned to Woody, clearly shocked at what he was saying. "I don't care what it amounts to. We need to get you looked at."

"I'm fine anyway. It's just a bump and some scratches."

"I hate to say it," Chase said, "but this doesn't look good for us at all if the cops end up involved. If Woody seems ok, and he does to me, then I think we should move on from here quickly."

"You have got to be kidding me," Sydney pleaded.

Suzanne then came walking through the door just as Sydney was finishing speaking."Kidding about what?"

"They don't want to take Woody to the hospital. They're worried about how it'll look if they find out how it happened."

"Well," Suzanne said, "it wouldn't look good. That's for sure. Woody, do you feel like you're ok?"

Woody nodded to the affirmative.

"Seriously? You too?" Sydney replied to Suzanne. "He was just attacked!"

"Yeah, after we walked into the house uninvited. Sydney, ordinarily I would run him right over there. But we don't have the luxury of time right now. And if we get tied up with talking to the cops, even if we can explain it away, then it just slows us up. And it'll make Scott look even guiltier. I say that we monitor him and make sure he doesn't show signs of serious injury. But otherwise, we need to push forward and avoid things that are going to stop us from doing what we need to do."

Chase nodded in agreement. "Exactly."

Sydney began pacing alongside the dining room table, her lips tight as she contemplated the argument that Suzanne and Chase made. She looked at Woody for his input.

Woody shrugged his shoulders before agreeing with them. "They're right, Syd. It's too important to risk losing the time. I'll be ok."

Sydney's shoulders relaxed as she let out a deep breath. "Fine, I guess you're right. I just wish we would've gotten more out of this trip here than we did. All we ended up with was a lump on Woody's head."

The four of them stared at each other for a moment. They all seemed to be in agreement that they were back to square one, when suddenly they heard the distant sound of Scott's voice.

"Um...guys? You might want to come in here and see this."

They looked at each other, as they came to the realization that Scott wasn't in the room with them. They quickly began to move towards the sound of his voice and followed it into what would normally be considered the living room of any other house. They instead found Scott standing in the center of what looked more like a command center.

"Holy shit," Suzanne said as she slowed her pace and took in the insanity of what she was seeing.

In the corner sat a desk with two laptops. Hanging on the wall, on either side of the corner above the desk, four monitors were mounted. A folding table sat in the middle of the room with two maps splayed out across it. One was a map of South Cuthbert Township. The other was of South Cuthbert University.

Chase immediately focused on two points of the maps, both circled in red. One was clearly 403 S. Martin Street, the KXP Fraternity house. The other circled area was easily recognizable, perhaps, only to him. It was the location as the one where Chris Wilbanks was found dead twenty-eight years prior. Written next to it in red were two symbols that would stand out to any member of a Greek Organization:

$$A\Omega$$

The first and last letters of the Greek Alphabet. The Alpha and the Omega. The Beginning and the End. Chase felt a pit in the bottom of his stomach and hoped that he was wrong about what he believed the significance of this to be.

His attention was then drawn to Scott. "Guys look at this." Scott was staring at the far wall in the room. The entire group now saw the real reason he had called them in here.

On the wall was a large cork board, adorned with photos and press clippings. Some were recent, pulled from stories published about Fran Coleman. Others were two decades old and related to the Chris Wilbanks murder. All of them were related to Chase and Scott Dempsey. Large photos of Chase and Scott both sat in the center of the board. Push pins were placed throughout, with red yarn attached to each, creating connected lines between all of the items on the board.

"Oh my god, someone in this family..." Woody began, his voice trailing off, unsure if his thought was based in reality or more of a conspiracy theory.

Suzanne was more certain and gladly finished Woody's sentence for him. "...blames Chase for Chris Wilbanks' death and is trying to pay him back by framing Scott for murder."

"This is it!" Scott exclaimed, stepping in front of the board and holding his hands out wide. "This is the evidence we need! This clears me!"

Suzanne, Sydney and Woody were all smiles, nodding their heads in agreement. Chase, however, was more quiet. He quietly studied the board before turning his gaze back to the map, then once more back to the board.

"Guys, I'm sorry. This isn't enough."

"What'd ya' mean, not enough?" Scott asked angrily. "This shows us everything!"

Chase shook his head "Scott, I'm sorry. But all that this shows, definitively, is that this person is interested in both cases. Someone could have the same type of board for the JFK assassination. That doesn't mean they killed him."

"Dad, this is very clear to me."

"Scott, it's clear to me too. But it's not enough to bring a crime investigation unit in here just yet and announce to the world that they did it."

"Well, we have to do something with it, Chase!" Suzanne joined Scott in his protest.

"If we go to the South Cuthbert Police with this information, all we'd be able to do is say 'hey, you might want to look at this angle too.' And then the eyes start looking back at us wondering how we know about it. Then it comes out that we were in this house and they'll start saying we planted it all to get the focus off of you."

The air immediately fell out of the collective sail of the group. They knew what Chase was saying was true.

Scott let out a loud scream and moved towards the wall with a motion that indicated he was about to punch it. Chase moved quickly and held him back.

"Easy, bud! We don't want to touch anything in this room. Listen, there are ways to get this info in front of the cops without drawing attention to ourselves. This is a good thing that we found all of this. We definitely want those computers searched. But we can't be the ones to do that. But we need to leave now. Ok?"

Suzanne nodded in agreement. She motioned to the rest of the group. "Ok, yeah, he's right. Let's get out of here. But, I want some pics of this first."

Chase paused for a moment, unsure if he wanted any evidence available that they were ever in the house. He knew, though, that as soon as the owner returns they would clear this room out. "Ok, yeah, go ahead and snap pics of everything." He took out his own phone and snapped a pic of the South Cuthbert Township map.

The group left the way they had come in and gathered out in the driveway.

"So, what's next?" Suzanne asked Chase.

"We need to go see Sully," he responded. "Hop in your car and follow me. I'll call him on the way."

CHAPTER 46

The air felt different to Sully as he walked across the stretch leading from the parking lot to Barness Union Hall. The students were gathered along the grass enjoying the fall day. Footballs were being tossed. Multiple hacky sack circles had been formed. On any other day he might have taken a moment to think that, despite all of the changes that have occurred with society and technology over the years, not much has changed when it comes to the need for college students to unwind on a warm Fall day. But today had more important things on his mind. He was oblivious to the activity around him. His mind was elsewhere.

For twenty-eight years he'd been trying to forget the night that had ostensibly changed his life forever, whether he would admit it or not. He thought he'd be able to get past the presence of Chase Dempsey's son on campus. But suddenly his memories were thrown back into the forefront, impacting him in a way he had never expected.

Now Chase was back on campus to help his son, and actively including Chris Wilbanks' death as part of his investigation. Sully knew it was only a matter of time before Chase found out the truth. It was a truth that had haunted Sully ever since that night. Yet he had never chosen to accept it, instead choosing to believe that it would never actually reach the light of day and force him to face it. He now suddenly found himself forced to make a decision on how to deal with it.

Without even realizing how far he'd walked, Sully looked up and found that he was approaching his office door. He paused for a moment and looked at the wall plate next to the door bearing his name, along with his title - Director of Greek Life. It had just become background scenery over the years. Something that he never really noticed as he passed by. But today he felt a pang of disgust inside of him and he thought about the past he had hidden in order to get him where he is today.

He walked in and dropped the full weight of his body into his desk chair. Leaning back, he let out a sigh and closed his eyes. He then thought back to a memory that he hadn't allowed himself to fully recall for nearly three decades. He thought back to the last time he saw Chris Wilbanks alive...and the moment that he died.

CHAPTER 47

TWENTY-EIGHT YEARS PRIOR
APRIL 7, 1993
South Cuthbert, PA

"Membership built from only those insistent on the Brotherhood of all men!

A demand for only the highest moral standard!

The predominant responsibility of love and acceptance among all members!

Judgment only by...only by..."

Sully could hear the sound of Chase Dempsey's voice echoing through the woods as he hid in the bushes. At least he assumed it was Chase Dempsey's voice. He had only met him a handful of times. But he was certain that the voice didn't belong to Chris Wilbanks. That was a voice he'd come to know by heart in recent weeks.

Sully had met Chris at a Kappa Chi Rho party earlier in the month. Sully, a Brother of Sigma Phi, was friends with a few KXP brothers and was able to secure one of the rare male invitations.

Sully had just pledged Sig Phi in the Fall of '92 and this Spring was proving to be an eventful one for him. He was very outgoing, very good looking and very loud. Once he was done pledging and was initiated as a Brother in Sig Phi, it wasn't long before everyone started to notice him. The sorority girls fawned all over him. The entrance to his bedroom may as well have been a revolving door.

His clear interest in the opposite sex, however, also made it very easy for him to hide what had become an equal interest in men. It was a detail that he'd benefited from throughout high school. He had grown up in a small town that was not known to be accepting of the gay community. So he spent his time hiding behind his tough, heterosexual exterior, while also becoming skilled at spotting like-minded individuals that were also interested in exploring their lesser known side.

He had hoped that college would be different. He expected that he'd be able to move away and be himself. But he instead encountered more of the same prejudices, and found himself once again leaning on his skills of deception and observation.

That night, at the party with Kappa Chi Rho, he did just that.

Parties at South Cuthbert most often resulted in the bulk of the party-goers gathering in the basement. Some danced. But mostly it was just wall to wall people standing around drinking. Drug use was common. But it was usually confined to upstairs bedrooms, out of the view of the other guests. But, more importantly, out of view of any cops that might bust the party. At the moment, Sully was fine with just a beer in his hand. He had smoked a bowl with his Fraternity Brothers before arriving and was feeling fine.

As he scanned the basement scene, it seemed like any other party. His expectation was never that he'd find a man to hook up with. But then the face of Chris Wilbanks jumped out at him from across the room. He was immediately taken by his blue eyes and with the way his long blonde hair hung down along the side of his face. It was apparent that Jen Somers, one of DZ's finest, was also taken by him and had already begun moving in. Sully decided to join the conversation and find out if it might turn into a competitive situation.

"What's happening, Somers?" he said, nestling in alongside her.

"Hey, Sully! How's your bod?" she asked with a bright smile on her face.

"Oh, like you don't know," he replied, winking at her and then glancing up towards Chris. He extended his hand to Chris with a smile.

"Hey, Mike Sullivan. Everyone calls me Sully." He eyed the Pledge Pin affixed to Chris' shirt. "So, you're one of the many Crow pledges this semester?" he asked with a smile. He was certain to make solid eye contact.

Chris laughed at the friendly jab. "Yep, sure am! The two of us are ready to take the Greek system by storm. Chris Wilbanks. You're Sig Phi, I see?" He asked as he reached out to shake Sully's hand, noticing the letters on Sully's hat. Sully returned the gesture and noted that it was a firm grip. He also noted the extended eye contact that Chris seemed to be partaking in. He was immediately attracted to Chris and he could tell right away that the sentiment was mutual.

Jen Somers didn't seem to notice the connection, or perhaps was already too drunk to do so. She excused herself nonetheless, giving Sully a kiss on the cheek and a squeeze on his ass.

"I'm gonna grab a beer. Catch ya' later?" she asked.

"Yeah...sure," Sully responded, continuing to shake Chris' hand and never breaking eye contact. One thing he had noticed over the years was that, in these situations, no one else seemed to ever really notice when two closeted gays were making a connection. It's just not something that anyone was ever looking for. And if they did, it was usually brought up more like a joke instead of an accusation. No one actually believed it was real. Sully would play along and people would be none the wiser.

The two chatted for a while. It was clear to each of them that they were interested in one another. They surreptitiously exchanged enough information for them to meet up later, where they could connect in private, with no concerns of being seen. From that moment on, the two of them made every attempt to continue doing so as often as possible. It was difficult, of course, with Chris pledging. So much of his time was taken up with pledge activities. And, as was customary with pledge classes, Pledge

Brothers were encouraged to spend much of their free time together in order to strengthen their bond. With only two members in their pledge class, that meant that Chris spent a great deal of time with Chase Dempsey, and he was not keen on revealing his secret to him. This meant late night rendezvous were required for Sully to get any quality time with Chris.

As time went on, he found his feelings for Chris getting stronger and stronger. By the time Hell Week rolled around, Chris could barely contain himself and didn't want to wait any longer to see him. Hell Week, however, meant that the Pledges spent every night sleeping on the basement floor of the Fraternity House. Late night meet ups were not an option. Unable to contain himself, he devised a plan to quietly disrupt the KXP drop-off night so that he could pull Chris away, if only for a few moments.

Drop-off night was a common practice. Sig Phi had done the same to him just a few months prior. Every Fraternity used the same spot in the woods just Southeast of campus. It was safe, remote, and not *too* far of a walk back for the Pledges. Knowing from his conversations with Chris that the event hadn't occurred yet for KXP, with one night left of Hell Week, he knew that tonight was the night for them.

It was a moonless night. Hiding in the woods undetected wouldn't be an issue. Sully could see the road from his chosen position. Occasionally headlights would pass by. His heart raced each time they approached, and a feeling of sadness came as they continued moving down the roadway. That is until he saw two cars begin to slowly pull over to the shoulder. He could see their silhouettes through the trees as they looked around for any onlookers before opening the trunks to let out Chris and Chase. Seeing that the two were brought over in separate trunks, he was quietly thankful that Chris wasn't sharing an enclosed space with Chase.

He listened closely as the KXP Brothers led the two into the woods, and watched as they positioned the two blindfolded men just off of the path before retreating back towards their cars. He counted the Brothers that came in and watched closely to ensure that the same amount had left. He didn't want to be seen by any Brother that might stay behind to make sure that the Pledges are safe. He knew, though, that if he had been seen, he could pawn it off as simply a Fraternity prank.

Once the cars pulled away, he immediately began making his way towards the two Pledges. Arriving at their position, he thought about removing Chris' blindfold so that he could see who it was. Instead he decided to have some fun with him. *He was just a pledge, after all*, he thought to himself with a laugh.

Sully pulled out a pocket knife and cut through the rope around Chris' waist. He then quietly led him away, leaving Chase alone in the woods with nothing but his thoughts. He was certain to be loud enough that Chase would hear at least enough movement for him to think it was a KXP Brother. He knew that Chase wouldn't dare remove his blindfold if that was the case. This meant that there was no danger of being caught.

Chris followed Sully willingly and without making a sound. Sull assumed that this was because he believed it was a KXP Brother leading him away. His plan was to lead Chris down the path, only far enough to be out of earshot of Chase, so that the two could steal just a moment together. He walked behind Chris, altering his voice at times and telling him to keep walking. The path grew darker as they moved deeper into the woods. It was darker than Sully had expected. He chose not to use the flashlight that he'd brought, for fear that they would be spotted wandering together.

At one point, Sully turned back to see how far the two had gone. To his surprise, Chase was nowhere to be seen. They must've walked further than he had anticipated.

It was then that the unthinkable happened.

The first sound that Sully heard was that of leaves rustling as Chris attempted to find his footing. Then came the guttural gasp that barely escaped Chris' lips. Sully turned back around just in time to see Chris Wilbanks falling over the edge of a ninety-degree vertical drop just off of the edge of the path. His eyes were wide as he rushed forward, attempting to grab for Chris. But he was too late. Chris was over the edge and out of sight before Sully could get to him. Next he heard the sound of branches breaking. Finally, there was the unmistakable sound of an impact below. It was followed by nothing but silence.

He stood in shock at the edge of the path, trying to see any sign of Chris.

"Chris?! Chris?! Oh my God, Chris are you ok?" he yelled down in a loud whisper, unwilling to let Chase hear him.

"Chris!" he called out again. "Fuck." he said to himself.

Sully saw nothing but darkness below. The pitch black night overtook any sense of sight that he might have had just minutes earlier. Pulling out his flashlight, he shined it down towards the bottom of the ledge, where he saw the image that he immediately knew would haunt him for the rest of his life.

Staring back at him, from twenty feet below, was the lifeless body of Chris Wilbanks. His body had twisted during the fall, landing backwards and head first. His feet were leaning against the dirt wall of the ledge. His head, still blindfolded, was positioned unnaturally to the right. It looks as though his neck was broken. A broken tree branch was also piercing through the front of his chest. Sully shined the light on Chris' face, hoping to see motion of some sort. He was met by only one one lifeless eye peering out of the bottom of the slightly shifted blindfold.

Wandering from side to side, trying not to fall himself, Sully searched for a way down the ledge, unable to find one. But he realized that it was no use. Even from twenty feet up, it was clear to him. Chris Wilbanks was dead. And it was his fault.

He fell to his knees. He wanted to scream, but was unable to make more than a few low noises, and quiet cries of 'No'.

It was then that the reality of what had just happened hit him. He knew that it was only a matter of moments before Chase would come wandering down the path calling for Chris - this time without a blindfold. At that point, he made the decision to allow his panic to overtake him. When faced with fight or flight, Sully turned and ran.

He raced through the woods, staying off of the paths and making his way out to the road as far away from Chase and Chris' entry point as possible. Once out of the woods, he jogged home to his dorm. He was fairly certain he hadn't been seen.

Sully quickly went into his room and collapsed. Barely able to breathe, he thought through the night's events. He felt that he needed to tell the police and that they should at least be tipped off on where to find him. *What if he was still alive?* Sully thought to himself. He hadn't gone down and checked. No, he was dead. He was sure of it. *But what if...?*

Sully picked up the phone and brought his fingers to within an inch of dialing 911, and then he froze. A thousand thoughts raced through his head surrounding the implications of telling the police. Not just for himself. But for Chris. Sully knew that if he came forward, it would only be a matter of time before the news would come out about why he was there that night. The entire world would then know that Chris was gay. It was a secret that Chris had gone to great lengths to conceal, and he would now have no control over the spread of that information. It wasn't fair to Chris. Chris was dead through no fault of his own. There was no sense in ruining his reputation in the wake of it. Sully told himself that it was now his responsibility to keep that secret for Chris...at all costs. Even if that meant living with the secret of how he died.

Sully thought back through his every action that night. He hadn't told a soul about what he was going to do. No one knew he had left. He didn't speak to anyone upon returning. And not a single person ever knew about his relationship with Chris. As far as the rest of the world was concerned, Mike Sullivan and Chris Wilbanks were barely acquaintances. And that was how it would need to stay. But then one thought occurred to Sully.

Chase Dempsey!

Sully realized that Chase would be questioned at length by the police, having been the last *known* person to be with Chris while he was alive. Chase had to have heard him approach them and lead Chris away. He would certainly tell the police that someone else was there. The Brothers of Kappa Chi Rho would

226

all be questioned. The timeline would be pieced together and it would become clear that someone was there and led Chris away *after* the Kappa Chi Rho Brothers left.

With nothing tying Sully to the scene, and Chase being the only one that could claim someone else was there, Chase would be the prime suspect.

Sully closed his eyes. Could he let another person be blamed for Chris' death? He thought once more about the prospect of the world finding out Chris' secret, and then his decision was made. He gently hung up the phone. Chase Dempsey would need to be blamed for the death of Chris Wilbanks.

CHAPTER 48

PRESENT DAY

The sound of his mobile phone ringing shook Sully out of a trance as he sat at his desk. Startled, he leaned forward and checked the screen. Chase Dempsey's name flashed across it. He thought about letting it go to voicemail, but decided against it. He took a deep breath and exhaled, attempting to relax his body before answering.

"Hey Chase, what's happening?"

"Sully, hey listen, I need to see you. We've got some new information. It's big. Where are you now? Can we meet?"

Sully sprang to his feet and began circling his desk.

"New info? Yeah, we can meet. Where are you? I'm in my office if you want to come here."

"I'll tell you when we see you. We're on our way to campus now. I'd rather not meet in your office, though, if that's ok. Too many reporters around."

"Ok, just park over in the Ward Center lot. I'll come meet you. You can't tell me this over the phone?"

"I'd rather not. This is big, Sully. It involves the Wilbanks Family."

Sully stopped in his tracks and fell back into his seat. His heart dropped at the sound of the Wilbanks name.

"Wilbanks?" he asked, trying to sound surprised. "You mean you actually found something?"

"Oh yeah, we definitely found something. I'll tell you about it when we see you. We'll be there in ten minutes."

"Ok, yeah...see you then."

Sully hung up the phone and slowly fumbled to drop it into his coat pocket. He ran his hands over his face as he contemplated what could be coming next.

He looked up to the ceiling and whispered to himself. "Well, Chase. I guess it's time for you to learn the truth."

CHAPTER 49

Chase placed his phone down in the center console and briefly glanced over at Scott. He could see a change in him. It was a look of confidence that he hadn't seen in his son since he had dropped him off at South Cuthbert two months prior. He knew from experience, however, that the feeling could be short-lived. There were many times while Chase was going through the same experience that he thought things were looking up, only to have it crash down over him like a wave three times his size. Most notably, when he was officially exonerated by the police, and even by the press, there were still members of the student population that didn't trust him. Lies were spread about him and his involvement. It made the rest of his time in school almost as hard as the time he spent being investigated.

It wasn't lost on Chase that they were now on their way to see Sully, the one person that was the most responsible for the spreading of those lies. But they now had a small window in which to get Scott cleared and avoid the same stigma being attached to him. In the most ironic twist he could ever have imagined, the one responsible for ruining his life was the one he was relying on to save the life of his son.

"Dad, are you sure this is a good idea?" Scott asked as the car powered into the Ward Center parking lot. "Shouldn't we just go directly to the police with this?"

Chase shook his head from side to side. "Nope, they'll never believe that we just happened upon this. There is too much room there for it to be thrown back on us. We need this to come from another source. From a trusted source. We need Sully to buy in on this."

"A trusted source? Do you actually trust him."

Chase paused for a moment, contemplating his answer.

"We have to," he reluctantly allowed.

"There he is now," Scott pointed across the lot where Sully was walking across the grass divider. "Well let's hope this works then."

Chase pulled up towards Sully, gave a quick honk to alert him of their arrival, and then pulled into an open parking spot. Sydney, Suzanne and Woody, who had been following behind, pulled into the spot alongside them. The group exited their cars and met Sully in the lane beside the back of Sydney's car.

"Hey, so what's up?" Sully asked with his arms outstretched slightly. "What's so important that we had to meet all clandestine like this?"

Chase glanced over at Sully. Something seemed off. He wasn't quite sure what, or even if he was just looking for a reason not to trust him. He decided that it was too important not to continue.

"We just came from the Wilbanks house," he said curtly.

Sully's eyes widened. "What were you doing there?"

"Following a hunch," Chase replied.

"And it turned out to be right," Scott chimed in. Chase glanced over at Scott and gave him a look that said 'let me handle this'. Scott knew the look well and stepped back.

Chase continued. "We found some potentially incriminating information there."

"How incriminating?" Sully asked.

"Well, that's the thing. On the surface, it seems clear that someone in that family is still blaming me for Chris Wilbanks' death. And, it would seem, is trying to punish me by framing Scott. There is a room in their house that's right out of some True Detective episode. It's got this crazy ass wall covered in news clippings that connect both of the cases. Maps of the township with the location of where Chris Wilbanks was found and of the campus with the Crow House circled. Could be very damning. But..."

"There's a but?" Sully asked skeptically.

"But number one, it's circumstantial on the surface. It'd require a deeper dive into their computers, and a warrant to get into their house, to really make it more concrete."

"And number two?" Sully pressed.

"Number two is how we ended up in the house...I wouldn't call it illegal. But it doesn't make us look good. Suz, Sydney and Woody knocked on the door. No one answered. The door was wide open though. So they stepped in calling out for whoever was in the house. And then..."

"And then some asshole attacked me," Woody chimed in.

Chase gave Woody the same look he'd previously given Woody. Although Woody didn't seem to register quite what it meant and just shrugged his shoulders back at him.

Chase again turned back to Sully and continued. "So then *that* person fled the scene. Nearly ran over Suz. Then Scott and I showed up and we looked around a bit and found that room that I just described. Long story short, there is some shit going on in that house that the cops need to see. We've got pics of it."

Suzanne handed Sully her phone. Sully scanned through the pictures. His face showed that he understood the enormity of what they had discovered. He handed Suzanne her phone back and stood quietly as he considered everything he'd just been told before continuing.

"So, am I right in assuming then, that you can't go to the cops with this information because of how you found it? And also because it won't look good coming from you? So you need someone else to put it in front of the cops."

"Yes, exactly," Chase nodded.

"And you want that person to be me," Sully added.

Chase held his hands out to his side. "Sully, you're the only one we can trust right now."

Sully ran his hand through his hair before resting it on the back of his head and exhaling forcefully, walking in a small circle, and then turning back to Chase. He looked at the group as a whole, and finally let his gaze fall on Scott and his helpless eyes. The two stared at each other for a moment. Then Sully turned back to Chase and let out another deep sigh.

"Listen, I'll help you. But there is something you need to know first."

Chase, happy to hear the news, smiled slightly but also looked a bit perplexed.

"Ok, what's that?" he asked.

Sully took a step back, and then motioned for Chase to follow him. "Let's walk for a minute. I'd prefer it if we talk in private."

Chase looked at Suzanne, who shrugged her shoulders and raised her eyebrows, signaling that he might as well follow. So he began walking alongside Sully as the two made their way down the middle of the parking lane.

"Chase there's something you don't know about Chris Wilbanks," he started. "It's actually something no one has ever known. No one, except for me at least."

As they walked along, neither of them noticed the black Mustang slowly rolling along in the lane perpendicular to theirs. It's engine hummed unassumingly as it neared their lane, obscured by the parked cars.

"What are you talking about, Sully?"

"Chase, I actually knew Chris pretty well," he responded. "In fact, he and I..."

At that moment Sully was interrupted by the roar of the Mustang's engine coming to life as it turned the corner and raced towards them. It was just feet away when Sully looked up and saw it.

Chase, with his head down as he attempted to make sense of what Sully had said, saw it a split second later. Before Chase had a chance to react, he felt the force of Sully's hands pressing on him and pushing him to the side. Falling backwards onto the ground behind the nearby parked cars, Chase looked up at Sully just in time to see the Mustang's hood make impact with him as it sped past.

Sully's upper body flung forward as his legs were taken out by the front corner of the car. He flipped sideways like a helicopter rotor. The car was twenty yards away before Sully landed on the ground, slamming his head on the concrete.

Further down the lane, Scott's arms were spread wide as he was forcing his Mother, Sydney and Woody into the area between the cars. The black Mustang swerved towards them, just narrowly missing them as it sped by.

"That was the car!" Suzanne yelled. "That was the same car from earlier!"

Suzanne, Sydney and Woody ran back into the open and watched as the Mustang powered out of the lot and sped off. Turning around, they were faced with the sight of Chase leaning over the unconscious body of Sully in the middle of the roadway.

Scott could hear his Dad pleading as he ran towards them.

"No! shit! Sully! Sully can you hear me?" Chase yelled. He saw blood pouring from the back of Sully's head. "Shit! Suz, get down here!"

Suzanne came rushing over and knelt down beside him. She yanked off her coat and turned Sully's head slightly, pressing her coat to his head and applying pressure.

Chase reached into his coat pocket, pulled out his cell phone and dialed 911.

"I need an ambulance in the Ward Center parking lot over at SCU. A man has been hit by a car. It's a hit and run. It was a black Mustang. Late 90's model. He's bleeding badly from the head. Please send someone...quick!"

Chase dropped his phone and helped Suzanne attend to Sully. The two looked at each other, and then both looked up at Scott. Without saying a word, they all knew that everything had now changed.

CHAPTER 50

The campus police were the first to arrive on the scene, with the ambulance just minutes behind them. Sully was unresponsive, but the paramedics were able to stabilize him within moments.

Everyone watched as they loaded the stretcher into the back of the ambulance.

"Are you taking him to Cuthbert?" Chase asked them.

"Yes, we'll be driving ahead. If you're going to head there yourself, then please follow the traffic laws and you can meet him in the ER."

"Don't expect that you're going anywhere just yet, Mr. Dempsey," a voice called out from across the lot.

Chase looked up to see Quinn and McKue walking towards them. "What are you two doing here?" Chase shouted back. "No one was killed here."

"No," Mckue agreed. "But it certainly sounds like someone tried to kill someone. You know anything about it?"

"Yeah, I do. I was one of the people they tried to kill. I already gave my statement to the Officer in charge. You can go talk to her and get the whole story," Chase replied curtly.

Quinn blindly pointed in the direction of the officer. "Yeah, the OIC showed us your statement. What I'm interested in knowing is what you're doing talking to Mike Sullivan. Seems odd that you're still hanging around campus here."

"Do you have any kids, Lieutenant?" Suzanne chimed in.

Quinn turned to her, surprised at the interruption, and paused for a moment before answering. "No, no I don't have any kids."

"Well, please know that when someone's children are in danger, then they'll do anything to protect them. We're trying to find more information about what might've happened to Colemen and Wilby. And part of that included talking to Mike Sullivan."

"You say you'll do anything. Does that include having someone run Mike Sullivan down?"

"Hey that car tried to run down Scott's dad too!" Sydney yelled.

"Yeah, so he says," McKue chimed in, with an air of suspicion.

"Listen, I've already told you guys everything I know. I'm going to the hospital with Sully. If you need anything more, you know where to find me."

Chase turned to the group. "We don't all have to go over there. But someone should. He should have someone there. I'm going to follow them over."

"What should we do?" Scott asked. His eyes told Chase how worried he was about the state of their plan and the fact that their best chance was literally just rushed to the hospital.

"I don't know. I'm not sure right now," Chase said. "Just sit tight for now. I'll call you guys. Wait to hear from me. Don't do anything until then."

Scott and Suzanne reluctantly nodded back to him in agreement.

Chase stepped into his car and pulled away.

Quinn and McKue watched as he left. Then Quinn turned to the group as he was preparing to leave. "Well, I'm sure we'll be seeing you."

"Wait!" Suzanne blurted out. Quinn and McKue stopped and turned back in surprise.

Suzanne hesitated a moment, looking at Scott before turning back to Quinn and McKue.

"I need to show something."

CHAPTER 51

Cuthbert County Hospital is the last place that Chase thought he would find himself returning to this week. Although he admitted that he was happy that neither of his recent visits here were to visit his own son. He thought back to all of the times that he considered hurting himself in college. He hoped that he could help Scott avoid even the possibility that he might see that as an option. He reminded himself that despite his feelings for Sully, and despite the fact that he needed him right now to help clear Scott, that Sully was still a human being in need of help. He deserved to be given that.

He pulled into the lot by the Emergency Room, parked and entered through the automatic doors. Approaching the reception desk, he was speaking before even arriving there. "I'm here to see Mike Sullivan? He was just brought here? Hit and run?"

The woman behind the desk quickly replied while pointing through the doors to her right. "Yes, he's in observation room 6. Through those doors, down the hall and to the right."

"Thank you," Chase answered as politely as possible as he quickly made his way by.

He briskly walked down the hall, fighting the urge to jog or even run. Arriving at Observation Room 6, he gently pulled the curtain back to peek inside and saw Sully lying in a bed. He was still unconscious. He then pulled the curtain back further to enter, and was met with a surprising sight.

Lynn Clowry sat quietly in the chair next to the bed with one leg neatly crossed over the other.

"Oh...Hi!" he said. "I didn't expect anyone else to be here yet. How did you...?"

"It's not that big of a campus. As soon as I heard I raced right over here."

Chase nodded, recognizing that what she said made sense. He'd been at the scene for long enough for word to spread like wildfire across the school grounds. News that the Director of Greek Life was just hit by a car does not travel slowly.

"How is he?" he asked.

Lynn looked over at Sully, and answered in a quiet tone. "Well, the doctor was just in. He said he probably has a broken leg and a concussion. He'll need some stitches. And they'll need to do some X-rays and other tests. But, at first glance, they expect that he'll recover."

"Well that's a relief. For sure." Chase exhaled and tried to relax.

"Why are you so interested anyway?" she suddenly asked. A look of contempt was now occupying her face. Chase was visibly surprised by the question.

"Excuse me?"

"What I mean is, you two clearly never got along. Why all of the sudden are you at his bedside?"

"Well, it's uh..."

"Complicated?" she asked. "I imagine it is. I mean, you've been relying on him to help clear your son. Can't be easy with the history between you two."

He nodded in agreement. "That's true."

Lynn nodded solemnly, then looked over at Sully. "That must be a tough position to be in."

"Well, to be honest, yes. It's very tough." Chase moved closer to the bed and stared down at Sully as well. "But he's got his own battle to fight right now. I can't force my own on him. I'll need to figure out my own way through this now. And besides, I feel like this is my fault."

"From what I understand, it's been quite a battle that you've had to fight yourself."

Chase looked at her. He thought to himself that Sully must've shared some of their history with her. He was hesitant to answer and decided to just share only the bare minimum.

"Yeah, it...uh...it was certainly tough for me."

"I imagine, it was also tough for that poor Wilbanks boy too...*and* his family. Such a shame. Never found the killer...or so I'm told."

Chase was growing uncomfortable with the conversation and was about to put an end to it, when the pleasant sound of a groan came out of Sully's mouth. The two looked down and saw Sully beginning to awake.

"Heeeeyyy, what's up sleepy head!" Lynn whispered sweetly. "How are you?"

"Hey buddy, ya doing ok?" Chase asked in a low voice.

Sully's eyes opened and he slowly turned his head and began to look around before propping himself up on his elbows.

"Where am I?"

Lynn placed her hand on his chest to stop him from sitting up further. "Hey easy there. You're in the hospital. You were hit by a car. You got banged up pretty good. Just lay back down."

Sully looked over at Chase. "Are you okay? Who *was* that?"

Chase smiled. "Yeah, yeah, I'm okay. Thanks to you!"

"Who was it?" he asked again. This time more forcefully.

"No idea." Chase responded. "But the cops are looking for the car."

Lynn then stood up and began walking out of the room. "I'm going to go tell the doctor that you're awake."

Chase nodded to Lynn as she left and Sully let his body fall back into a prone position. He winced and raised his hand to his head as it landed on the hard hospital pillow.

"Man, I am in...oh man this hurts!"

"Yeah, well that car got you pretty good. You were literally airborne. But just relax, okay? Doctors are going to get you patched up."

"I need to finish telling you, Chase," Sully said, reaching out and grabbing Chase's forearm.

"That can wait man. Just rest for now. We can talk later."

"No, it can't wait. We..."

The two were interrupted by the Doctor walking in. Lynn was just a few steps behind him.

"Well look who rejoined the living!" the Doctor joked as he walked in. "How are you feeling?"

"I've felt better," Sully replied.

"Well let's get a quick look at you." The Doctor moved in and performed a quick check on Sully. Lifting his eyelids to examine his pupils and looking again at his head wound.

He held up his pen in front of Sully's face. "Take a look at this and try to follow it as I move it." Sully followed the pen, never taking his eyes off of it.

"Well you're tracking well. Tell you what, we'll have someone in here in a few minutes to get this head stitched up and then we'll take you for an X-ray for this leg and that noggin' of yours."

"Thanks, Doc," Sully said. "Appreciate it."

The doctor looked at the group before nodding his head. "Great, see you soon. It's great to see you awake!"

The doctor turned and left, and Sully turned to Lynn. "Lynn, would you mind stepping out for another moment? I need to speak to Chase alone."

"Oh right, sorry!" she said in surprise. "I'll...uh...sure I'll just go take a quick walk."

Lynn fumbled for a moment with the bag that she had on the chair and then stood to leave. Chase and Sully watched as she left. Sully waited to make sure she was out of earshot, then turned to Chase.

"Ok, so what's up?" Chase asked.

"It was me," Sully said flatly.

Chase was clearly confused. "What was you?"

"The night Chris died..." Sully added.

Chase felt the bottom drop out of his stomach and his face grew long. He was now silent with his eyes open wide as Sully continued.

"It was me. It was all me. You told the police there was someone else there that night when you were blindfolded. That you heard someone lead Chris away. It was me. I was the person that you heard. I cut the rope that was tied around Chris' waist. It was me that you heard."

"You were there?" Chase asked before shaking his head. "That's impossible. Why would..."

Sully interrupted him and continued recounting the events of that night.

"I led him away from you. I took him deeper into the woods. I wasn't trying to..." his voice trailed off before continuing. "I was just trying to pull him away for a bit. So that we could be...together."

"You were together with him when he died?" Chase asked. A puzzled look was on his face.

"No I mean...well yes, we were together. But, Chase, what I mean is...we were *together*."

A look of recognition came over Chase's face as he fell back into a chair.

"Oh my God, I had no idea," Chase moved his glance from Sully, to the floor, and back again. "But how..."

"I was just trying to pull him away for a bit. Trying to get a moment alone. It was dark. He was still blindfolded, and I...I swear I only took my eye off of him for a moment. Chase, I swear it was only for a moment."

Tears were beginning to gather in Sully's eyes. Chase leaned in. A mix of anger and denial was displayed on his face. "What happened," he said with gritted teeth. "Tell me what happened!"

"I only looked away for a moment and I didn't see that the path was turning. He lost his footing and fell over the edge. I shined my flashlight down on him. His blindfold was shifted to the side a bit. His eye...I could see that he was dead. I could see that he was dead."

Chase dropped his head into his hands. Each hand grasping onto a tuft of hair as he tried to make sense of what he'd just heard.

"I'm sorry. I...," Sully searched for the right words, "There's nothing I can say to make it right. I know that I..."

"You killed him," Chase interrupted in a whisper. "You killed him and you let the world think it was me."

"I didn't...Chase it was an accident. I swear." Tears were now flooding in Sully's eyes.

"And blaming it on me ever since. Was that an accident?"

Chase felt his phone vibrating in his pocket. He ignored it.

"It's unforgivable, I know. But Chase, you needed to know the truth. If someone from the Wilbanks family is trying to get revenge on you, then you deserve to know the truth so that this can be sorted out. They're going after the wrong person."

"I deserved to know the truth twenty-eight years ago!" Chase yelled. "I dealt with years of crippling anxiety. Shit, I'm *still* dealing with it!"

"I'm sorry... I" Sully's voice trailed off. The sudden sound of the curtain being pulled back was a welcome one to to him. He wanted to defend himself. But he knew that what he did was indefensible.

An orderly poked his head in and looked at the two of them.

"Knock knock!" He said in a delightful voice as he entered and began organizing Sully's cords. Sensing he had just walked in on something, he announced, "I hope I'm not interrupting anything. I am going to take you down the hall so that you can have that head stitched up. We'll have you back in a jif. Sound good?"

Sully paused for a moment to gather himself and wipe the tears from his face. "Yeah...sounds good," was all he could manage to get out.

"Yeah, I was just leaving anyway," Chase said as he stood up and left the room, not even looking at Sully.

"Chase..." Sully called after. Chase only raised his hand, motioning to Sully to stop. He never turned back. He wanted nothing further to do with Mike Sullivan.

CHAPTER 52

Lynn Clowry sat patiently, and reluctantly, in the waiting area of the Cuthbert County Emergency Room. Being asked to leave the room so that Sully could speak to Chase alone was, to her, a slap in the face. She has spent all of her free time devoted to helping Sully and felt that the two had developed a trusting relationship. The fact that there was something that he couldn't say in front of her was surprising, to say the least. She especially didn't like that bastard Chase Dempsey spending time alone with him. Who knew what kind of lies he could put into Sully's head? *Well, I'll know soon enough,* she thought to herself.

She looked up to see Chase making his way down the hall towards the exit. She began calling out to him. Though he seemed to be oblivious to anything around him. He only acknowledged her once she caught up to him and touched him on the arm.

"Hey, everything ok there? Is he alright?" she asked.

"Why don't you go ask him," he responded angrily without stopping. "That is if you think you can trust anything he tells you."

Lynn stopped walking, surprised at his response, and watched as Chase left the ER and made his way into the parking lot.

Turning her head back in the direction of Sully's room, she paused for a moment before heading down the hall. Arriving at the Sully's room, she yanked the curtain to the side to reveal that Sully had been moved. She assumed temporarily. She adjusted her gaze to the chair where she had left her phone. It was still face down.

Walking over and taking it in her hand, she looked at the screen to see that it was still recording, just as she had left it.

She pressed stop and saved the recording. She then pulled the curtain back into place, sat in her chair, and hit the Play button.

Lynn Clowry was about to learn that the anger she had held for the past twenty-eight years, and the target of her revenge, had been drastically misplaced.

CHAPTER 53

"So was I right? Or was I right?"

"Mrs. Dempsey, it's safe to say that you were definitely right."

Suzanne was standing with Lt. Quinn on the shoulder of the roadway outside of the Wilbanks home. Once Chase had left for the hospital, Suzanne had promptly ignored his views on whether or not they should involve the police in what they found. With Sully now unconscious and on his way to the ER, there was no telling how much time they would lose if they waited for Sully to be healthy enough to help them.

She filled in Quinn and McKue on the events of their trip to the Wilbanks house, and their reasoning for doing so. Knowing that a press conference and potential charges were on the horizon, she reminded them of the potential impact it would have on the case, both in the court and in the court of public opinion, once it became clear that they didn't follow every lead and led the investigation to a predetermined outcome.

Detective McKue was difficult to convince. Lt. Quinn, however, only needed a moment to acquiesce to Suzanne's request. He had seen enough cases thrown out as a result of poor police work in the early stages of the case. When a case has this much potential to become high-profile, he wasn't about to roll the dice on the chance that this tip would result in nothing. If what she was describing was true, then it made for a potentially case-breaking situation. He called the D.A. and immediately got a warrant based on the idea that, having known someone was inside the home and may have seen the room, the longer they waited, the more time the Wilbanks would have to clear the home of any and all evidence.

Within an hour, a team was descending on the house. No one was home and the forensics team was now at work collecting evidence and deciphering what they had found. A digital forensic scientist had already broken the password encryption of the computers and was currently combing through the data on the system.

"Thank you for staying out here and away from the house, Mrs. Dempsey. I'm sure you understand, especially since you've already been in there once, that we can't allow you on the grounds. But you were definitely right. It is sincerely...what did you call it?" he asked Woody.

"Crazy town." Woody dutifully responded.

"Yes...it's crazy town in there."

"Right?" Suzanne agreed. "And like I said, it might be circumstantial on the surface. But that is worth digging into. I swear you're going to find something in there."

"Well, we'll see. But Mrs. Dempsey, question for you. Do you know the Wilbanks family at all?" Quinn asked her.

"No, I actually don't. Why?"

"Well, the house is owned by an Evelyn Wilbanks. We were just wondering, since you've clearly been looking down this rabbit hole already. I thought the name might jump out at you."

Suzanne thought for a moment. "No it doesn't," she said, shaking her head. "Chase has never really liked speaking much about it. He never mentioned Chris Wilbanks' family at all."

Lt. Quinn held out a framed photo of a young woman and young man. It was an older photo and had aged quite a bit. "What about this? Does anyone in this photo look familiar to you?"

"Well, that's Chris Wilbanks right there," she said, pointing at the male. "I remember him obviously from when he was killed. His picture was everywhere. He looks a bit younger there. But it's definitely him. I don't recognize the girl though."

"Can I see?" Sydney asked, stepping in and leaning in to better see the photo.

"Is that Lynn Clowry?" she asked.

"I'm sorry, did you say Lynn Clowry?" Lt. Quinn asked, as Scott and Woody both leaned in to see the photo.

"Lynn Clowry, yeah" she responded. She's Sully's assistant. "Guys, isn't that her? I mean she's much younger here. But I swear that's her."

Woody and Scott both leaned in over each of her shoulders. "Oh my God, yeah I think it is!" Woody chimed in.

"Yep," Scott agreed. "That's unmistakable. That's her face. I'd put money on it,"

Suzanne looked at the image more closely, recalling the run-in she had with her just two days prior. "Oh my God, that is her." She turned her attention to Lt. Quinn. "Wait, are you saying that you think this image is actually of Evelyn Wilbanks?"

"We believe it may be, Ma'am," Quinn responded. "Initial investigations, from what we're seeing in there, we believe that this woman is Evelyn Wilbanks, Chris Wilbanks' sister. We also have seen multiple identifications and passports in there for a woman by that name that matches this description." He paused for a moment before continuing. "The passports are using different names though. One name is Evelyn Wilbanks. The other name...is Lynn Clowry."

"Oh my God," Suzanne's eyes went wide. "Lieutenant, you need to get your people over to Cuthbert County Hospital."

Before even explaining why, she pulled out her phone and called Chase. The call went straight to voicemail.

"Chase, it's me. I'm with South Cuthbert Police now. Listen to me. Lynn Clowry is Evelyn Wilbanks. She is a Wilbanks, Chase! She's his sister! Lynn Clowy is Chris Wilbanks' sister!"

CHAPTER 54

"Well, that didn't go as well as I had hoped," Sully thought to himself as the orderly rolled his bed down the hallway. He'd spent years pushing the events of that night deep down inside. Never allowing himself to admit the truth, even to himself. He'd had brief pangs of guilt over the years and did occasionally think of what he might say to Chase, if given the chance. But he never once expected that it would actually come to fruition.

Even when Chase came back in his life two days ago, he still didn't believe that he'd need to admit the truth. He saw Chase's face and instinctively went back to his old ways. Blaming Chase for something that he had no fault in. With each attack, Sully felt the pangs of guilt rise up inside of him. He even felt guilt for feeling a sense of relief after revealing the truth to Chase. It certainly felt good to finally say it out loud. But having done so, he realized that he had just dropped a monstrous weight onto the shoulders of Chase Dempsey.

Chase now had the knowledge that the past twenty-eight years could have been lived blame-free. His college years and post-college years could have been made infinitely easier had he not had a need to recover from years of anxiety, as well as a need to overcome the stigma of being suspected of murder.

"Mr. Sullivan, we are going to have you as good as new shortly," the orderly reassured him.

"That's good to hear," he responded with a fake smile. Although internally he was wondering how far Chase was from 'good as new' now that he had just shared his secret with him.

"Ok, here we are. Observation Room Number 6!" the orderly announced as he turned the corner into the room to find it empty.

"Oh man, everyone leave you? Well I'm sure they'll be back soon," the orderly said with a smile as he wheeled the bed into place.

"I'll leave you alone and someone will be back shortly to take you down for X-Rays."

"Great, thanks for your help," Sully said with a forced smile as he watched the orderly leave.

Sully laid there for a moment, thankful for the silence. However, a moment later, that silence was broken as Lynn Clowry walked in. Sully was surprised to see that she was now wearing hospital scrubs and pushing a wheelchair.

"Hey there, welcome back," she said with a smile as she turned around and pulled the curtain closed again.

"Hey, what's with the scrubs? You have an accident?" he asked.

"Well," she said, tilting her head to the side and smiling. "Let's just say that somebody did. So, all stitched up?" she asked as she came to the side of Sully's bed and reached both hands into her messenger bag.

"Yep, twenty-seven of them, I'm told."

"Good," she said.

Suddenly, with one swift motion, she pulled her hands from her bag and lunged at Sully, placing a knife to his throat and holding a .22 caliber pistol to his cheek. "But I'm afraid you're going to need more than stitches when I'm through with you."

"Jesus Fucking Christ! Lynn, what the fuck are you doing?!" he said in a muffled tone. His eyes were wide with fear not.

"Shhh...quiet there, my friend. I'm bringing what you've got coming to you," she growled. "If you think that you're in pain now, you just wait. It's going to get much worse. Now you listen to me. You are going to get into that wheelchair over there, and then you and I are going to leave this hospital together, nice and quietly. You hear me?"

"I can't leave here. My leg, it's, it's..." he stuttered.

"It's bruised at best," she said dismissively. Her face now had a look of anger that Sully had never seen on her before. "If it's anything more than that, I'd be shocked. I didn't really hit you *that* hard with my car." A slight smile creeped across her face as the reality of the situation slowly sunk in with Sully.

"H-hit me? You? That was you?" Sully's face contorted as he slowly started putting the pieces together.

"Ah yes! There it is! I see the light going on in your head right now," she said. "It's amazing the things you can learn about someone unexpectedly."

Sully glanced down as he saw the shimmer of light reflecting off of the shiny metal of the knife held against the shine of his throat. Lynn tilted her head lower to bring his attention back to her.

"Do you like that knife? I've had it for about twenty-eight years now. Bought it for a very special purpose. I was saddened when I had to use it on Coleman first. But I suppose it was all in the same vein. No pun intended. Well...maybe a little."

Sully's face did nothing to hide his shock.

"Ah, bet you didn't see that one coming, did you? Neither did Coleman. Wilby did, unfortunately. But I'll deal with that later. Alright, get up and let's get moving. And don't even think about making a single noise or trying to signal anyone. I have absolutely zero compunction about shoving this knife through your ear hole in the middle of the hallway, just to keep your head steady while I put a bullet through it. That is exactly the level of crazy that you are dealing with here. Got it? Now get in the wheelchair!"

Moments later, Lynn was pushing a wheelchair-bound Sully down the hall. The two looked right at home in their environment. No one even gave them a second look. Even if they did, they wouldn't notice the knife that Lynn had penetrated the back of the chair with as a reminder to Sully of the danger he was in. It poked through just enough for him to feel the tip penetrating his skin.

Lynn thought back to the nurse she had beaten when she caught her stealing these scrubs from the supply closet. She'd beaten her to a bloody pulp. Though she definitely didn't need to beat her so badly. The woman had walked in on her taking the scrubs and needed to be dealt with. Simply knocking her unconscious would have sufficed. But beating her half to death felt good. She viewed it as a pregame warmup to what she was about to do to Sully - the man whom she now knew was responsible for her brother's death.

"You are doing great, Mr. Sullivan," Lynn said to Sully in an effort to keep up the appearance of a nurse kindly transporting her patient. "We're almost there."

Lynn could see the waiting room just a few yards ahead, and beyond that, the exit to the parking lot. She fought the urge to pick up speed and kept her pace as she wheeled Sully past the reception desk. She was now just feet away from the automatic doors, and had triggered the sensor, causing the doors to part in front of them. A few more feet, and they'd be home free. That is until she heard...

"Excuse me! Excuse me!"

Lynn kept moving, pretending not to hear.

"Excuse me, Miss!"

Keep moving, she told herself. But she couldn't avoid it. The owner of the voice had caught up with her, and tapped her on the shoulder.

"Excuse me, you dropped this," she found a Security Guard saying to her, holding out a Hospital ID. It was the ID she'd just a few minutes prior taken off of the woman she'd beaten to within an inch of her life. Glancing down at it, she saw a spot of blood from the incident.

"Oh, well thank you. I'm going to need this, for sure!" She said with a pleasant smile.

"Sure thing," he replied with a smile. "Happy to help."

"You have a nice day now," she said, turning around, only to find Sully looking at the guard with wide eyes.

"Oh get that head forward, Mr. Sullivan," she said, pushing the wheelchair forward. "That's not going to help that neck pain."

A few minutes later the two found themselves at the door of Lynn's black Mustang. She'd parked it in the parking garage to limit the chances that anyone would notice it there. Especially any Police that may have been funneling in and out of the Emergency Room. She had assumed there was an APB out for the car after it was involved in a hit and run.

She yanked the knife out of the back of the wheelchair and poked at Sully. "Get in," she told him, forcing him into the driver's seat. Moving around to the other side of the car, she slid into the passenger seat and pointed the gun at him.

"Okay, start driving."

"Where are we going?"

"Oh, it's a place that I think you'll be very familiar with, Sully. It's high time for some retribution."

CHAPTER 55

Chase sped out of the Cuthbert County Hospital parking lot. His heart was racing and his breath was shallow as he seethed with anger. He now lived in an entirely different world than the one he occupied just moments ago. A myriad of thoughts careened through his mind. None of them were able to claim top billing for more than a few seconds.

More than half of his life had now been revealed to be a complete lie. For nearly thirty years he had been reliving the events of that night. What were the sounds he had heard around him? Who else was there? How did Chris wind up at the bottom of an embankment just a few hundred yards away from him?

For twenty-eight years he had allowed himself to believe Sully's attacks and blamed himself for the death of Chris Wilbanks. He believed that he could have done something to stop it. For Twenty-eight years he had endured the stigma that came with being the one and only suspect in Chris' death. The mental anguish. The sleepless nights. The endless anxiety-filled hours and uncontrollable panic attacks.

And now he learned that it was actually Sully who was to blame. Sully may not have killed him. But he was to blame. He was there. He knew. He knew all along and he told absolutely fucking no one. Sully let the police investigate him. What if they had decided to press charges? Would Sully have stepped forward? It was clear to Chase that he would not have done a thing. Sully would have allowed him to rot in jail.

The anger was boiling up inside of Chase. As his breathing increased, he could feel himself begin to hyperventilate and he began to worry that it would lead to a panic attack. He needed to release his anger and share it with the one person he knew that he could lean on right now. He reached for his phone to call Suzanne. She was the one person that believed him through all of these years. His one outlet. The only one he could turn to.

Turning on his phone, the first thing he saw was that he actually had a voicemail from Suzanne. He pressed play and listened.

"Chase, it's me. I'm with South Cuthbert Police now. Listen to me. Lynn Clowry is Evelyn Wilbanks. She is a Wilbanks, Chase! She's his sister! Lynn Clowry is Chris Wilbanks' Sister!"

"Holy shit! What?!" he said to himself as he yanked the steering wheel and pulled over to the side of the road.

He listened to the voicemail again to be sure he'd heard it correctly.

Everything fell into place inside of Chase's head. It all made sense. She had always blamed Chase for the death of her brother, and when she saw that Scott was going to school at SCU, she saw an opportunity to exact her revenge.

But, of course, it was now clear that she was completely wrong in her thought process. Her anger should have been directed at...

"Oh my God, Sully!"

Chase threw the car into gear and quickly turned back in the direction of Cuthbert County Hospital. He had only made it a few miles away from there. But the drive back seemed much further.

He pulled up underneath the overhang outside of the Emergency Room doorway and ran into the hospital. Completely ignoring the pleas from the receptionist to stop and come back, he was back at Observation Room 6 within just a few seconds. Yanking back the curtain, he found nothing but an empty bed. Sully and Lynn were both gone.

He turned and frantically searched for someone that looked even remotely like they worked at the hospital. "Excuse me! Excuse me!" he yelled as he ran up to the desk outside of the room. "The man in that room, Mike Sullivan. Has he been moved to another location?"

The woman behind the desk checked her computer. Chase fought the urge to ask her to hurry up.

"Ummmm, no. It looks like he was brought back already after getting his head stitched up. Is there something I can help you with?"

"Did you see them leave?" he asked.

"No I didn't notice, but..."

The nurse behind the desk was then interrupted by the sound of the receptionist coming towards them. The Security Guard was trailing closely behind.

"That's him right there!" she yelled, pointing directly at Chase.

Chase pulled his badge out and flashed it at the Security Guard.

"Excuse me, can you tell me if you saw the man that was in that room over there? Did you see him leave this hospital with a woman?"

The Security Guard thought for a moment before slowly answering."A lot of people come and go from here, I suppose."

Chase sighed. He needed the answers to come much quicker. "This man would have needed help getting out of here. He would have either had to have limped out or been pushed out in a wheelchair."

"A lot of people get wheeled out of here sir, I don't know what else to tell you. The only people I've seen leave here in a wheelchair were wheeled out by hospital personnel. That's the policy here."

Chase was growing frustrated. He was about to walk off when he was startled by the sound of the Nurse behind the desk slamming down the phone and calling out to everyone around her.

"I need someone to cover for me here! Janet Webb was just found down the hall in the supply closet. Bloody and unconscious."

Everyone jumped into action and began to move away from the conversation with Chase. As the Nurse behind the desk began leaving the area, Chase caught up to her and grabbed her by the arm. She yanked it away instinctively.

"Excuse me, sir, I need to go!"

"Wait, I'm sorry. Did you say she was found in the supply closest?"

"Yes, that's what I said." She started to walk away again when Chase once again stopped her, this time more gently.

"Are there scrubs kept in the supply closet? Someone beat her up and took scrubs from there?"

"Yes, there are scrubs there. Now please, I need to go!"

The Nurse ran off down the hall and Chase found himself standing alone in front of an empty Observation Room 6. Glancing back over at the Security Guard, he recounted his insistence that no one could leave this hospital in a wheelchair without being accompanied by hospital personnel.

"Son of a bitch."

Racing past the receptionist once more, Chase sprinted outside and jumped into his car. Speeding out of the parking lot, he dialed Suzanne's number. She answered without saying hello.

"Thank God! Did you hear my message?"

"I did. Suz listen. I think she's got Sully."

"What are you talking about? Where are you? Isn't Sully in the hospital?" she asked.

"I just left the hospital. He's not there, Suz. I'm telling you, she's got him. It was Sully, Suz. Sully was the one responsible for Chris Wilbanks' death. He was the one I heard that night! She thought it was me. But it was actually Sully! It was Sully and she knows it now!"

"Oh my God, *he* killed him?"

"No! No he didn't kill him. Chris fell. It was an accident. Shit it's too long of a story. But I think she knows it all now and they are both gone now."

"Oh my God, she is gonna kill him, Chase. Where the hell would they even go?"

Chase thought back to the map that he saw while inside the Wilbanks house.

The Alpha and the Omega.

"I know exactly where she's taking him."

CHAPTER 56

"Membership from only those insistent on the Brotherhood of...blah, blah, blah. What a load of shit! How do you guys push that shit on people? It's all bullshit. It means nothing. They're just words." Lynn Clowry was visibly upset as she sat pointing her gun at Sully from the passenger seat of her car.

Sully didn't quite get the reference she was making, but he hazarded a guess that it was in relation to a Greek organization. Every one has it's set of landmarks or core values, and that sounded like something one of them would use. One thing he knew for sure, though, was where she planned to bring him.

"Ok, pull over here," she told him. He was nearly one step ahead of her. As soon as they turned down Oakburne Road he recognized where they were. He knew it was no coincidence that he had just told Chase about the part he'd played in Chris Wilbanks death. And now all of the sudden she had lost her shit in a way that he'd never seen from her before. Part of him wondered if Chase was involved in this. But he was confused as to what her connection to Chris could be.

He pulled the car over to the side of the road and glanced at the path leading into the woods. It was the very section of woods where he'd last seen Chris Wilbanks alive. The last time anyone saw him alive.

"You should've just kept your mouth shut, Sully," she said as she exited the car. He watched as she walked around the front, keeping her eyes and the gun on him the entire time. Arriving at the door, she yanked it open and continued. "If you had kept your mouth shut, you'd be sitting in the hospital recovering from a terrible hit and run. Sorry about that, by the way. Well, I was sorry. I wasn't trying to hit you. I was trying to hit Chase Dempsey. You just happened to be in the wrong place at the wrong time. Oh and that was admirable, by the way. The way you pushed him out of the way? So off brand for you! I was impressed!"

"You are fucking insane, you know that? What the fuck are you even doing this for?"

"Ha, you don't even have a clue, do you?" She motioned with her gun. "Just get out of the car. Let's get moving."

Sully slowly shifted his body to stand up. He was still in pain from being hit, but at this point his adrenalin was taking over.

"I suppose this is happening because you're so good at keeping a secret," Lynn continued. "Otherwise I would've done this years ago. And it sounds like you were keeping a lot of secrets actually! I never would've guessed that you and Chris...together? I sure never knew that about him. But I'm not sure how I didn't notice that about you after all of these years. You always seemed to be more of a ladies man. I would not have guessed you like both."

She looked him up and down, noticing a tear in his shirt. "Tear a stretch of that shirt off. Big enough to blindfold yourself. If we're going to do this, let's do it right."

"Are you shittin' me? Would you please tell me why we are here?" Sully asked her.

"Oh all in good time my dear boy," she replied. "Just do it. You'll find out soon enough."

Sully did as he was told, tearing the shirt and tying it around his head to cover his eyes. "Nice and tight," she told him. "I want you to experience the same thing he experienced that night."

"It's tight, ok?" he said, yanking on the knot in the back with both hands. Pain rushed through his skull as he did so.

He heard her feet moving around him and shuttered as she pushed her gun into the small of his back. "Start walking."

"You hit me with your car! Would you please cut me a break?" he yelled.

"Oh stop it with that already! I think you can push through the pain. After all, it's what I've had to do for almost thirty years. Push through the pain. Although, my pain and anger was clearly directed at the wrong person. I can't believe that you were right under my nose after all of these years. Even more so that you let Chase Dempsey take the fall for all of this. You really are a pussy."

"Is that what this is about?" he asked as the two moved deeper into the woods. "Chris Wilba...?"

Before he could finish speaking, he felt the butt of Lynn's gun slam against the back of his head. Pain surged through his entire body.

"You get my brother's name out of your fucking mouth," she growled at him.

Sully reached his hand up to his head and felt fresh blood seeping out of his previously stitched up wound.

"Brother? Chr..." he stopped himself from saying his name again, hoping to avoid another blow to the head. "He was your brother?"

"Just fucking keep walking," she ordered while shoving him forward.

Sully began moving forward. Small steps. Unsure of what was in front of him. Although he knew exactly where she was taking him. And with each step his concern grew deeper that within a few minutes he'd end up dead at the bottom of that embankment, blindfolded, just like Chris. Images of that night flashed in mind as he walked. Years of denial. Swaths of lies. All crashing down on him in one swift wave of retribution.

"Stop here," she eventually told him. He stopped walking immediately, remembering that one step in the wrong direction here could be fatal.

"It's time to answer for your sins, Sully," she said, spinning him back around in her direction. "I want to hear what happened that night."

"It was all an accident, Lynn, I swear," he said. "I was just trying to get some time alone with him, and he fell."

"He fell?" she screamed. "He fell and you just left him there?!"

"There was nothing I could do!" He yelled, fighting back tears. "He was dead already. I decided it was better to let Chase take the blame than to have him die and let the world find out he was gay. He wouldn't have wanted to be outed like that."

"Well that was mighty noble of you. Of course, unlike him, you were able to continue living your double life. You know, I thought I was over it. I thought I'd gotten past it. When I started working for you, I was in a good place mentally. But then fucking Scott Dempsey showed up and, sure enough, it all came rushing back. Then it occurred to me, maybe this was my chance. Maybe I could finally get my revenge. If Chase Dempsey was forced to watch his son go through the same hell that he went through, but this time with an actual murder conviction, well that would be much more satisfying than just killing Chase. Unfortunately it required me to involve Scott and some unsuspecting Pledge Brother's of his. They all seemed like good kids. But it was necessary for me to put that aside."

"My God, you really are insane," he shouted.

"Well, I gotta tell you though, it was all much easier than I thought it would've been. I mean, stealing Scott's student ID was easy. You can accomplish anything with some friendly flirting. Especially with a horny eighteen-year-old. But I honestly found killing Coleman and, well, trying to kill Wilby, much easier than I thought. I'll admit though. I was a bit surprised by Wilby. I didn't expect him to be there when I came up the stairs. I got sloppy there. But, overall, I've got a bit of a knack for it, I think. In fact, I think I've developed a taste for it," she said as she playfully poked Sully's forehead with the barrel of her gun.

Sully's head was pounding. Just the tapping of the metal on his forehead sent a pain rippling through his skull.

"Sorry, buddy. That hurt?" Lynn asked. "Ya' know we met once before, you and I. I was just sixteen and came up to visit

Chris. I remember he introduced you as a friend. I remembered you when I came to interview for this job twenty years later. You didn't seem to recognize me though. You probably don't even remember what name I went by back then, do you?"

"Lynn, that was a long time ago, I can't even..."

Before he could finish Lynn spun him around and shoved him a step forward, taking hold of the back of his shirt.

"Pull up your blindfold!" she yelled.

Startled, Sully immediately did as she said.

"Now look down!" she said tersely

Sully slowly lowered his eyes, followed by the rest of his head until a twenty foot drop revealed itself before him.

"I imagine the last time those eyes stared down there, you saw a much different view. Am I right?"

Sully didn't answer.

"Am. I . Right?" she asked again. Her anger was clear.

"Y-y-y-yes. Yes, you're right."

"That was the night he died, correct? The night you KILLED MY FUCKING BROTHER!"

"Damn it, I didn't kill him, Lynn!" Sully screamed.

"What's my name, Sully? Huh? What is it? Better remember before I shove you over the side, like Chris!"

Sully tried to remember. But his mind was blank. He was about to admit as much when he suddenly heard another voice call out from in the woods.

"Eve!"

Sully and Lynn both turned to see Chase Dempsey standing a few yards away.

"You went by Eve," he said matter of factly. "I remember meeting you when you came to see Chris. When did you become 'Lynn', though?" he asked, making air quotes. "Why not just go by Evelyn? Too formal?"

"Ding, ding, ding!" she said with a smile. She was looking at Chase while keeping her gun trained on Sully. "Glad to see somebody around here paid attention. But it's definitely been a long time since I've gone by Eve Wilbanks. I couldn't quite fly under the radar around here without being known as the sister of a dead former student. I started going by Lynn Clowry a few years later when I started attending South Cuthbert as a Freshman. Clowry is my Mother's maiden name. It made life much easier for me. So tell me, Chase, how did you know to come here?" She still had a strong grip on Sully as she dangled him over the ledge.

"The map in your house. The Alpha and the Omega," he replied. "The beginning and the end."

Lynn nodded in agreement. "Fitting, wouldn't you say? This is where it all started. It should be where I finish it all off."

"Lynn, listen..." Chase said, stepping forward.

"Don't you come any further!" She yelled, pointing the gun at Chase, while simultaneously shaking Sully above the drop with her other hand. "I will drop him like the piece of shit that he is."

"Easy Lynn, you don't want to do that," Chase reasoned with her. "Killing him isn't going to bring back your brother."

"No, nothing is going to bring him back. Not ever! But it'll make me feel better. That's for sure."

Chase saw movement out of the corner of his eye and turned his head slightly to see SWAT team members move swiftly through the woods. Lynn immediately took notice as well.

"Nobody comes any closer!" she screamed, shaking Sully again. "I swear I will drop him! And trust me. He knows for a fact that the fall will kill him."

Chase took the opportunity to take a few small steps forward until he was just within a few feet of the two of them, and just along the ledge himself. He had a clear view of the inside wall of the ledge below Sully. He could see the roots of a nearby tree jutting out from the side. Making eye contact with Sully, it was clear to Chase that he could see the same.

Sully didn't need any prodding. Instead of leaving his fate in Lynn's hands, he leapt straight down off of the ledge.

Surprised at the motion, Lynn was pulled forward and nearly went over herself. As she regained her balance, Chase could see her angling her gun downward towards the embankment below in one last attempt to exact her revenge. He lunged forward and wrapped his arms around her, taking them both over the ledge.

Twenty feet felt like a hundred. Chase could feel Lynn struggle as they fell. He heard the sound of her gun firing. Suddenly he felt an impact and a pain in his shoulder. Then there was silence.

Chase looked around him and saw that they'd reached the ground. The gun was lying ten feet and he was lying on top of Lynn Clowry. Her eyes were wide open. Her lips moved slightly. Looking down he saw that a broken tree branch was piercing his shoulder. He hadn't been shot as he had first thought. The two had landed on a fallen tree.Following the path of the branch, he found that it had impaled Lynn's shoulder and entered the front of his.

He rolled to the side, dropping a few more feet before finally hitting the ground. Wincing from the pain, he looked at the bloody branch sticking out of her shoulder.

A noise from above took away his attention. Turning his gaze up to the top of the ledge, he saw SWAT team members lifting Sully to safety. Sully had grabbed hold of the tree roots below him, saving him from the same fate that Chris Wilbanks had suffered years before. Chase could see blood soaking the side of Sully's leg as they pulled him up. Lynn's shot had met its mark. But it wasn't quite on target. Sully sat down at the top of the ledge as they attended to him. He looked down at Chase. The two exchanged a nod, recognizing that the nightmare was over.

A moment later Suzanne and Scott came running up to Sully's side.

"Oh my God, where is he?" Chase heard Suzanne asking before she looked down in fear. He smiled up at the two of them and saw Suzanne's shoulders relax as she embraced Scott.

"Is she alive?" Sully yelled down, reminding Chase of what lay next to him. He slowly pulled himself to his feet, and looked down on Lynn Clowry. Her eyes met his as she began to speak softly. Chase leaned in closer to hear her.

"My brother," he heard her say. "he...deserved...better."

Chase looked up to see the SWAT team coming around the bend with paramedics in tow. He returned his glance to Lynn.

"He was my brother too," he told her, "and yes, he absolutely deserved better than this." He then looked at the first responders as they drew closer. "She's all yours."

CHAPTER 57

"Just relax and lay back, Mr. Sullivan. It's time to get you back to the hospital." A paramedic was patiently attempting to coax Sully into a prone position. But the adrenaline rushing through Sully's body had a different agenda.

"I walked all the way into the woods on a broken leg. I don't need to lay down on a stretcher," he protested.

"Relax, Sully," Chase told him, as a Paramedic finished adding dressing to his shoulder. "How many people get to take two ambulance rides on the same day?"

"Yeah, very funny. Where's your ambulance ride?"

"Oh, I just called an Uber," he said. He considered adding a smile. But he didn't want to convey that he was suddenly ready to forgive him.

Sully, seemingly understanding the vibe that Chase was giving off, turned to the paramedic and asked quietly, "Hey, would you mind giving us a second before you lift me in?"

The paramedic looked over at Chase, then nodded. "Sure, but don't take too long. We need to get you both in for treatment." he said before stepping away.

Sully turned his head back towards Chase, pausing before speaking. "Hey, I need to tell you...I'm sorry. You must hate me."

Chase walked over and sat down on the rear bumper of the ambulance. He winced slightly as the pain from his fall began to settle in. "Listen, I'm not going to act like I'm all hunky dory with all of this. But I genuinely am sorry that you had to endure the pain of losing Chris without being able to actually tell anyone. And I feel bad that you two were in a position where you couldn't tell anyone about your relationship. I wish that you two could have publicly been together. No one should need to go through that just to be with the one they want to be with. I...I'm just sorry. If people were more accepting back then...well..."

"He might still be alive today," Sully added.

"Yeah, basically."

"Well, I'm not going to pretend that the only reason for everything you did back there was to help me. I mean if that was even a reason at all. But regardless...thank you. I owe you. I...I really don't even know how to ever express the feelings I have about what I did to you, and I don't blame you if you never forgive me. I'm actually going to resign my position at the school. I don't deserve to be leading these kids into adulthood. Not the way I went about living mine."

Chase stood and paused for a moment before taking a deep breath and exhaling before he spoke. "Well, I honestly don't know how long it'll take for me to get over what you did to me. Or if I'll ever get over it. I just don't know. I haven't had time to really process it yet."

He glanced over towards Scott, who was leaning in for a hug from Sydney and reaching his other hand out to Woody for high five. He then turned back to Sully and continued.

"But you might want to think twice about resigning. I have a feeling that you're just what these kids need right now. They need someone that understands what's at stake in life, and that actions have consequences. I think that...and I mean this sincerely...your recent experience puts you in a unique position to successfully put them on the right path."

Sully lowered his head, fighting back the tears he felt welling up in his eyes. Taking a deep breath, he looked back at Chase. "Thanks, I'll take that into consideration. But, I...uh...don't know if the Police are going to think the same, much less the University."

Chase, finally allowing himself to crack a smile, put forth a surprising offer. "Yeah, well, from what I hear, it sometimes helps when a highly respected member of a neighboring Police Department puts in a good word, it could be helpful. I don't know if Universities react the same way. But, it's possible."

Sully lowered his head. "I can't thank you enough," he told him as he fought back tears. "I'll definitely think about it."

"I hope you will," he said with a nod, before waving over to paramedics to signal that Sully was now ready. "Now get going," he told Sully. "You need to go get that head checked out."

"Eh, it's probably just a bruise," he said with a smile before calling out to the paramedic. "Ok, are we going or what?"

Chase laughed as he looked past Sully towards Scott, Suzanne, Sydney and Woody approaching him.

"Hey there!" he called out.

"Hey Dad, how ya feeling?" Scott asked. He broke into a jog in his Dad's direction.

"Never better," Chase responded as Scott came closer. "How 'bout you, bud? You feeling ok?"

"Yeah, I am. Thank you, Dad," Scott told him. "You really came through. You kept your promise."

"That's what Brotherhood is all about, right?" Chase replied with a smile.

Scott reached out for a fist bump, which Chase returned. "Care to show me the secret handshake?" Scott asked with a smile

"Hey, you're not *in* yet! You've still got the rest of pledging to go through. Buuut, I'd say that the past few days have been your own personal Hell Week. You can handle anything those guys have to throw at you now."

Scott looked around towards his Mom, Woody, and Sydney. "And thank you to all of you, actually. You've all done more than I ever could've ever imagined. I'll never forget this."

Sydney wrapped her arms around Scott and reached up for a kiss. "I just hope that they can find enough at Lynn's house to tie her to the murders and fully clear Scott,"

"We'll know soon enough," Lt. Quinn chimed in as he approached. "Our guys have been combing through there and they won't stop until they've got every ounce of evidence. And I spoke with some of the SWAT team that said they'd heard everything she had told you and Mr. Sullivan. That will be helpful for sure. But, more importantly, we also found a knife on her. We'll have our guys match that. We think there's a good chance it could be the murder weapon."

Their attention was drawn across the road as a stretcher carrying Lynn Clowry was carried out of the woods. Her chest was bandaged and she was wearing an oxygen mask.

"She gonna make it?" Chase asked Quinn.

"I'm not a doctor," he replied. "But, yeah, it does seem like she will."

"We need an ID on her. We need someone tying her to the scenes," Chase didn't take his eyes off of her as he spoke.

"Well, might be your lucky day, and Will Bonnetti's for that matter," Quinn responded while turning to Scott. "We just got a call from the hospital. Your friend is awake. We'll be heading over there shortly to see if he can ID Ms. Clowry."

Suzanne motioned to Chase. "Well I think we'll all be heading to the hospital as well. So maybe we'll run into you there."

"I'm sure you will," he said. "But in the meantime..." Quinn extended his hand towards Chase.

"... Lieutenant Dempsey...thank you for your help here today. It won't go unnoticed."

Surprised by the gesture, Chase reached out his good hand and shook Lt. Quinn's. "Thank you, Lieutenant."

Quinn continued, "Maybe one day we'll get to coordinate on a case in a professional capacity."

"Possibly," Chase replied with a smile.

CHAPTER 58

When Will Bonnetti awoke, he was surprisingly lucid. The doctors had surmised that, as a defense mechanism, his body had simply shut down all unnecessary functions while it worked on healing. They did not want any immediate visitors, aside from the family. However, two visitors were given permission to speak with him immediately. Lt. Quinn and Detective McKue had shown up with one question - Did Will Bonnetti see the face of his attacker? Wilby answered confidently to the affirmative. They followed up by asking if he could tell them who it was. Wilby nodded slowly, turned to them and said, "It was Lynn Clowry".

Quinn reached into his coat pocket and pulled out a photo of Lynn Clowry. He held it up so that Wilby could see it. "Is this the person that attacked you?" Will nodded his head once more, and confidently answered, "Yes, that's her. Lynn Clowry attacked me."

He went on to explain that after leaving CJ's apartment, he and Coleman decided to go to 403 to see if anyone was partying there. They arrived to find no one around. But he started to feel sick and went up to the bathroom. When he came back down, Coleman was nowhere to be found. He walked into the kitchen just in time for Lynn Clowry to ascend the basement stairs. The last thing he remembered was a pain in his side as she thrust a knife into his side. Then everything went black.

Quinn and McKue thanked Wilby and his family for their time and then left. When they arrived back at the Station, they were informed by Forensics that the knife found on Lynn Clowry was determined to have traces of Coleman and Wilby's blood on it. It was now official. Scott Dempsey had been exonerated of all wrongdoing.

EPILOGUE

TWO WEEKS LATER
Initiation Night

Tonight, this Pledge Class would become the 75th class to be initiated into the Brotherhood of Kappa Chi Rho. Never before, however, had there been a class like this. Never before had there been a group of young men that have come together to protect their own in the same way that this group has. They started as a group of twelve. Tonight, eleven Pledge Brothers would be initiated and become Brothers of Kappa Chi Rho.

All of the remaining members of the Pledge Class, with the exception of Robbie Goldberg, were in attendance. After the events surrounding Coleman's murder, word had spread to the Brotherhood that Robbie had given information to his Mother about the case to be published in the South Cuthbert Daily Local. Once Scott was found to be completely innocent, the Brothers of Kappa Chi Rho voted unanimously to blackball Robbie. He was kicked out of the pledge class and would never be allowed to be a part of the Kappa Chi Rho.

The atmosphere was decidedly jovial. They now knew that Wilby's life was no longer in danger. He, in fact, had recovered enough to attend. They also now knew that the innocence of Scott Dempsey was no longer in question.

The thought remained, however, in the back of their collective mind, that they had lost one of their own. Coleman would be with them in spirit, and in fact he would be initiated along with his Pledge Brothers. It was decided by the Brotherhood that he would posthumously become a Brother of Kappa Chi Rho. They also unanimously agreed that the next day the members of the Pledge Class would visit Coleman's parents home to present to them his Brother pin and a sweatshirt displaying the letters 'KXP' across the chest. Two items that Coleman had looked forward to for two months and had been robbed of the opportunity to ever experience.

But, despite their loss, they now had reason to celebrate as well. And celebrate they would. Every member of the group had a smile on their face as they gathered around. They shared stories about their fallen Pledge Brother as they patiently waited for the ceremony to begin.

Scott Dempsey stood and took in the scene in front of him. He made sure to have a feeling of gratitude. He held onto that feeling throughout the ceremony, including the moment when he was sworn in as a Brother of Kappa Chi Rho by his Father, and now Brother, Chase Dempsey.

Made in the USA
Middletown, DE
27 July 2021